BLACKKERCHIEF DICK

Discover books by Margery Allingham published by Bloomsbury Reader at www.bloomsbury.com/MargeryAllingham

Blackkerchief Dick
Dance of the Years
Mystery Mile
No Love Lost
The Crime at Black Dudley
The White Cottage Mystery

BLACKKERCHIEF DICK

A Tale of Mersea Island

MARGERY ALLINGHAM

BLOOMSBURY READER

LONDON · OXFORD · NEW YORK · NEW DELHI · SYDNEY

This edition published in 2013 by Bloomsbury Reader

Bloomsbury Reader is a division of Bloomsbury Publishing Plc,

50 Bedford Square, London WC1B 3DP

First published by Hodder and Stoughton Ltd 1923

ISBN: 978 1 4482 0702 2
eISBN: 978 1 4482 0693 3

Printed and bound by CPI Group (UK) Ltd, Croydon, CR0 4YY

Dedicated
To
Hal Grame

In The Hope That He Will Be Satisfied
That I Have Done My Best to Fulfil
The Promise I Made to Him to Tell the
Story of Anny and to "Tell True."

Contents

Chapter I

"Dangerous! Why there's no trade from here to the Indies more dangerous than ours. I've been about a bit, and mind you I know."

Mat Turnby shifted his large body to a position of greater ease, tilted slightly the rum cask on which he was sitting, and leaned back against the fully-rigged mast, balancing himself carefully in accordance with the gentle roll of the ship.

"Oh, I don't know about that, Mat," remarked a wiry, black-bearded man, who squatted on a coil of rope some six feet away. "I've been on this ship two years now, and how many fights have I had with the Preventative folk? Three! How many hands did we lose in the lot? Eleven! That's not danger!"

"Ah!" said the other, wisely nodding his head, "maybe, maybe, Blueneck, but it's some nine months since we last went foul them coastguards, and since then we've been coming and going as though the damned old Channel belonged to us. Such scatter-brained tricks don't pay in the end."

"You be careful what you're saying, Mat Turnby," piped a shivering, miserable little man, who was trying to protect himself from the cutting February wind with a ragged, parti-coloured blanket which he continually wrapped and unwrapped about his skeleton-like shoulders, "You be careful what you're saying. All kinds o' things on this ship have ears," and he nodded once or twice significantly.

The big man moved uneasily on his unstable seat, but he answered boldly enough.

"I saying? Here, you mind what you're saying, you snivelling rat! Saying? I'm not saying aught as I am ashamed of—I say these daring tricks don't pay in the end—and—and—they don't," he finished abruptly.

"Oh! it's not for the likes o' us to talk about what the Captain does," said the little man whiningly. He snuffled noisily and unwrapped and wrapped his blanket again. "Not for the likes o' us," he repeated.

"Who's saying aught of the Capt'n?" roared Mat, bringing the cask to the ground with a thud. "Who's saying aught of the Capt'n?"

"Oh! no one, no one at all," said the shiverer, considerably startled. Then he added, as the big man slid back against the mast once more, "But if no one did—that's all right, ain't it? If no one did, I say."

Mat swore a round of obscene oaths under his breath and there was silence for a minute or two.

They were nearly at the end of the trip. Indeed, another two hours or so would see them safely at anchor in the safest of all smugglers' havens—the mouth of the River Blackwater, and their cargo easily and openly landed on Mersea Marsh Island.

The shivering little man smiled to himself at the thought of it. The warm kitchen at the Victory Inn, the smoking rum-cup, and the pleasant sallies of the fair Eliza appealed to his present mood, and he sniffled again and rearranged his blanket.

The green white-splashed water lapped against the boat and a big saddle-backed gull flew over, screaming plaintively.

Mat began to talk again.

"I wonder why we do it," he said slowly. "There ain't anything in him—a weak, ugly little Spaniard, no——"

Blueneck interrupted sharply.

"Hush," he said, "No good ever comes of talking about Blackkerchief Dick, whatever is said."

"Who said I was talking of the Capt'n?" said Mat quickly.

Blueneck looked uncomfortable, but he replied steadily, "Ah! Mat Turnby, you be careful!"

Mat laughed.

"I reckon you've got enough to do lookin' after yerself—wi'out worrying about me, master Spaniard," he said good-naturedly.

Blueneck shifted his position slightly.

"I reckon we git paid more than most sea-faring folk," he said.

Mat snorted.

"Oh, yes," he growled, "paid! We're paid all right, but how are we treated?"

Blueneck grinned.

"Like princes of the blood on the island," he laughed.

"Oh, yes, on the island," Mat's voice rose, "but I say—on the brig? How then? Like dogs, men—like dirty, heathen, black-skinned dogs! And what I ask is, why do we do it? Are we men to be afraid of a brown-skinned drunken little pirate of a Spaniard? Just because he owns a brig or two and smuggles as much rum in a year as any other man in the trade? What has he got about him that we should turn wenches and follow him, like the scum he thinks us? Save that he has a mighty plaguy way of turning fine words and——"

"The knife!"

The little man who had spoken huddled his blanket closer and shuddered again. The wind dropped for a moment and a tremor ran through the full sails, as though they also had shivered.

Mat Turnby laughed, albeit somewhat uneasily.

"The knife?" he said. "Lord, what's a knife to a man who holds one of these?" He pulled a heavy flint-stock pistol out of a pocket in the voluminous skirts of the sleeveless and brightly-coloured coat which he wore over a rough homespun guernsey, and held it on the palm of his open hand.

Blueneck smiled grimly.

"A precious great deal when the hand that holds the knife is Blackkerchief Dick's," he said.

Mat Turnby laughed again, contemptuously.

"Are you flesh and good red blood, or mud and pond slime, that you fear the foolish word of a Spanish sot? I tell you no knife held in a mortal hand can stand against a bullet from this."

"Ay, in a mortal hand," said he of the blanket, fearfully looking behind him.

The big sailor swore.

"Lord," he said, "I knew not that I had come aboard a ship manned with a crew of beldames. I tell you this great captain of yours would be laid as flat as Mersea mud with one little lead ball from this."

He stroked the pistol lovingly.

"Maybe," said Blueneck stubbornly. "But whoever fired that shot would die by—the knife."

"Ah! that's tremendous likely," sneered the other, "him on his back with a good ounce of lead in that wicked head of his."

Blueneck shrugged his shoulders.

"You can laugh now, Mat Turnby," he said, "but you won't always laugh at what I tell you. No, not by a long way, that you won't."

He hugged his knees to his chin, and let the heavy lids fall over his eyes.

This apparent indifference seemed to irritate Mat more than words for, bringing his hand down on his knee with a mighty slap, he swore loudly for several seconds. Then suddenly breaking off short he burst into a short, sharp laugh.

"Well!" he said, "It's time the Spanish swine knew that there's someone aboard who ain't afraid of him, no, neither him nor his knife. 'Struth! am I to cower down to a Spaniard?"

He stretched his huge limbs and showed his large yellow teeth as he smiled rather sourly.

"No, by the Lord, not I," he went on. "Let him cross me if he dare, and he'll see good Suffolk blood is a match for thin Spanish sap any day. Ho! ho! ho! let him cross me if he dare! Ho! ho!"

The laugh died away on his lips as from just behind his ear came another. It was soft, rich, musical, and wholly unpleasant.

At the first sound of it the three men sat rigid and when it had ceased there was no sound for several seconds, save for the water lapping against the side and the scream of the gulls overhead.

Blueneck was the first of the sailors to recover. He lifted his eyes cautiously to the direction from which the laugh had come.

He saw what he feared and expected. Up against the other side of the mast, directly behind Mat Turnby, stood a slight figure, dressed extravagantly in the French style of the day, a dandy from the Brussels frill at his throat to the great silver buckles of rich workmanship which adorned his tanned shoes. But it was not these things which stopped the three sailors so suddenly in their talk and caused them to sit aghast.

The most remarkable thing about the newcomer was his face—long, lean, brown, and unhandsome, it yet had a character at once interesting and repulsive. The finely-marked eyebrows met across the low, well-tanned brow in almost straight line, and the hair—oiled and curled—showed as black as the silk kerchief which covered the greater part of head and neck. The eyes beneath the lids, fringed with heavy lashes, smiled and glittered disconcertingly. The whole face was smiling now, viciously, almost fiendishly, but yet smiling and with some enjoyment.

Blueneck's eyes dropped before that terrible smile and, as they travelled slowly downward, suddenly dilated, and he shivered as though a snake had touched him.

The figure by the mast had moved a little more round, and his hand was visible. It was at this that Blueneck stared.

Among the small, white, much-beringed fingers and round the slender wrist, from which the lace ruffle had been pushed back a little, slid the thin, blue blade of a Spanish stiletto. Through the thumb and first finger it slipped, over the blue vein of the white forearm—mingling its brightness with the flashing jewels on the third and fourth fingers—and so round again, all without any apparent effort or even movement of the hand. It was an exhibition to be admired and praised, yet Blueneck and the shivering little man at his side shuddered and looked away.

Mat Turnby, on the other hand, had not seen anything. He sat quite still, the pistol lying idly in the palm of his great hand, staring fixedly in front of him.

A hand, white and slender, slid over his left shoulder and away again—the pistol vanished. Still Mat did not move.

"A very pretty toy, and a useful, my friend," said the same soft voice just behind Mat's ear.

The big sailor pulled himself together with an effort, stood up, then turned towards his captain.

Blueneck and the little man in the blanket also rose.

Blackkerchief Dick had not changed his position. The big pistol and the slender knife lay side by side on his small white palm, and he still smiled as he spoke again:

"Now my noble son of an ox," he began pleasantly, his white teeth shining, "if it so happened that this day you had to die——" A hasty flush spread over the giant's face, but otherwise he made no sign. Blackkerchief Dick continued, "If, I say," he repeated, "that this day you had to die, which of these beautiful toys would you choose as a means to death?"

He held his open hand a little nearer to the sailor.

Blueneck stared at him fascinated, and the little man with the blanket sniffed audibly.

Blackkerchief Dick's eyes left Mat Turnby for a moment and rested on the shivering little creature. "Sniff thy way aft, Habakkuk Coot," he said quietly. The little man stared at him, shivered, sniffed again, and seemed unable to move.

Slowly the Spaniard's arm lifted the pistol in his hand.

Habakkuk sniffed again and his eyes dilated with terror; a white finger raised, crooked round the trigger, and pressed. There was an explosion. Habakkuk remained standing for a second, then fled down the hatchway, a jagged hole through his blanket.

Blackkerchief Dick smiled and, turning to Mat, continued. "As I said, Matthew Turnby, if this day thou hadst to die, which of these weapons wouldst thou choose? Thou seest I know the manner of either," he added, and, suddenly darting out his hand, he plunged the knife between the big sailor's arm and body, so that the sleeve of the man's guernsey was skewered to the body of his coat. Still Mat Turnby neither moved nor spoke. Laughing slightly, the Spaniard drew out the knife and resumed the one-sided conversation.

"Nay, Matthew Turnby, you do but jest in keeping the thin Spanish sap in my veins so long awaiting for an answer," he said with a sneer and a smile. The sailor swallowed noisily, but said nothing.

"The drunken sot of a pirate must be taught not to cross thee, Matthew," went on the Captain, and his smile vanished, leaving only a weary expression on the lean features. "Lord! man, if thou wilt not choose, faith, I must for thee."

"Surely, Capt'n,—you jest—surely."

The words came like a flood from the big man's open mouth.

An expression of surprise spread over the Spaniard's face. "I jest?" he said. "Nay, faith, good Matthew, I jest?" he repeated. "Lord, man, when didst thou get that into thy ass's pate—nay, nay, of a certainty, I do not jest—which wilt thou have?"

Mat Turnby's face grew purple, but he did not speak; his tongue protruded slightly from his lips.

Blackkerchief Dick looked at the weapons critically as they lay side by side in his hand.

"Ah," he said at last, holding the pistol in his left hand. "This we see, Matthew, is discharged. I beg thy pardon, signor, for pressing a choice I could not give thee. As it is, you see, but the knife remains," and he dropped the pistol into a capacious pocket.

Mat Turnby's hand clutched at his throat and he stepped back a pace or two.

Blackkerchief Dick followed him, the knife swinging lightly between his thumb and forefinger. Blueneck stood watching, his eyes fixed on the Spaniard in unholy fascination. Further and further back stepped the big sailor, Dick keeping always the same distance from him, until he reached the side of the boat. There he stayed, breathless with fear. Slowly the Spaniard came nearer and nearer to him, and the thin, blue blade ceased to swing.

"So thou wouldst teach that 'drunken pirate' that all men are not afraid of him. Eh? Is that so?" The voice seemed to grow more caressing at every word and the big sailor's eyes shut. Suddenly they opened again and looked down.

"Look!" Dick was saying. "Look, Matthew, son of Sussex clay, see how fair my blade looks against thy fur-grown hide." He tore at the guernsey and pulled it open, showing the great hairy chest beneath. The terrified sailor made one lunge forward, as though to grasp the lean brown throat, but he was too late. Swift as lightning the small, white hand shot back and then forward, and the thin, blue blade vanished in the wretched man's body just over the collar-bone, cutting the jugular vein. The great body stiffened and then, gradually relaxing, dropped at the Spaniard's feet.

Blueneck stifled a cry and stepped forward.

Slowly the Spaniard pulled out the steel, wiped it carefully on the brightly-coloured, sleeveless coat, then slipped it into his belt.

"Over with the dog," he said shortly to Blueneck, as he walked off quietly up the deck.

Blueneck hailed one of the frightened crew who had watched the scene from the deck-house roof, and in silence the two lifted up all that was left of the great sailor, and pushed it over the side. The body splashed in the green water and somewhere near a cormorant shrieked to his kind the news of fresh prey, and the ship, her sails bellying out to the wind, sped on towards the island.

Chapter II

"Anny!"

"Ay, Hal!"

"Do you love me, lass?"

"Oh now why will you keep plaguing me, Hal? How many times have I told you so on this same wall. You know I do."

"Can I kiss you again, then?"

"Ay, Hal."

There was silence for a minute or so, and the gulls fishing for eels in the soft black mud came in closer to the shingle-strewn strip of beach, taking no notice of the two figures on the sea wall, so still they stood.

"When we get married, lass," the young voice sounded clearly in the quietness and the gulls flew screaming, "we might keep the Ship ourselves."

The girl at his side cut him short with a bitter little laugh.

"Ay, Hal," she said sadly, "when we get married—that's a tremendous long way off, I'm thinking."

The boy put his arm round her waist unchecked.

"I don't know," he said, and his voice sounded hopeful, "I don't know, lass. Gilbot's leaving the place in my hands more than ever, and who knows but what some day he'll be handing it over to me altogether."

Anny joined in his laugh and her hand slid up and caressed his broad, scarlet-shirted shoulder.

"Ay, and then I'll be serving our own rum, and you and Captain Fen de Witt will settle the price yourselves—oh, Hal! lad, that'll be happiness."

"Why, Anny, girl, ain't you happy now? Gilbot's been more than good to both of us. It isn't every landlord who'd bring up a couple of orphans in his inn and look after them the way he has us."

The girl pouted her full red lips.

"It isn't as if we didn't work for him," she said.

"Oh, Anny!" Hal's honest blue eyes clouded for a moment, "you didn't serve the liquor till you were fourteen, you know, and he even let me study a bit before I started to help."

"Ay, maybe, but your folk left some money to him, didn't they?"

"Nay, lass. They died aboard Fen de Witt's schooner, the *Dark Blood,* coming down from the North. You know that; I've told you so some twenty times."

"Ay, you have, but I like to hear you praise Gilbot, Hal, your eyes shine so, and you seem almost angry with me—I like you angry, Hal."

The boy laughed.

"Saucy minion! when we are married you will not wish me angry. Faith, lass, you would not make another Ben Farran of me, surely?"

The girl shuddered.

"Peace, prithee," she said. "I do not like to hear you jest so. Oh, that he had died with my father."

"Marry, sweetheart, fie upon thee speaking of thy grandsire so," Hal laughed merrily.

The girl looked about her uneasily.

"Hush!" she said. "I would not have him hear us."

The boy's laugh rang out again and he bent as he kissed her, although her height was unusual in the island, for he was very tall.

"Look, Anny, lass," he said laughingly, "see how far we are from the *Pet,*" and he pointed ahead of them to where an old mastless hull lay moored in a little bay, about a quarter of a mile from where they stood.

Anny glanced up at him and he stopped to look at her. Although they had lived in the same house since they could remember, he was never tired of gazing at that wonderful face of hers, and praising it till it reddened to the colour of the rough, canvas shirt to which he pressed it.

It was plump and oval in shape, white, but delicately touched with a colour in the cheeks, and her hair of that intense blackness which seems to absorb the light, curled over her low forehead. But her eyes were wonderful. Of a deep sea-green, they caught light and shadow from her surroundings. The girl was certainly a beauty and of no common type.

Hal caught his breath.

"Anny," he said, his young eyes regarding her solemnly, "you are as beautiful as the sea at five o'clock on a summer's morning. Look, sweetheart, over there, see—your eyes are as green as that sea, and your hair black as yon breakwater that starts out of it."

The girl laughed, well-pleased, but she looked over at the old hull again quickly.

"Will we go back now?" she asked at last.

The boy looked at her, astonished.

"Go back!" he said. "Why, what for—art not tired, surely?"

The girl shook her head.

"Nay," she said, "but——" she stopped and looked at the hull again.

Hal followed the direction of her eyes before he spoke again. Then he laughed.

"Why, Anny, you are afraid to pass your grandsire's boat."

Then, as she did not speak, he took her little chin in his brown hand and raised her face to his.

"What are you feared of when I am with you, sweetheart?" he asked.

The girl shivered slightly.

"They say," she began hesitatingly, "that Pet Salt is a witch."

Hal's face became grave.

"Ay," he said, "they do say so, but, Lord," and he smiled, "they said the same of Nan Swayle."

"Ah! but that's a lie," said the girl hotly.

Hal laughed.

"Ay," he said, "and maybe so is the tale of Pet Salt. Anyway, thy grandsire seems to thrive beneath her care, be she witch or no. Fie, Anny, for shame," he added, "you would not haste back yet. Master French will not thank us if we get in so soon, stopping his love-talk with Mistress Sue."

Anny wrapped her shawl a little closer about her head and shoulders, and slipped her arm through the boy's, and they walked on for a while without speaking.

About three hundred yards from the old hull Anny stopped.

"Look!" she said, "he's on deck."

Hal looked in the direction she pointed and saw the stubby figure of old Ben Farran, a long telescope to his eye, leaning against the remnant of what had once been a neat deck-house. Lumber of different kinds—mostly empty rum kegs—lay strewn all round him, while, from the shattered stump of the main-mast to the painted ear of the fearsome green and red dragon which served as a figure-head, was stretched a clothes-line, on which a few rags leaped and fought in the cold breeze.

Hal studied him critically for a few moments.

"He's not so deep in liquor as usual," he said at last.

"Oh! poor Pet Salt!" exclaimed the girl involuntarily. "I wonder where she is?"

"Stowed away safely under hatches, I reckon," said Hal, with a laugh.

"You should not jest, Hal. I have not known him able to stand so, these three months. I fear he may have kilt her. He would if she could beg him no more rum."

"Oh! what soft heart it is," said the boy gently. "How long ago was it that you shivered when I spoke her name, and now you fear for her—shall we go back?"

The girl hesitated for a moment, then she said, "Nay, she may have need of help, poor soul. Come with me, Hal."

"Come with thee, lass! Think you I'd let you go alone—thy grandsire sobered?" His voice rose in indignation as he put his arm about her shoulders protectingly.

They came within twenty yards of the boat before the swaying figure on the deck became aware of them. Then, however, to their extreme surprise he hailed them affably, and called to Hal.

"Hey, you boy there, be your eyes good?"

"Ay, none so bad, sir."

"Ah, I doubt it, come up here, will 'ee, and see if you can make out this craft." Then, his eyes falling on the girl, "Is it that slut Anny you have with you?"

" 'Tis Anny Farran, sir," she said, speaking for herself.

"Ah! you run down to Pet Salt, girl, she may need thee."

Anny climbed up the rope-ladder which dangled over the side, and Hal after her.

"Is Pet Salt sick, grandsire?" she ventured timidly.

Anny had been a serving-maid at the Ship Tavern some three years and her acquaintance with profane language was not limited, but she quailed visibly and the red blood mounted from her throat to the ebony curls on her forehead before the stream of abuse levelled at the head of the unfortunate woman in the hold. She fled down the hatchway and Hal stood looking after her, undecided whether to follow his love and protect her from the aged witch below deck, or to remain and attempt to pacify the wrathful man by the deck-house.

Ben decided for him.

"Here you are," he said fiercely, "take this telescope. Now"—as Hal took it from the old man's unsteady fingers—"what do you see?"

The young Norseman, his yellow hair curling over his ears, and one dark blue eye screwed to the rim, swept the glass to and fro once or twice, then he held it still.

"She's a brig," he said at last.

"Ah!" assented the old man.

Hal looked again. "Light's very bad," he remarked.

"I could ha' told you that—here, give me the thing." Ben regained possession of the glass and, unable to hold it steady, broke into another flood of profane language, cursing the woman, Pet Salt, again and again.

"She has vexed thee, sir?"

The young man put the question timidly.

"The ronyon burnt my rum-cup," Ben Farran gulped with rage.

"Oh lad! the defiling of good, Heaven-sent rum with burnt eggs and honey!"

He spat on the deck at the thought of it.

The boy grinned, but he said nothing.

Once again the old man handed him the telescope.

"Now look! Be she Captain Fen de Witt's *Dark Blood?*"

Hal began to understand the old drunkard's interest in the brig. If this was the *Dark Blood,* the whole of the East end of the Island would run rum for a night or so, and as he guessed Ben's stock was getting low.

"Nay," he said at last, " 'tis not she. Why, Master Farran, Captain Fen de Witt isn't expected for a week or more."

The old man mumbled curses for a while before he spoke.

"Ah! but who be she?" he said, pointing out to the horizon.

"Why," said the boy in some surprise, " 'tis someone making for the West."

The old man seized the glass.

" 'Tis impossible with the tide out like this," he said.

Hal strained his eyes.

"Ay," he said, "but she's trying it."

"But I tell thee, lad," Ben's voice rose shrilly, " 'tis impossible. Why, down there in the fleet there ain't no more 'an four feet o' water when the tide's like this."

"Ay," said Hal, "I know there ain't, but she's trying it," he added stubbornly.

"Why, so she be," Ben Farran put the glass at last safely to his eye and spoke in amazement. "But she won't do it," he added with a certain enjoyment. "She can't do it. There's only one man as I've heard of who'd try it," he continued, "and it ain't likely to be him at this time o' day."

"Ah!" said Hal, "and who's that?"

"Dick Delfazio—him as they call Blackkerchief—but it ain't likely to be him, as I said."

Hal nodded.

"I've heard of him," he said, "lands his stuff at the Victory, don't he?"

The old man grunted.

"I don't know that," he said. "All I know is I don't see any of it. Lord," he added, as he had another look through the glass, " 'tis the *Coldlight,* though—sithering fool. He'll lead the preventative men on the Island after him one o' these days."

"He'll never get down to the fleet with the tide like this, whoever he is," said the boy, staring out curiously at the white-sailed craft.

"Ah! you're right there," said Ben. "Curse the fool, he'll get her stuck fast in the mud and have to stay all night. Lord!" he added, "when these wars be over there'll be a deal more care taken in the trade, take my word for it. Why, this ain't smuggling, it's free trading."

But the boy was not listening to him; his eyes were fixed on the *Coldlight,* now well in view.

"Look!" he said suddenly, "look, she's turning."

"Eh? What? Eh? So she is!" ejaculated the old man in a frenzy of excitement. "Do 'ee think she be coming here—eh?"

Hal spoke slowly, his eyes on the brig.

"Ay," he said, "you're right, she's making for East—who did you say she was?"

"The *Coldlight*—the *Coldlight,* lad, commanded by the finest man in the trade—oh, my boy, the Island will swim in good Jamaica this night," and he dropped the telescope, which fell clattering to the boards.

Hal picked it up and turned to give it to the old man, but he was off, tottering to the hatchway. There, kneeling on the deck and poking his head down, he called whiningly, "Pet! Pet! my own, will you come up and hear what I have to tell you? Great—great news, Pet." Receiving no answer he tried again while the boy stood looking at him.

"Pretty old Pet, queen of my heart, Pet, my Pet, come up."

Still no answer, save for the patter of raindrops on the boat.

"I'm sorry I beat you, Pet—although I'm damned if I am, the ronyon!" he added to himself. Still all beneath the hatches was silent as the grave.

Swearing softly the old man crawled over to the ladder and began to descend.

Hal heard him reach the bottom and stumble off.

The boy looked out to sea, where the brig was making slowly for the Eastern Creek. He stood looking at her for a second or two and then sprang round suddenly as though someone had called him.

Where was Anny? In the excitement of watching the brig he had forgotten her. His face flushing with remorse he raced to the hatchway and was just in time to help his sweetheart, pale and frightened, up on to the deck.

"Oh, Hal, how he has beaten her!" she said, as she moved quickly over to the rope-ladder and climbed hastily down without once looking behind.

"Could she speak to thee?" he asked as he slid to the ground after her.

"Ay," she nodded her head fearfully.

"Did she curse thee much?"

"Ay!" she nodded again.

Hal smiled.

"Art afraid?" he enquired tenderly.

Anny looked up at him before she pulled his arm about her waist.

"Nay," she said, "not while I have thee, Hal."

He kissed her before he spoke again.

"I suppose Ben was plaguing her to meet the *Coldlight* and beg a keg?" he said.

Anny nodded again. Then she said quickly. "Come, lad, we must back to the Ship if company be expected."

"Wouldst rather serve rum to the company than walk to the shore with me, lass?"

The grip round her waist tightened and she laughed.

"If thou wert a wench, Hal, thou wouldst be a jade," she said. "Come, Master Gilbot will be scuttering this way and that, and Mistress Sue, loath to leave Big French, will have the skin flayed off everyone in the place if we're not there to help her."

"Thou'rt a great lass, Anny," said the boy smiling. "When we're married there'll not be an inn in the country to equal ours."

The girl laughed happily.

"Ay, when we are married, Hal," she said.

Chapter III

"Oh, I called her Mary Loo,
  And she shwore that she'd be true,
  Until I took to rum and went to shea,
  Then she goed along wi' he,
  And forgot all love for me,
  Sho I stayed wi' me rum and me shea,
Sho I stayed wi' me rum and me shea."

Gilbot, landlord of the Ship, sat before a roaring fire in his comfortable kitchen, singing in a quavering, tipsy voice, and beating out the accompaniment with an empty pot on one podgy knee.

It was six o'clock in the evening, and already the tallow dips had been lighted. They cast a flickering, friendly glow over the scene, the long, low room, stone-flagged and small-windowed, the ale barrels and rum kegs neatly arranged side by side on a form which ran nearly all the way round the wall, and the two long, trestled tables, flanked with high-backed seats which were now unoccupied, but were presently to be filled with the best company that the East of the Island could provide.

Besides Gilbot, who appeared happily oblivious of all around him, four other persons sat in the Ship kitchen; two old men threw dice for pence in one corner, while in another, between two rum kegs, sat a girl. She was about twenty-three years of age, and, although her appearance was not of that uncommon type so marked in Anny Farran, yet she had a certain quiet comeliness and gentle expression which made her almost beautiful. At least the handsome young giant who lounged near her in an ecstasy of shyness appeared to think so, for he eyed her so intently, his mouth partly open, that she was forced to pay more attention to the garment she was patching than was strictly necessary. They sat in perfect silence for some ten minutes before the young man plucked up courage to speak. When he did, his voice came uncomfortably from his throat, and he reddened to the roots of his hair.

"I reckon I'll be going up West now, Mistress Sue," he said, as he half rose to his feet and looked towards the door.

"Oh!" there was a note of real regret in the girl's voice, "must you go so early, Master French?"

Big French sat down again quickly.

"Nay," he said shortly, and there was silence again for another minute or so.

She stitched busily the while.

"Is it great business you have in the West, Master French?" she said at last, her eyes still on her work.

French discovered suddenly that it was easier to talk to her if she was not looking at him.

"Ay," he said. "Blackkerchief Dick will get in to-morrow."

Sue sighed.

"Ah!" she said, "you have a fine life, Master French, travelling to and fro the way you do."

Big French beamed delightedly.

"Ay," he said, "a fine life, but dangerous," he added quickly, "very dangerous."

The girl looked at him appraisingly.

"But you are so strong, Master French, what have you to fear from footpads—you're in more danger from pretty wenches, I warrant," she said, as she shot a sidelong glance at him.

French reddened and smiled sheepishly; then he suddenly grew grave and his grey eyes regarded her earnestly.

"Wenches, Mistress Sue?" he said, "nay! one wench—that's all."

It was Sue's turn to redden now and she did so very charmingly, and French, noting her confusion, immediately bethought him of his own, and he sat fidgeting, his eyes on the tips of his untanned leather boots.

"I'll be forth to Tiptree market this week if Blackkerchief Dick's brought aught but rum from Brest," he said at last, "and if there be aught you may be wanting from thence, Mistress——?" His voice trailed off on the question as he studied his boot-toe attentively.

She smiled as she laid a brown hand on his arm, thereby causing him much nervous disquietude.

"Come back before you go—er—Ezekiel,"—Big French started pleasurably at the sound of his Christian name—"and if I have bethought me of aught we need from Tiptree, I will be glad if you will get it for me," she said.

Big French took the hand that was resting on his sleeve in one big fist and his other arm slid round the girl's waist unhindered.

"Sue," he said softly, "will ye——"

"Sho I stayed wi' me rum and me shea,"

sang Gilbot, suddenly waking up from a doze he had fallen into. "Shue," he called, "more rum, lass."

The girl jumped up to obey him, and Big French swore softly under his breath.

Two or three seamen entered the kitchen at this moment, and, after saluting Gilbot, called for drinks and settled themselves in the high-backed seats on either side of the fire. They began to talk noisily of their own affairs.

Sue opened an inner door and called for more lights.

Gilbot, happy with his rum, continued to sing.

Big French rose slowly to his feet. He was an enormous figure, some six feet five inches tall and proportionately broad; his face as the light from the dripping candles fell on it showed clearly-cut and very handsome. He wore his hair long and his chin had never been shaved, so his beard was as silky as his hair, curly and of the colour of clear honey. He walked over to the door after exchanging greetings with the rowdy crew at the fireside, and lifted the latch. On the threshold he was met by Hal and Anny.

They had walked briskly and the cool air had brought the colour to the girl's face and, as she stood there, the men at the fireside, instead of clamouring for the door to be shut and the draught stayed, sat looking at her in silent admiration.

Hal Grame, standing just behind her, was the first to speak. He stepped forward, shutting the door behind him.

"Blackkerchief Dick, aboard the *Coldlight*, will be putting into the Creek inside of an hour," he said.

Big French looked at him for a moment.

"Blackkerchief Dick coming here?" he said at last.

Sue came forward to listen, and several men left the fireplace and joined the little group near the door.

"Ay," said Hal, "he couldn't get down the fleet with the tide like this."

"Ah!" said French.

"He couldn't rest in the Channel for twelve hours or so, now could he?" continued Hal.

"Ah, you're right there, lad," said one of the men pressing forward. "Blackkerchief Dick would risk most things, but he's no fool."

Big French scratched his head thoughtfully.

"Ah," he said slowly, "he's no fool, that's right enough." Then he looked at Sue furtively out of the corner of his eye. "He'll be coming up here I reckon," he said.

Sue shrugged her shoulders.

"Well," she said, "we've rum enough for any foreigner, and, if we ain't as fine as the Victory, our liquor's as good."

"Eh, what's that?" Old Gilbot pricked up his ears, the pewter-pot half-way to his lips.

"Not as fine as the Victory, lass? Who says we ain't as fine as the Victory, any day? Eh? Anywaysh," he added, his face hidden in the nearly empty tankard, "anywaysh, we've prettier wenches."

"You're right, host—here, rum all round and drink to the wenches," Big French, his hand in his breeches pocket, spoke loudly and the coins jingled as he planked them down on the table, and the two girls hastened to draw the rum.

"The wenches!" shouted French, one big foot on the form and

his tankard held high above his head.

"The wenches!" roared the company.

"The wenches!" piped Gilbot happily from his corner.

This pleasant ceremony took some minutes, and Sue and Anny stood together smiling at each other, neither giving a thought to the little dark-skinned, white-handed Spaniard who was sailing under full canvas towards their home.

"I'll go down to the hard to meet Blackkerchief," said French at last, wiping his beard with a green handkerchief.

"I'll with you." "And I." "And I." Most of the company rose and followed the young Goliath to the door.

"Goo-bye," said Gilbot, waving his pot. "Come back soon."

The men laughed and promised.

"The owd devil," said one man to another as he shut the door behind them. "The owd devil hasn't been sober these four years." And they went off laughing.

"What manner of fellow is that they call Blackkerchief Dick?" said Anny, as she collected the empty tankards from the tables.

"A devil," said one of the men at the fireside.

"Oh!" Anny was not impressed. She had met many strangers who had been described to her as devils, and not one to her mind had lived up to the description.

"Oh!" said Hal, as he piled fresh logs in the open grate, " 'tis only a foreigner, some Spanish dog or other."

The man who had spoken before shook his head.

"Ah, you be careful, lad. Dick ain't the chap to make a foe of in a hurry," he said.

Anny paused for a moment.

"Is he a big man, sir?" she asked.

Sue interposed quickly.

"Not as big as Master French, I reckon," she said defiantly.

The man laughed.

"Big as French?" he said. "Lord! he ain't no bigger than you, Anny."

"Oh!" the two girls looked at one another and laughed.

"Marry, I reckon he's a devil without horns then, Master Granger," said Sue.

Granger spat before he spoke again.

"I don't know about horns, Mistress," he said, "but I reckon his knife is good enough for him—ah! and for me too for that matter," he added.

Anny laughed again.

" 'Twould not be enough for me, anyway," she said, fixing a stray curl over her ear as she spoke.

Sue looked at her strangely. It was impossible not to like this beautiful, wild little creature, in whom her uncle, Gilbot, had taken such an interest. Yet she could not help wishing that the younger girl had been more careful. She was so young, so very beautiful, and the company which came to the Ship was not the best in the world.

She shrugged her shoulders. It was not her business she told herself, but her eyes followed Anny almost pityingly as the little maid moved across the room to speak to Gilbot.

"Master Gilbot," Anny said. "Should we prepare a bedchamber for the gentleman?"

Old Gilbot looked at her over the rim of the tankard; then he took one of her hands.

"Thou art a pretty wench, Anny," he observed solemnly. "Will 'ee fetch me another stoup of liquor, lass?" he added, brightening up in anticipation.

Anny did as she was told and then repeated her question.

"Eh? Bedchamber? Eh? What?" said the old man, his brows screwed into knotted lines, and he seemed troubled; after a few minutes, however, "Oh! ask Hal," he said, his face clearing. "Ashk Hal, everything."

He looked across at the boy affectionately.

"Shly dog," he murmured, "keeps me in liquor all day long sho he can get the Ship. Ho-ho-ho!" he laughed, shaking all over. "Shly dog—shly dog."

Hal laughed with him and then discussed with Anny and Sue the various arrangements for the reception of the visitors. Having settled everything to their satisfaction they joined the group about the fire, where the talk was still running on the Spaniard.

"Wonderful fighter," one man was saying. "Oh, a wonderful fighter, take my word for it."

"Ah, you're right," said another. "I saw him kill a man with a knife throw, one time. From right the other side of the room it was. That was in a house in Brest, in '59," he added reminiscently.

"How old do you reckon him?" said the first man curiously. "I've not known him more'n a year or so."

"Well," the other man's tone was dubious, "He says he's thirty, and I shouldn't say more; no, I shouldn't say so much—though it's wonderful the way he manages them foreign dogs he mans his brig with."

Hal joined in the conversation.

"They're a rough lot I expect," he said.

The men round the fire laughed.

"You're right there, lad," said one. "Keep your eye on the rum and lasses to-night. Wonderful rough lot they are," he added. "Oh, wonderful rough!"

Hal flushed.

"I reckon the lasses can look after theirselves," he said gruffly.

Anny put her hand on his shoulder.

"Ay," she said, "maybe we can, but where's the need of us troubling when you're by?"

"Bravo, Anny, lass. The girl has wit as well as beauty," said the man addressed as Granger from his seat in the chimney corner, whence he had moved to make room for Sue.

"Ay, a fine wench," said Gilbot, waking for a moment; the others laughed and the talk continued cheerily.

"Evening to you all," the speaker was a man, dressed in the usual fisherman's guernsey and breeches. He stood in the doorway, looking in on the company round the fire and smiling affably.

Hal looked up quickly and seeing who it was rose at once to meet him.

"Evening, Joe," he said cheerily. "Come, sit down; what'll you drink?"

Joseph Pullen smiled and took the seat offered him, and named his choice.

Anny was up in a moment to serve him, and his eyes followed her as she flitted hither and thither, with a smile for one and a jest for another, laughing happily the while. He looked across at Hal.

"Ah, you're a lucky one, mate," he observed in a hoarse whisper.

The boy smiled.

"Amy been at you again?" he enquired.

It was well known that Joe and his wife, Amy, were not a happy couple.

The other looked round him.

"She's a shrew and no mistake, Hal," he said softly.

Hal laughed.

"You're right," he said, "but cheer thyself," he added, as Anny brought a tankard. "Look'ee, Joe, did ever you set eyes on a man called Blackkerchief Dick?"

"I did that," Joe's face appeared red above the pot, "and I set eyes on one of his mange-struck crew as well," he said fiercely.

"Ah, and who might that be?" Granger enquired.

"A black-bearded old Spanish villain called Blueneck. Yes, and what's more, I set eyes on him kissing my wife."

A roar of laughter greeted this outburst, and Joe looked discomfited.

"I stopped it, of course," he remarked.

Another roar shook the building. Joe reddened again.

"I don't see why you're a laughing," he said gruffly.

The men round the fire laughed again.

"I can manage my wife better nor any man here and I'm willing to prove it with these," he said, putting up two bony fists.

The laughter died away and no one spoke for a moment or so. Then Joe, all his anger vanished as suddenly as it had come, remarked, "Blackkerchief Dick, eh? Where did you hear of him? I didn't know he ever came up East."

"Nor don't he as a rule," said Hal, "but he has had to put in here owing to the tide. I reckon he'll up here soon."

"Ah, will he now?" Joe's eyebrows rose expressively, then he put down his mug. "Did you say he was putting in here—crew and all?" he asked, wiping his mouth.

"Ay," said Hal, "I reckon so."

"Ah," said Joe again, "I'll be going back to home," he announced suddenly.

Then, as some knowing smiles appeared on the faces in the firelight; he added, "Ah, you can laugh, but take my word for it, you keep your wenches clear of Spaniards. They have wonderful ways with women." He walked to the door. "See you afore the night's over, Hal," he called cheerily as he went out.

Under cover of the laughter which burst out as he shut the door behind him, Anny whispered to Hal, who was making up the fire, "I would not change thee for the King o' the Spaniards, lad," and he turning suddenly to look at her knew that she spoke truth.

Chapter IV

"Marry! Fortune favours her lovers! Greetings, Master French. Damn my knife! there is not another on the Island I would rather see than thee at this moment."

Blackkerchief Dick stepped out of the open row-boat which had conveyed him from the *Coldlight* and gave a small, white hand to Big French, who assisted him on to the board pathway which was laid over the soft mud.

"Greetings to you, Captain," said the young man, and then added slowly, "you're somewhat before your time, ain't you?"

Blackkerchief Dick broke into a storm of curses.

"Ay," he said at last, "Ay, too early for the tide and so forsooth compelled—I, Dick Delfazio, compelled mark you—to put in at this God-forsaken corner"—he took in the marshland with a comprehensive wave of a graceful arm, and continued sneering— "which is as flat and empty as a new-washed platter."

The big man at his side smiled.

"Nay prithee, Captain," he said, " 'tis none so bad."

The Spaniard turned to him fiercely, but Big French went on quietly. "If you be a wanting to stay the brig here for the next tide," he said, "best to take her up the Pyfleet round to the back o' the Ship—plenty o' water up there," he added.

Blackkerchief Dick shrugged his shoulders.

"The Pyfleet?" he said. "Surely that is Captain Fen de Witt's haven? I would not take advantage of his hiding-place."

The smile on the big man's face vanished.

"Lord, Captain!" he said quickly, "you cannot leave the brig in open channel all the night. The preventative folk may not be very spry hereabouts, but they ain't all dead yet—no not by a long way they ain't."

The Spaniard replied with another shrug.

"As you wish," he said, and then with a smile, his teeth flashing in the dusk, he added: "But that I need thee to-night, Master Hercules, I would not so easily have yielded."

Big French flushed, but he spoke quietly.

"Ah, and what will you be wanting to-night, Captain?" he said.

"Passage in thy cart to the Victory, friend," replied the Spaniard.

"Oh!" Big French spoke dubiously. "Why do you not rest at the Ship?" he enquired.

"The Ship?" the thin lips curled in contempt. "Dick Delfazio stay at a wayside tavern? This moon hath made thee mad, friend French."

Big French sighed involuntarily and the Spaniard laughed.

"A wench?" he asked.

"Nay," the blood suffused the young man's handsome face and he spoke shortly.

"Well, take me to the Victory," repeated the Spaniard.

An anxious snuff sounded at his elbow as he spoke. He turned quickly just in time to seize Habakkuk Coot by the neck of his guernsey.

"You evil-smelling son of a rat," he began slowly, giving the little man a shake at every word, "get thee back to the brig and tell Blueneck I would speak to him."

With the final word he jerked the wretch off the board pathway and watched him flounder in the deep oozing mud.

"Haste thee, dog," he said, touching him lightly with the blade of his knife.

Habakkuk screamed and floundered on for the row-boat, where he was hauled in by several of his comrades. The boat then pushed off for the brig.

"You have a wonderful way with your crew, Captain," said French, looking after the boat.

"Ay, of a truth." the Spaniard laughed. "Cannot Dick Delfazio rule a pack of mangy dogs?"

French looked at him narrowly, and then took up the conversation where he had left it.

"The Ship is no wayside tavern," he said, "the folk be simple but the liquor good and the wenches pretty, and they are waiting for you to come—the maids in their best caps, and the canary warming on the hearth."

Dick looked at him for a moment.

"Master French," he said, keeping his glittering eyes on the other's face. "Master French, 'tis strange that thou shouldst be in this part of the Island so ready for my coming, Master French," he added, his voice assuming the soft caressing quality for which it was so remarkable. "Dare I suppose that it was not to meet me that thou camest to the East? That it was to the Ship thou camest, eh? Master French?"

Once again the big man blushed to his ears, but he laughed.

"Ay, Captain," he said, "you are right there. 'Twas not to meet you I came to the East. Prithee tell your men to take the brig down the Pyfleet and come with me to the Ship."

The Spaniard laughed strangely.

"Friend French," he said, "are thy horses lame?"

The young man looked at him for a moment before he spoke.

"Ay," he said at last. "Wonderful lame."

Blackkerchief Dick threw back his head and laughed heartily.

"Thou art a brave man, French," he said, but continued quickly. "There is such a lameness as can be cured to-morrow for a trip to Tiptree, eh, friend?"

"Ah!" said the big man nodding his head sagely, " 'tis a wonderful strange lameness that they have."

Dick nodded.

By this time the row-boat had once more come to the plank across the mud. Blueneck, a shadowy figure in the darkness, stepped out and came towards them.

Dick gave his orders briefly.

"Take the brig up the Pyfleet," he said; "any of these fellows will pilot thee," he added, pointing to the group of Mersea men on the wall. Then as an afterthought, "And bring five kegs from the hold to me at the Ship Tavern."

A certain amount of enthusiasm among the volunteer pilots was noticeable after this last remark, and Blueneck smiled as he replied, "Ay, ay, Capt'n."

Blackkerchief Dick and his friend Big French the smugglers' carter turned, climbed the wall and walked together down the lonely road to the Ship Tavern without speaking.

"Marry!" said Dick, stopping after they had walked for some five minutes, his hand feeling for his knife. "What's that?"

Big French stopped also and, standing side by side in the middle of the road, they listened intently. Apparently just behind the hedge on their right a human voice, deep and throaty, said clearly, "Rum—rum—rum—rum," the sound trailing off weirdly on the last word.

The Spaniard crossed himself, but his hand was steady.

"Is't a spirit?" he said.

"Nay," Big French's voice came stifled from his mouth.

The Spaniard drew his knife. "Then I'll have at it," he said.

Once again the stifled monosyllable broke from the younger man's lips.

Blackkerchief Dick looked at his guide quickly. By the faint light of the winter moon he saw the man's face was distorted strangely—once again the ghostly voice behind the hedge said distinctly, "Rum—rum—ru——"

"Ho! ho! ho!" roared French, his laughter suddenly breaking forth, "Peace, Mother Swayle," he shouted, "by our lakin! you had us well-nigh feared with your greeting."

The Spaniard sheathed his knife.

"If 'tis a friend of thine, Master French," he said shrugging his shoulders, " 'tis of no offence to me. Though by my faith," he added, as a dark figure in flowing garments bounded over the hedge and stood by the roadside, " 'tis strange company you keep."

The tall, gaunt woman addressed as Mother Swayle shrank back into the hedge.

“Who is it with thee, Big French?” she said in her deep tired voice.

“Blackkerchief Dick, new landed by the wall,” said French.

“Ah! I know naught of him—Peace, good swine—farewell, Rum!”

There was a note of finality in the last word and Big French started to walk on. “Rum,” he said over his shoulder, and added to Dick in an undertone, “ ’Tis only a poor crone—peace to her—her wits’ diseased.”

“Oh!” the Spaniard felt the pocket of his coat and pulled out a silver dollar. “Here, mother of sin,” he said as he tossed it to her, “buy thyself rum withal. Almsgiving is a noble virtue,” he added piously to French, as they prepared to walk on. Hardly had the words left his lips when his silver dollar hit him on the back of the head with considerable force.

“May you burn, you mange-struck ronyon,” the deep voice grew shrill in its intensity. “All men are villains and you are a king among them.”

With a foreign oath the Spaniard turned about.

“Rum—rum—r-u-m,” the voice faded away and they heard the patter of feet down the road.

Blackkerchief Dick laughed sharply.

“It is well for Mother Swayle that she lives in the East,” he said, his eyes glittering. “Were she in the West she would take my bounty, if not——” he laughed unpleasantly.

Big French looked at him anxiously, uncertain how the fiery Spaniard had taken the old woman’s vagaries.

“The old one was ducked as a witch in the merrymaking at the Restoring of the King,” he said at last. “She was not quite drowned,” he continued, “so the folk—wenches mostly—look up to her and as I said, Captain, her wits’ diseased.”

Dick shrugged his silken-coated shoulders.

“ ’Tis no matter,” he said with a wave of his hand.

Big French sighed in relief and they walked on in silence for a minute or so. They were now some four hundred yards from the Ship. The high building with its great thatch showed a dark outline against the cold, starlit sky, but all the uncurtained lower windows showed the warm glow within and from the partly open door the sound of singing came out to them on the cold breeze.

The two unconsciously hastened their steps. When they reached the gate of the courtyard the words of the song could be heard clearly above the noise of laughter and banging of pewter.

"Pretty Poll she loved a sailor"

Gilbot's voice was piping a little in advance of the rest.

"And well she loved he,
But he sailed to the mouth
Of a stream in the South
And was losht in the rolling sea,
And was losht in the rolling sea."

Dick straightened his lace ruffles at his throat.

"The dogs seem merry," he observed as he kicked open the door, and stepped into the candle-lit kitchen of the Ship.

All eyes were immediately turned on him, and he stood perfectly still for some seconds enjoying to the full the impression he was making.

The Ship's company was used to the simple finery of Captain Fen de Witt and his men, and most of them had been to the Western end of the Island and had seen strangers who had come, it was whispered, from London itself, but Dick's magnificence was wholly new to most of them, while even those who had seen him before were surprised at the contrast which his glistening figure made with the sombre background of the Ship kitchen's smoke-blackened walls.

Hal stood staring at him as long as any of the others, and Mistress Sue let the rum she was drawing fill up one of the great pewter tankards and spill over on to the stones before she noticed it, so intently did she look at the stranger in the doorway.

Gilbot alone took no notice of the visitor. He sat happily in his place by the fireside, his head thrown back a little and his eyes closed, beating time to imaginary singing with his empty pot.

Joe Pullen was the first to speak. He had just entered by a side door and apparently was entirely unimpressed by the Spaniard or anyone else.

"Evening," he remarked, as he walked over to the most comfortable seat in the chimney corner and sat down. "Evening to you too, sir," he said, noticing Dick for the first time—and then he added, peering out of the fireplace—"Mistress Sue, a rum if you please."

Blackkerchief Dick, noting that the spell was broken, swaggered forward into the firelight.

"Greeting, friends," he said courteously, and then after looking round curiously his eyes rested on Gilbot. "Is this mine host?" he asked.

Gilbot's eyes opened slowly and his jaw dropped as he saw for the first time the splendidly-garbed figure.

"Eh?" he said at last. "Washt?" He tried to rise but gave it up as an impossibility, his brow clouded and he turned his tankard upside down on his knee.

Dick stood looking at him, a slight smile hovering round his mouth and twitching the sides of his big Jewish nose.

Gilbot's face cleared as suddenly as it had clouded.

"Ashk Hal," he said triumphantly, and leaning back once more he closed his eyes.

The Spaniard shrugged his shoulders.

"You Mistress," he said, turning to Sue who dropped a curtsey. "Can I have a bedchamber here this night?"

Sue replied that all was ready for him, and Dick, having assured himself that everything was to his liking, put his hand into his pocket and drawing out a handful of gold and silver coins tossed them lightly on the table.

"Drinks all round, I pray you, Mistress," he said to Sue.

There was a slight stir among the company, and the Spaniard was regarded with still more respect.

Sue stood looking at the coins, her hands on her hips. "'Tis much too much," she murmured.

Blackkerchief Dick laughed.

"Marry! Then, Mistress, 'twill do for the next lot. I pray thee haste, my throat is parched," he said.

Sue, her eyes round with admiration, curtseyed again and ran to the inner door.

"Anny, lass, come hither I prithee," she called, and then hastened to obey the Spaniard.

Anny stepped in unnoticed a moment or two later, and busied herself with the tankards.

Dick was sitting with his back towards her and she did not see him.

"Here, lass," said Sue, seeing her, "the foreigner would drink sack—wilt get it for him?"

There was not much call for Canary Sack at the Ship, so Anny was some minutes finding and tapping a cask. When she returned from the cellar, a flagon in her hand, the talk had become more animated and one or two lively spirits had started a song, but above the noise a voice penetrating although musical was saying loudly, "Marry! Master French, do you never drink aught but rum in the East that a gentleman is kept waiting ten minutes for a cup of sack?"

French's deep tones replied slowly.

"Nay, Captain, very little else but rum; sack be only for gentlefolk."

Anny hastened forward.

"Here's for you, sir," she said briskly, and then stopped, awe-struck before the Spaniard, dazzled by his appearance.

Blackkerchief Dick stretched out a white jewelled hand for the tankard without looking at the girl.

"Thank thee, Mistress," he said carelessly, lifting it to his lips.

Still Anny did not move and Hal Grame, looking up from the rum keg which he was tapping, cursed the Spaniard's clothes with that honest venom which is only known to youth.

"Ah, a good draught!" The Spaniard put down the pot and touched his lips with a lace-edged handkerchief.

"Mistress, another by your leave," he said suddenly. Then his gaze, too, became fixed, his dark eyes taking in every detail of her face.

"God's Fool!" he exclaimed. "Mistress, you are wondrous fair."

Anny blushed and, her senses returning to her, she curtseyed and taking up the empty tankard tripped off with a gentle "As you wish," as she went.

Blackkerchief Dick stared after her for a second or two before he turned to French.

"By my faith, Master French, you have no poor skill in choosing a wench," he said.

Big French laughed and reddened.

"Oh!" he said carelessly, " 'tis not she but the other I would have favour from."

The Spaniard darted a look of misbelief at his big companion, but he said nothing for Anny had returned and was standing before him a brimming tankard in her hand.

Blackkerchief Dick took the wine and set it by untasted, but retained the brown hand which was even smaller than his own, and held it firmly.

"Mistress," he said, and Anny thought she had never seen such bright, merry eyes, "would you deem it an offence if I asked you your name?"

Anny smiled and curtseyed as she pulled away her hand.

"There be no more offence in asking my name than in holding my hand, sir," she said. " 'Tis Anny Farran, an you please so."

"Anny, a good name and a simple," said the Spaniard, choosing to ignore the first remark. "Now tell me, fair Anny," he continued, "hast ever been told how beautiful thou art?"

The girl looked round. No one in the noisy company round the fire was listening to them and a gleam of mischief twinkled in her eyes before she dropped them as she turned again to the Spaniard.

"Nay, sir," she said. "Neither has my mirror."

"Then 'tis a right vile and lying thing, Mistress," said Dick, "for by my knife," here he drew the slender thing from his chased silver belt and held it up to the light, "I never saw a comelier lass than thee."

Anny looked at the knife curiously.

" 'Tis a pretty weapon you have, sir," she said innocently.

Dick laughed.

"Pretty," he said, "Ah, fair Anny, I would not send the blood from those bright cheeks of thine by telling thee what this same dagger and this right hand have together accomplished."

"Oh, never mind the wenches, Captain, let's have the story," said one of the group at the fire, the company's attention having been drawn to the Spaniard on the appearance of the knife. Blackkerchief Dick stood up.

"Sack for everyone," he said grandiloquently as he threw another handful of coins on the trestled table. And then as the tankards were passed round, "To the fairest wench on the Island, Fair Anny of the Ship," he said, lifting his tankard above his head.

The toast was given with a will. The Spaniard was in a fair way to win popularity.

" 'Tis a fine gentleman, Hal," whispered Anny to her sweetheart under cover of the general hubbub.

"Ay, a deal too fine," replied the boy putting a pot down with such violence that all the others rattled and clinked against one another with the shock.

Anny laughed.

"Thou art very foolish, O Hal o' mine," she said softly.

"There be more tales to tell o' this dagger than will suffice for one evening."

The Spaniard's voice was once more raised in a flaunting tone. "Let it be enough," he continued, "to say that it hath some ninety lives to answer for."

There was a general gasp at this information and a slow smile spread over Blackkerchief Dick's face as he noted their amazement.

"It will be wonderful old I reckon?" Joe Pullen put the question quietly, but as though he expected an answer in the affirmative.

"Nay," the Spaniard smiled again, " 'twas of my own killings I was talking," he said.

"Oh!" Joe Pullen leant back and closed his eyes as though bored with the conversation.

This procedure seemed to irritate the Spaniard, for he said suddenly, "Look, friend, 'tis a fair weapon," and he threw the glittering thing at the man in the high-backed seat with a seemingly careless jerk of the wrist. The dagger shot through the air a streak of glistening steel, and fastened itself in the wood half-an-inch above Joe's head.

Sue shrieked, but there was a murmur of admiration at the feat from the men looking on.

Lazily Joe Pullen sat up and wrenched the blade out of the soft wood; he studied the dagger carefully.

"Ah!" he said at last, an expression of polite interest on his face, "a wonderful fine throw that, sir," and then added, the knife poised delicately between a clumsy thumb and forefinger, "I wonder now could I do that?" He raised his hand and appeared to be taking aim directly at the Spaniard's head.

"And was losht in the rolling sea,"

murmured Gilbot; his head fell forward on his chest, and his pot slipping off his knee fell clattering on the stones. The noise woke him and he looked up just in time to see Pullen, knife in hand, standing in the middle of the room.

"Eh? eh?" the old man's voice had the remnant of a note of authority in it. "Put down t' knife, lad. Ain't no good in knives." His head fell forward on his chest again. "Why not shing happy shong?" he mumbled.

Joe grinned. "Ah," he said slowly, "maybe the old n's right." He handed the knife to the Spaniard who took it without a word. "I might have hit you—I ain't a very good hand wi' knives," said Joe pleasantly.

The Spaniard smiled graciously. "Doubtless you will learn," he said, his jauntiness returning, and then continuing, "fair Mistress Anny, will you see these tapped?" and he pointed to five rum kegs which Blueneck, Habakkuk Coot, and one or two others of the *Coldlight's* crew had just brought in. "Rum all round," he said, "and the charge to me."

By the time his last command had been obeyed the company in the Ship was more noisy than before, and, answering to the call for a song, old Gilbot, having been assisted to his feet, leaned his back against the nearest ale barrel and quavered forth in a voice which evidently had once been very tuneful:

"Oh, no one remembers poor Will
Who shtayed by hish mate at the mill;
He ground up more bonesh
Than barley or stonesh,
And more than old Rowley could kill."

"More bones, more bones," roared the company as the rum flowed more freely.

"More bones! more bones!
And more than old Rowley could kill."

"Ah, ha, may the Lord bless ye, fine gentleman, and could ye spare a drop o' rum for a poor woman to take to her man who's dying o' the cold."

This request uttered in a high-pitched whining voice coming from just behind the half-opened door startled the revellers and they paused to listen, all eyes being fastened on the door. They watched it open a little further, and round it just below the latch appeared the head of an old woman. The face, red and coarse, smiled leeringly and the grey elf locks above it were matted and ill-kempt.

Anny, who was standing near Blackkerchief Dick, caught her breath.

"Lord! 'Tis Pet Salt," she whispered as she shrank against the table.

The Spaniard dropped a hand over hers unnoticed by anyone save Hal. "Why shudderest thou, wench?" he said softly. Anny slipped her hand away.

" 'Tis naught," she said.

"Will 'ee spare a little rum, fair gentlemen?"

The old woman came a little further into the room disclosing a body so bent and twisted as to be hardly human. She came nearer, the firelight flickered on her, and a murmur rose from the company, she was so ragged and scarred. The Spaniard looked at her critically, then he turned to French.

"You have strange crones up this part of the Island, friend," he observed.

French laughed.

"Oh, this one won't treat your almsgiving the way Nan Swayle did," he said.

At the sound of the name, Nan Swayle, an extraordinary change came over the terrible old figure in the firelight. She straightened herself with a fearful effort and her small eyes blazing with fury broke forth into such a stream of horrible epithets that the rough company of the Ship looked at one another shamefacedly.

"Peace, hag," the Spaniard strode out from the crowd and touched the old woman with the top of his forefinger.

Pet Salt stopped and seeing the gaudy figure in front of her fell on her knees and holding up a fat, begrimed hand, recommenced her whining.

Dick stood there for a second or two, and then turned his head. "Blueneck," he said, "bring out a small rum keg."

The old woman fell snivelling at his feet.

The Spaniard kicked her gently.

"O mother of many evils," he said, "get thee out of this room with thy keg, methinks the air stinks with thee."

Blueneck stepped forward, jerked the woman to her feet, and put the rum on the floor beside her. Mumbling blessings, thanks, and curses, she stumbled out of the open door, the keg clasped in her arms.

Dick watched her go and then turned to Sue. "Mistress, I would wash my hands," he said, looking at the tip of his forefinger.

Sue ran to get water and the company began to break up for the night.

"Good night to 'ee," shouted Hal, as Joe Pullen went out, "may thy wife be sleeping sound."

"Would she were sleeping with a heavenly soundness, mate," replied the other as he shut the door behind him.

The crew of the *Coldlight* went off in a body to their ship rolling and singing happily.

Sue and Hal assisted the old landlord to his room, a nightly duty of theirs, and Anny flitted about getting candles for the visitors.

Dick looked at Big French as they stood for a moment alone together before the dying fire.

"Methinks thy horses will not have recovered from their lameness by to-morrow, friend French," he said, as Anny, two lighted candles in her hand, appeared at an inner doorway.

French followed the direction of the other's eyes, then he shrugged his broad shoulders.

"As you wish, Captain," he said carelessly, and wondered why the Spaniard should laugh so triumphantly at his answer.

Some minutes later all was still in the Ship Tavern. Hal Grame alone stood before the fast-greying embers in the kitchen, thinking miserably. For the first time since he could remember his childhood's sweetheart had forgotten to kiss him as she bade him good-night.

Chapter V

"An excellent repast, fair Mistress, and one I warrant you well-appreciated."

Blackkerchief Dick pushed the empty platter from before him, leaned back in his seat, and looked round the room with approval.

It was six o'clock in the morning; and although only a faint greyish light was beginning to steal in the windows and the air was cool and slightly rum-tainted, the kitchen in the old Ship Inn presented a cheerful and lively scene of domestic bustle. The fire, though newly-lighted, blazed brightly and the logs, some with the hoar-frost still glittering on them, crackled and spat merrily.

Hal, his boyish face glowing after a hasty splash at the well-nigh frozen pump, hastened to and fro from the scullery to the kitchen, bearing great trays of newly-washed tankards, while Sue, a little paler than on the preceding night, but all the same retaining most of her usual good-humour, her sleeves rolled high above her elbows and a sail-cloth apron tied about her waist, appeared from time to time in the open doorway between the kitchen and the back scullery, whence the pleasant smell of cooking emerged.

Gilbot was yet abed, but his seat with its old hay-stuffed cushions was put in readiness for his coming, in his favourite corner by the fireplace.

One of the long trestle-tables had been pulled out into the wider part of the room clear of the high-backed seats, and it was here, one at either end of the table, that Blackkerchief Dick and Big French sat in tall, wooden, box-like chairs, finishing the first meal of the day.

Anny waited on them.

This morning she was more beautiful than on the evening before. At least so thought the Spaniard as he watched her trip to and fro with a wooden platter, or an earthen pitcher of home-brewed ale in her hands. Her cheeks seemed to him to have more colour in them, her little bare feet, as they pattered over the stones, more elasticity and lightness of touch, and her wonderful, shadowed green eyes, more mirth and gaiety than he had noticed before. As she moved about she sang little snatches of old songs in a lulling, childish voice, tuneful and sweet.

> "My father's gone a roving—a roving—a roving,
> My father's gone a roving across the raging sea,
> With a feather in his stocking cap,
> A new son on his rocking lap,
> My father's gone a roving and never thinks o' me."

The Spaniard's white fingers kept time to the simple refrain almost without his knowing it; he caught himself silently repeating the words after her, and he laughed abruptly and then looked round him so fiercely that none dared ask the jest.

It was absurd, he told himself, he, Blackkerchief Dick, smuggler, chief of all the Eastern coast, Captain of the *Coldlight*, and owner of six other good sailing-vessels in the trade, to waste his time humming tunes after a serving-wench, a pretty lass of some seventeen years, who served rum to a pack of greasy fishermen in a wayside tavern on the almost uninhabited end of a mud Island, when there were women in France, in Spain—he shrugged his shoulders, and to take his thoughts off the girl he ran his mind over the events of the preceding night.

"Friend," he said suddenly, wiping his lips with a dainty handkerchief, "that same woman who so vilely returned my alms yesternight, what say'st thou is her name?"

Big French sat up and yawned.

"Oh!" he said, "that was Nan Swayle."

At the sound of his voice Anny, who had been attending to the fire the other side of the room, came forward and stood at the end of the table looking at the pair with wide-open, serious eyes.

"Nan Swayle," the Spaniard rolled the name round his tongue thoughtfully. "Ah, didst say she had been ducked as a witch?"

Big French laughed.

"Ay," he said, "at the Restoration of the King, and a mirthful figure she made, Captain, her thumbs and great toes tied crossways—so," and he chuckled at the thought of it.

Anny leant forward, her face flushed and her eyes bright. "A cruel jest, Master French, to so ill-treat a poor woman as far from being a witch as you an angel."

Blackkerchief Dick regarded her excited little form and earnest eyes with open admiration.

"Marry, Mistress," he said, "what a friend thou art to Mother Swayle! May I ask what she has done for thee?"

Anny dropped her eyes before the Spaniard's smile.

"She was ever good to me, sir," she said.

Big French grinned.

"Ay, Anny," he said, "Nan Swayle's goodwill is about all which thy grandsire has ever given you, isn't it?"

The girl flushed and Sue and Hal stepped forward to listen.

Dick looked puzzled.

"Thy grandsire, Mistress?" he enquired.

Anny reddened again.

"'Tis an old story, sir," she murmured.

"Prithee, Master French," the Spaniard turned lazily and looked at the young man. "Prithee tell it."

French shrugged his shoulders.

"'Tis naught," he said carelessly, "save that in their youth old Ben Farran—the lass's grandsire—and Nan Swayle, a sweet wench they say she was then—'tis strange what rum will do to a woman's face—well, Captain, they were, as you might say, sweethearts."

He raised his eyes to Sue at the last word, but she was engrossed in the Spaniard, and looking away again he went on. "Well,

Captain, Ben was a sailor—on the *Eliza* he was—and there he got the taste for rum pretty bad, and Nan, she couldn't get the stuff for him so when Pet Salt came along—Pet o' the Saltings she was then with her begging tricks—the old devil left the one for the other. That's all," he concluded.

"Ah!" the Spaniard smiled, "a pretty story," and then turning to Anny, "and so, Mistress, Nan Swayle hath a soft heart for thee, eh?"

"Ay, sir, she is very good to Red and me," Anny said demurely.

"Red? and who might Red be?" The Spaniard looked up quickly. "A lover?"

Anny blushed again.

"Nay, sir, my little brother," she said softly. "He lives with Mother Swayle."

"So!" the thin, straight eyebrows on the olive brow rose in two arches. "I thought thy mother died when thou wast born?"

Big French broke in quickly.

"Ay," he said, "she did. The lad, Red, a fine child, and one I love, was brought home from the South by young Ruddy, the wench's father, the trip before his last—drowned he was, peace to him."

"Oh!" the eyebrows straightened themselves. Blackkerchief Dick turned once more to Anny. "And so my little beauty hath only Nan Swayle to take care of her," he said smiling at her kindly as though she had been a child.

"Nay!" The word escaped from Hal Grame's lips before he had time to stop it. Immediately the Spaniard's glittering black eyes were turned on the young Norseman. They took in every detail of his appearance, the coarse scarlet homespun shirt, the white throat, and girlish pink and white face crowned with golden-yellow elf locks, and the deep blue eyes which faltered and fell before the Spaniard's as they bent on the boy in an amused stare.

"Indeed, sir, and who else?" Blackkerchief Dick spoke negligently, the smile still on his lips.

The boy blushed and would not meet the other's eyes.

"We look after our wenches at the Ship," he said gruffly.

Dick laughed.

"Of course you do, O knight of the spigot," he said genially. "Believe me, sir, I had no meaning to cast a slur upon the fame of your house."

"Ah, 'tis well, then," and without looking up Hal began to clear away the delf from the now dismantled table.

Dick watched him march off with a tray of dirty crockery in his hands, then he shrugged his shoulders.

"Marry, what a joskin!" he said at last.

Anny opened her mouth to speak but checked herself and laughed instead.

Dick looked up at her.

"Mistress," he said, "might I beg thee to hie to the gate and tell me if thou see'st aught of my rapscallion mate, Master Blueneck?"

"Ay, sir."

Anny was half-way to the door when Sue ran after her.

"I'll with thee," she said.

Dick looked after them.

"A marvellous pretty wench but wondrous evilly-clothed," he said.

"What, Sue?" Big French spoke in great surprise. The Spaniard smiled.

"Cunning dog," he said under his breath. "Nay, 'twas the other I meant," he said quietly.

"Oh!" Big French laughed. "The lass has to wear her mistress' cast-off," he said.

"Indeed. Her mistress'? Is Sue, then, mistress of the Ship?"

"Mistress Sue," said French, laying stress on the first word, "is niece to Master Gilbot."

"Eh? eh? What's that?" said Gilbot, who had just come in, looking up at the sound of his name. "Plague on you all disturbing me." And then, looking round, "Where's Hal?"

"You are out of humour this morning, host," observed the Spaniard good-humouredly.

"No." Gilbot's voice quavered more than ever. "Ain't had time to get happy yet, that's all."

"Oh!" Dick looked up, his eyes twinkling merrily. "Will you drink a stoup of sack with me, mine host?"

Gilbot brightened visibly.

"Be happy to," he said quickly, and then called loudly for Hal, who presently came in flushed and still a little sulky.

Dick gave the order, and the boy obeyed, sullenly, slopping a good gill of the wine over the side of the tankard, as he handed it to the Spaniard. Then suddenly, as though realizing the absurdity of his childishness, he drew it back, and, mumbling something about not quite the full measure, filled it up again, wiped the pewter with the skirt of his sacking apron before he once more offered it to the Spaniard, who stood looking through the open door without apparently having noticed the boy at all. Now, however, he took the tankard, drained it at a draught, and threw down a silver coin by way of payment.

"Marry, master tapster," he said approvingly, "I do not look to find a sweeter cup of sack any place from here to the New World—another I prithee," and added, as Hal set it before him, "An' I grow this partiality for sweet sack, Hal, methinks I shall needs have to borrow the belt of that merry knight, John Falstaff, whom I saw in a foolish piece at the playhouse when last I visited London, that city of evil stenches."

Hal did not follow the jest, but in spite of this and his present ill-humour, he was forced to laugh with the spry little Spaniard who chuckled so mirthfully, and whose bright, sparkling eyes were dancing as they glanced at him over the tankard's rim.

At this moment Anny entered the kitchen and Dick seeing her raised his rumkin.

"To the health of Mother Swayle's charge," he said smiling.

Gilbot looked up suddenly.

"Mother Swayle?" he said in surprise, and then added confidentially to Dick, "Terrible old woman—in liquor nearly all the day—oh disgusting." He finished his draught, smacked his lips, and wiped them with the back of his hand. "Ah, you're right, sir, wonderful sack we sells," he remarked.

The Spaniard suggested that he should take another and Gilbot cheerfully accepted.

"Master Blueneck is coming up the road, an' it please you, sir," said Sue, coming in from the courtyard.

"Ah, I thank thee, Mistress," said the Spaniard courteously as he turned to help Anny lift an unusually heavy log on to the crackling fire, but Sue curtseyed and blushed as though he had looked at her with the same fire in his glance as lurked in the one which he bestowed on the younger girl, and her lip trembled as he turned away. All this which he saw and a great deal more which he thought he saw made Master Ezekiel French bite his honey-coloured beard and swear many oaths and curses against the slim, white-handed little foreigner who chatted so gallantly with the wenches of the Ship.

Blueneck entering at this moment was surprised to see his master talking so earnestly with a chit of a child who, as he rightly guessed, had not more than seventeen years to her credit.

"The brig is due to start in five minutes if we mean to catch the tide, Captain," he said.

"Ah, Master Blueneck," the Spaniard turned affably, "and if we missed the tide what terrible mishap would that be?"

The sailor shuffled uneasily.

"You're merry, Captain," he said.

"Ay, Blueneck, I am, indeed, so merry that I cannot abear to have a man with a face as long as the yard-arm about me. Here, my young host," he hailed Hal from the fireplace. "Give this dog some of thy famous sack, make him light-hearted as I." And he turned once more to the two girls and Big French.

"Master French," he said, "I trust to meet thee at the Victory this even, with thy three horses in the courtyard, and a trip to Tiptree in thy mind."

French looked pleased and would have entered into business details with the Captain, but the other cut him short.

"Marry, Master French," the Spaniard's tone was reproachful, "you would not pester me with tales of rum kegs and silk bales when I have but three minutes to bid farewell to two fair beauties even though it be but for three days."

"Three days?" Sue spoke in pleasure, French in surprise, and Blueneck in genuine alarm.

The Spaniard looked up.

"Yes," he said carelessly, "methinks this Eastern end of the

Island more suited to my needs than the West. In three days' time I shall return, and rest me at the sign of the Ship for a while."

Big French looked at him in amazement and Blueneck swore under his breath at his master's eccentricities.

Sue smiled.

"All will be ready for you, sir," she said. "I thank you."

The Spaniard bowed, sweeping the floor with his big hat. "Farewell, Mistresses," he said gallantly as they curtseyed, rather abashed at his Spanish courtesy.

"And now, Master French," he continued, "if thou wilt accompany me to the wall we will discuss that little matter of a trip to Tiptree."

French looked at the debonair little figure half-irritated by the underlying note of command in his voice, but on the other hand half-charmed by an indescribable air of perfect freedom which seemed to be exhaled from him.

"I'm coming, Captain," he said, and nodded to the girls before he turned to follow Blackkerchief Dick, who with another bow marched out of the open door, Blueneck after him.

Sue went to the door and watched them going down the road; Big French, a handsome figure in his blue coat, strode beside the slight, gaudily-clad little Spaniard whose head hardly reached a foot above the carter's belt, while Blueneck trudged alone behind. "Ah," said she, her eyes fixed on the small almost insignificant figure in the distance, "what a gallant gentleman!"

Anny laughed.

"Maybe," she said, "but I don't hold with gentlefolk," and she walked across the room to where Hal was adding up the yesterday's reckonings.

"Hal," she said, as she sat down beside him, "I did not kiss thee last night when you bade me goodnight."

Hal kept his eyes fixed on the slate in front of him, but he ceased to take any account of the figures thereon.

"Hal," said Anny again coaxingly. "Thou didst not kiss me when I said good-night to thee."

The boy did not raise his eyes and the girl moved a little closer to him.

"Hal," she said plaintively. Still he did not move. "Hal," said Anny again—"Oh, very well," she added, a catch in her voice, "if thou wilt not——" and she rose to her feet.

"What do you want, maid?" said Hal gruffly, albeit somewhat hastily.

Anny sat down again.

"I owe you a kiss, Hal," she said softly, twisting her fingers together as they lay on her lap.

"Well?" Hal's tone was still gruff.

"You owe me a kiss, Hal," she said without looking at him.

"Well?" The boy drew crosses and rings round the side of the slate.

Anny sighed.

"You were adding the reckonings, Hal, and I want to pay mine," she said.

"I'm sorry I doubted thee, Anny, but the Spaniard is so fine," said Hal, a moment or two later, all debts having been squared.

Anny laughed happily.

"'Tis not you but Big French who should be afeared of the Spaniard," she said, looking over towards Sue who was still staring through the open door.

As though aware that she was being spoken of the girl turned round.

"Anny, lass," she called. "Come, I would talk to thee."

Anny rose.

"Foolish one," she whispered to Hal as her lips brushed his ear.

Hal watched her go lightly across the room and then returned to his reckoning much comforted, but he reflected as he worked that whether she had paid him back or not Anny Farran had certainly forgotten to kiss him on the night that Dick Delfazio, the Spaniard, first came to the Ship Inn.

Meanwhile Sue and Anny stood together in the doorway deep in talk.

"But, Anny," Sue was saying, as she held out the skirt of her gown for the other's inspection, "think you 'twill serve another wintertide?"

Anny looked at it for a moment; then she displayed her own.

" 'Tis much better than mine, Mistress Sue," she said.

"Oh! but you need not look so neat as I," Sue spoke quickly and without thinking. But, seeing the other girl's lip tremble, she put an arm round her slim shoulders.

"Nay, I did not mean to speak so," she said kindly, "I was thinking but of myself; see, lass, when Master French next goes to Tiptree he shall bring me a new length of flannel from the market, and I will give thee this gown for, truly, thine is very old."

Anny looked up and smiled; the gift of one of Sue's old gowns was an event for her.

"Thank thee kindly, Mistress," she said, as Sue shook out the folds of the faded purple homespun frock and tightened the lacing of the corsage.

" 'Tis not so bad," she said.

Anny looked at it with pleasure and she laughed happily. "Nay," she said, "it will suit me well, I thank you, Mistress."

Sue bent and kissed her.

"You're a good wench, Anny," she said, "in spite of yourself."

Chapter VI

"Sit where you are, Joseph Pullen, and hold your peace, and be thankful you have a wife who knows your mind without you for ever speaking of it."

Mistress Amy Pullen, her kirtle hitched up at one side to give her greater freedom in the discharge of her household duties, strode across her small kitchen, an earthenware bowl of cold, fatty broth in her hands, and two small children hanging at her petticoats.

The kitchen, which was very small, served also as a general living-room for the Pullen family, and this evening, four or five days after Captain Dick had first left the Ship Inn, it was crowded. Joe, debarred from his favourite seat by his wife, who liked the whole of the fire to cook at, sat in a corner on a heap of miscellaneous lumber, a net which he was mending spread around him. In addition to the two little mites who hung on to their mother as though life itself depended on it, three other children were in the room: one baby of a year or so was nursed by another, a pretty, fair-haired little girl of eight or nine, who sat on a roughly made-up bed built into the wall opposite the fireplace. She amused the child by making quaint shadows on the wall with her hand in the flickering twilight, and save for the clatter of the cooking, the baby's happy gurgles and half-spoken words of delight were the only sounds in the warm little room. The third child, a boy of ten, even now remarkably like his father, sat on the lowest rung of a wide wooden ladder, which led to two little rooms above the kitchen, with a skip of small onions at his side and a knife in his hand. As he peeled the onions the tears ran down his cheeks and he sniffed at intervals.

Joe looked up over his net at the boy.

"Tant, hold thy peace," he said.

The child sniffed again.

"I can't hold it, 'tis these," he said, wiping his eyes on his jersey sleeve, and indicating the skip with one dirty little foot. Joe grunted and the child went on peeling, his tears falling faster and his sniffs becoming more and more frequent. At last Joe looked up again.

"Put down the knife, lad, and leave the onions if you can't peel them without setting up a snort like a hog every other second."

The boy, only too glad to be relieved of his task, obeyed with alacrity, and got up looking lovingly at the unlatched door that led out on to the road. He had not made a step in that direction, however, before his mother, who had been listening, turned from the fire. "Tant, sit down and finish them onions," she said sharply, and then turning to her husband who was assiduously attending to his net, she said, "Isn't it enough, Joe Pullen, for me to wear myself to skin and bone feeding you, looking after your children, cleaning your home? Isn't it enough I say for me to do everything for you, to work like a common drudge, to keep you idle, without you forbidding my son to help me?"

Her voice grew more and more shrill, and her words came faster and faster until her speech became almost unintelligible.

Joe looked up cautiously from his work.

"O peace with ye, Amy," he said impatiently, the easily-called colour mounting up to his fair hair and his blue eyes growing darker.

"Ay, that's it."

Mistress Pullen was a tall, well-made woman, and her eyes screwed themselves into slits of fury as she swung round, platter in hand, upsetting both children at her skirts, who began at once to whimper with fear.

"Ay, that's it, I must hold my peace! I, who slave day and night to make you happy, must hold my peace! Hold my peace forsooth!" she continued, breaking into a sharp laugh. "Look you, Joe Pullen, where would you and your children be without me? Tell me that.

Oh! you sithering rat, you ungrateful mass of rum-sodden food, where would you be without me?"

Joe vouchsafed no answer and the good lady, her wrath abating as suddenly as it had arisen, contented herself with a few muttered questions as to the possibility of Joe and his family remaining for an instant on the earth without her, turned again to the fire, shaking off the yelping little ones who tried to clasp her knees.

Tant continued to sniff over his onion peeling unmolested.

Called by her mother, the little fair-haired girl, who played so happily with the baby, left her game and, placing her charge carefully on the bed, set out six earthen bowls on the plain boarded table, which took up most of the space in the middle of the little room, and summoned the family to supper. Not until every one was seated did Mistress Pullen lift the great iron pot off the hook on the chimney beam and, resting it on the edge of the table, dole out to each person an allowance, which varied in quantity according to age. In the same way she distributed chunks of coarse home-made bread, and then seeing everyone served finally she sat down to her own meal.

The Pullens ate without speaking, quickly, noisily, and with evident relish, dipping the bread in the broth and eating the sodden lumps with their fingers. Mistress Amy held the baby on her lap, feeding the little creature with sops from her own bowl.

When all the broth had been disposed of, more bread and an earthen jar of honey was brought out and the meal continued.

Inside the little kitchen all was warm, one might almost say stuffy, for, in spite of the big fire and the number of people inside, the door was shut fast and the one little window which the room possessed was not made to open. However, the noise that the rain, swiftly driven over the marshlands by a fierce wind, made on the glass, and the hissing drops that descended the wide chimney, all helped to make the kitchen as desirable as it could be.

"Joan Bellamie was a-saying that the Captain of the *Coldlight* hath come back to the Ship, Joseph. Have ye heard aught of it?" Mistress Pullen looked across the table at her husband as she spoke.

Joe dropped his eyes before her gaze.

"Oh, yes," he said casually.

"Oh, yes, indeed!" Amy's voice rose again. "And ye did not think to tell me, did ye? Here I work the live-long day, and you so surly that you will not tell me the common gossip of the Island! I'd like to meet another woman who'd rest with ye." Then she added more quietly. "Did any of his crew return with him, perchance?"

Joe shifted uneasily in his chair, and reached out for another piece of bread before he spoke.

"They did not," he said shortly.

Mistress Pullen took a deep breath.

"And to think I have lived with a liar fit for the burning all these years!" she exclaimed. "For it was only this very day that I saw Master Coot (and if ever there was a snivelling sucking-pig 'tis he), with my very own eyes and he told me that the brig was that minute moored in the Pyfleet, and every man of her crew aboard. I'm ashamed of ye, Joseph, to lie before the children the way you do."

Joe shrugged his shoulders.

"Ah, well, my girl," he said significantly, "as far as we're concerned they ain't on the Island, see?" And he rose to his feet and stepped across to the fireplace.

Mistress Pullen opened her mouth to reply, but at this moment a violent knocking at the door interrupted her.

Joe looked across at his wife.

"Whoever will it be?" he said.

"If you had any sense at all you'd go and see instead of standing like a sheep thunderstruck," said the lady, getting up from her seat, her baby on her arm. Striding over to the door, she opened it wide and then stepped back in astonishment, letting a blast of cold wind and rain into the overheated room.

"Well, come in whatever you are," she said at last to someone outside as she held the door wide open to let them pass. "If you're not welcome ye can always go again."

A strange bedraggled little figure stepped into the candlelit room. He was about nine years old, scantily clothed in a pair of sail-cloth breeches, so large for him that the waist was fastened about his neck with a coarse string, and the knee-latchets flapped loosely over his little bare muddy feet, which were torn and scratched with thorns, and blue with cold. Round his shoulders he hugged what appeared to be the remains of a woman's kirtle, the ragged hem hanging down to his knees and little rivulets of water dripping off the frayed ends on to the bricks. His face was like his feet, blue and muddy, but two sparkling blue eyes and a shock of red hair gave a certain charm to an otherwise insignificant countenance.

Mistress Pullen shut the door behind him before she turned to look at her visitor. As soon as she had done so, however, she whisked her baby over to the other side of the room, exclaiming as she did so, "Mother of Heaven! 'Tis Red Farran, the witch's brat. Out of the house with him. He can't stay here bewitching the whole of us."

The little creature looked up at her, his face puckering. "Not a witch's brat," he said, and then putting his grimy little fists to his eyes began to cry bitterly.

Joe Pullen's fair-haired daughter made a step towards the pitiful little figure, but her father's hand on her arm restrained her.

"You stay still, Alice, unless you want to wake up one day and find yourself a grey girl or a coney," he said.

Alice obeyed, rather frightened, and Tant stood by her, his arm round her, while the two smaller children hung as usual to their mother's skirts. The whole Pullen family entrenched behind the table stood looking at the weeping little stranger for some seconds before anyone spoke again. At last Joe, his natural kindliness overcoming his superstitious fears, stepped round the table and took the child by the hand.

"Why did ye leave Nan's cabin, this time o' night, lad?" he asked him.

The boy looked fearfully behind him, and Joe, noting the movement, himself turned round in some apprehension. However, nothing untoward being there, Red began to speak through his sobs.

"Pet Salt and Nan is fightin' horrid," he said.

Mistress Pullen, her curiosity getting the better of her discretion, came a little nearer.

"Pet Salt?" she said. "How did Pet Salt come to be up there?"

"She comed to beg some meal-cake," the child began. "She said she wanted it for Ben."

"Oh!" Mistress Pullen sniffed and looked at her husband significantly. "And wasn't it for Ben, manikin?" she said.

The child looked up.

"No," he said eagerly. "No, that's why they is fighting, Mistress, because 'twas not for my grandsire. No, Nan saw the old ronyon eating it herself."

Joe threw back his head and began to laugh.

"Oh! ho! and did you run away because the two crones were fighting, lad?" he said.

The child nodded and his tears began to flow again. "And they's hurt Win?" he blurted out.

"Win? Who's Win?" said Joe curiously.

"Oh, peace with you worrying the brat," said Amy. "Prithee, child, did Nan Swayle lay hands on Pet Salt because she had eaten the meal-cake Nan had made for thy grandsire?" she questioned eagerly.

The child shook his head.

"No, Mistress, 'twas not made for grandsire, 'twas all we had left, but Nan said that if Ben wanted it he must have it and we go hungry. So she was vexed at the ronyon's eating of it herself."

"Oh! art hungry now?" the question escaped Joe's lips before he had time to stop it.

The child looked up eagerly.

"Ay," he said, his eyes straying to the remains of the food on the table. "Ay, will ye give me some?"

Joe immediately stretched his hand for the remnant of the loaf of bread and the child's face brightened with expectation, but Mistress Pullen stepped forward.

"Mother of Saints! have I wedded a loon? Would ye have the household entirely bewitched, Joseph Pullen, that you'd feed a witch-child under our very roof?" she said, as she snatched the bread from his hand and replaced it on the table.

Joe looked sheepish and little Red began to cry again. Mistress Pullen reddened and sniffed fiercely.

"If he hungers he better go to his sister at the Ship," she said tartly. "Heaven knows what with her Captain and her other men she ought to glean enough to look after her brother."

Joe turned on his wife in honest indignation.

"Amy! how dare ye speak so of Hal Grame's lass?" he said. "I'm not going to have my mate's sweetheart spoke of so."

Mistress Pullen shrugged her shoulders.

"Maybe you like the lass yourself," she sneered, and then added fiercely, "anyway, you ought to be ashamed of yourself letting a witch's brat stay in the room with your own children. Out of the house with him, you loony."

Joe looked at the forlorn little boy and then at his wife.

"Maybe I better go with the child," he suggested casually.

Mistress Pullen turned on him, withering contempt in her glance.

"Ay," she said, "maybe you had. Lord, what an unnatural beast you are preferring to go to a rumshop in the company of a bastard brat, than to rest in peace at your own fireside. Oh, go by all means and the devil with you. You fool, do you think Nan Swayle has forgiven the ducking you gave her at the Restoring of the King?"

And with this parting shaft, Mistress Pullen, baby on arm, strode across the kitchen and climbed up the wide ladder to the rooms above.

Joe looked about him undecidedly. Then his glance fell on the boy.

"Who's Win?" he asked, suddenly remembering his question of a minute or two before.

The little boy began to cry again, and opening his kirtle-cloak, disclosed to the fisherman's astounded eyes a little black kitten nearly dead with fright and drenched with rain.

"This is Win," said Red, "him's hurt!"

Joe stepped back in horror.

"The witch's cat," he ejaculated.

Red looked up.

"No!" he said, "only a little one, look, only a very little one." He held it up for Joe's inspection. It certainly looked a very small and harmless animal. It was much too frightened to move, and the wet fur clung closely to its emaciated body.

Joe came a little nearer and then reached for his coat and cap which hung behind the door.

"Come, lad," he said gruffly, "we must get on to the Ship."

The child looked round the warm, bright room longingly, but he followed Joe out into the rain without a word.

The man carefully latched the door behind him, and they walked on in silence for a minute or so fighting their way against the storm.

It was bitterly cold, and Joe looked down at his little companion anxiously; the child was stumbling along, the kitten tightly clasped in his arms; once or twice he nearly fell.

Joe looked round him cautiously, although had there been any-one by they could not have been seen, then he bent down.

"You'll not tell Nan if I carry ye a bit, lad?" he asked. The child promised eagerly, and Joe swung him up in his arms.

"Here," he said, pressing a soft lump into the child's hands. "Even if you're a witch's brat ye mustn't be hungered."

Red bit into the bread that Joe had slipped into his pocket in his wife's absence, and hugged the well-nigh suffocated kitten a little closer to his breast, while Joe, his head bent before the wind and rain, pushed on to the Ship.

Chapter VII

A little more than an hour after Joe Pullen and little Red Farran left the cottage, Mistress Amy sat by the fireside, sewing. The five children were asleep upstairs and everything was quiet. Opposite her in the chimney corner, his heavy rain-sodden boots smoking in the heat, sat Blueneck, his unshaven chin resting in his hands. On the table lay the woollen cap and heavy coat which he had thrown off on entering. The water which dripped off the skirts of the coat made a little puddle on the clean red and yellow bricks of the floor.

"You're a kind man, Master Blueneck, to come trudging all this way in the soaking rain to cheer a poor woman whose husband is too surly to tell her of the doings of the Island," said the lady looking up from her mending, after a silence of a few minutes.

"Ah, Senora."

Mistress Pullen blushed with pleasure at the sound of the foreign address.

"Where on the Island is better company than yourself?" said the sailor gallantly, leaning a little forward so that the firelight played on the brass earrings that shone amongst the short oily curls hanging down the sides of his face.

Mistress Pullen giggled and applied herself industriously to her needlework.

"I warrant me you're not so well served at the Ship as you were at the Victory, Master Blueneck?" she said without looking up.

Blueneck laughed bitterly.

"You're right, Mistress," he said, forgetting the "Senora" to Amy's disappointment. "The Ship is none so bad a tavern, as taverns are nowadays, but 'tis of a truth much inferior to the Victory."

"I wonder that the Captain rests him there then?" said Mistress Amy, glancing under her lashes at her visitor.

"Marry, so do I." Blueneck's tone was almost querulous. "Why look you, Mistress," he added, "is it not bad for our trade for us to tarry so long at one place, ay, more especially when 'tis here in the East where the creeks are as unknown to us as to the excise men themselves?"

"Of a truth 'tis bad indeed," Mistress Pullen spoke with conviction, "I wonder the Captain has it so," she remarked, again glancing sideways at him.

Blueneck looked into the fire for a moment before he spoke. "Methinks the Captain is bewitched," he said at last.

"Bewitched!" Mistress Amy, her thoughts flying at once to her other visitor of the evening, spoke in some alarm.

Blueneck shrugged his shoulders.

"Anyway, I never saw him so before," he said, "and I've sailed aboard his ship these ten years."

"But whoever would bewitch him?" asked Mistress Pullen looking up innocently, as though no hint of the affairs of the Ship had reached her.

"A marvellous pretty wench," said Blueneck, and then he added hastily, "but of no comparison with thee, Senora."

Mistress Amy laughed.

" 'Tis a flatterer you are," she said, "but I never heard of a pretty wench of the Ship, Master Blueneck; will she be one of the Island girls?"

Blueneck looked up.

"Ay," he said, " 'tis a lass called Anny Farran."

"Oh!" Mistress Pullen's eyebrows rose, and she pursed up her lips. "That child!"

Blueneck looked at her curiously.

"Hast heard aught against the lass?" he asked.

Amy looked about her carefully, then leaning a little forward opened her mouth as though to speak, but as though another thought had crossed her mind she drew back and shaking her head said piously, "But who am I to take away a poor slut's character? 'Tis not my nature, and I pray you, Master Blueneck, that you will not urge me, for my very conscience revolts against it." She paused. "Though, mind you, I could an I would," she went on, "but then, as I said, the story will do the lass no good."

"You make me curious, Senora," said the sailor in his best manner.

But Mistress Pullen for a very good reason, namely, that she could not think of a convincing story on the spot, was not to be prevailed on, and the conversation flagged for a time. At last she broke the silence.

"Then the Captain of the *Coldlight* is much attracted by this—this—this wench?" she asked.

"Attracted!" Blueneck looked up excitedly. "I tell you, Mistress, I never saw him so before—of course, you will understand, Senora, there have been other women—how could there not be? But never has it been so that he has lost his delight in the trade. No," he added, "it has not been like this these last ten years, and before then he was but a lad. Without doubt the maid has bewitched him."

Mistress Pullen began to be interested.

"Have there been very many other women who loved the gallant Captain?" she said, her respect for the Spaniard growing at every word.

Blueneck threw up his hands.

"So many, Mistress, I could not name them all."

Mistress Amy thrilled with interest, but her face fell at her next thought.

"And now he is enamoured with an Island wench?" she said, feeling that the Captain had somehow lowered his standard of romance.

"Ay," said Blueneck, "but 'tis a new affair this time; before it was the wenches who sighed for the Captain and the Captain who laughed and was merry, but this time it is the wench who is merry and the Captain——" he laughed, "oh, the Captain is bewitched," he said.

"Indeed!" Mistress Pullen looked surprised. "I wonder that Mistress Sue would brook the affair in her uncle's house."

"Ho! ho! ho!" Blueneck laughed, his earrings glittering in the firelight. "Mistress Sue? Why, Mistress Amy, that lass would give her ears to get a fair look from Blackkerchief Dick. I warrant you Master French is well-nigh mad at her neglect."

Mistress Pullen sighed at the waywardness of youth and went on with her sewing.

"Ah, and that's another thing," said Blueneck. "Did you know that Master French was prevented from going to Tiptree last Tuesday?"

"Prevented! Were there excise men on the Stroud?" Mistress Amy spoke quickly, voicing the fear of all the Island smugglers.

The Stroud, a narrow bridge-like road across the mud, was the one connection the Island had with the mainland, and once the officers of the law held it, there was no telling what dangers would be involved.

Blueneck smiled.

"Nay," he said, "they will be as foolish as ever they were. Nay, there was some talk about the goods, and the Captain swore that he would not rest another night at the Victory, and that if Master French wanted aught from him he must come to the Ship and fetch it. So he had to return."

"Indeed, and when will he be going again, Master Blueneck? for I was wishing to get me a piece of ribbon for my new kirtle-top," said Mistress Pullen, her interest reviving.

The Spaniard looked at her smiling. "Would you allow me to get it for you, Senora?" he said in as exact imitation as he could manage of the Captain's manner.

Mistress Amy looked at him in surprise.

"Why surely you're not going to Tiptree, Master Blueneck, are you?" she said.

"I would go to London, if you wished aught from thence, Mistress," said the sailor loftily.

Amy looked at him in admiration. "If only Joe would speak so," she reflected.

The sailor seeing the impression he had made rose to his feet, narrowly escaping the chimney beam.

"To-morrow," he said, "I shall ride to Tiptree and bring the fairest dame in the Island a ribbon," he reached for his cap and coat and buttoning them on made for the door.

Amy followed him, thanking him. They exchanged farewells, Mistress Pullen blushingly consenting to a kiss, and parted.

As soon as his footsteps had died away, Mistress Pullen slipped a cloak over her head and moved to the window, through which she could see a faint patch of light about two hundred yards away.

"Ah!" she said to herself, "Joan Bellamie will be yet awake, what a deal I have to tell the ronyon," and she slipped out, shutting the door behind her.

Chapter VIII

"Anny, lass, I would speak with thee; wilt harken?"

Hal put the question timidly as he looked across at his sweetheart.

They were alone in the Ship's kitchen; Hal re-sanded the floor while Anny sat on the window-ledge cleaning a pair of old brass candlesticks. It was four o'clock in the afternoon, and the cold, watery sun shot a few last rays of yellow light over the Island before it sank down behind the mainland. Inside the kitchen it was warm and beginning to get dark, for the fire had been allowed to die down to a few smouldering red and white embers, and it was yet too early to light the dips. Outside in the yard Anny could see her little brother talking to old Gilbot, who had wrapped himself up in a seaman's jacket, and had stepped out to taste the air.

The old man was fond of children, and Anny sighed with relief as she saw the strange pair—Red still wore his costume of the night before—take hands and after some animated talk walk off together down the road in the direction of the sea, laughing as they went.

Hal made up the fire with logs which he had been drying on the hearth, crossed the room and stood beside the window-ledge just in front of the girl, before he spoke again.

"Will you harken to me?" he repeated.

Anny looked up smiling. "Harken to thee, Hal?" she said.

"Why certes, thou needst not look so solemnly; why should I not harken to thee?"

The boy did not speak for a moment but stood fidgeting before her.

Anny put down the candlestick which she was cleaning, and slipping off the window-ledge led him over to the fireplace, where she sat down on one of the long, high-backed seats and pulled him down beside her.

"Do you want to tell me you don't want to marry me?" she asked half-jestingly, half-anxiously, as she leaned her little round head with its long black plaits on his shoulder.

Hal turned to her in great astonishment.

"Marry, lass! How can ye be so cruel as to judge me so?" he said. "Of course not!"

"Oh, the saints be praised for that," said the girl quaintly. "Lord, how you fear'd me, Hal," she added, kneeling up on the seat to kiss him.

The boy put his arm round her.

"Anny," he said quietly, his face grave and old for one of his years, "you're terrible young yet, seventeen ain't you?" The girl nodded, uncertain as to what was coming yet. "Ah! well, you ain't had time to grow wise, have you?" he continued, still holding her on the seat beside him.

"I reckon you ain't had much more, Hal," she said laughing. "You're but eighteen, ain't you?"

Hal blushed.

"Ay, maybe," he said, "but I know what I'm telling you."

Anny kissed him lightly on the forehead.

"I'm harkening," she said.

Hal opened his mouth to speak and then shut it again; then he withdrew his arm from about her waist and stood up.

Anny looked at him in astonishment not unmixed with fear.

"Why, what in the world is the matter with ye, lad?" she said. "You don't want to go for a sailor, do you?"

The boy shook his head violently, and Anny began to feel alarmed.

"Whatever will you be worrying about next?" she said.

Hal stepped towards her, and, putting a hand on her forehead, pushed her head back until she looked into his eyes.

"You—you—you're not loving the Spaniard, lass?" he blurted out, ashamed of the words as soon as he had spoken them.

Anny looked at him for a moment uncertain whether to be offended or to laugh.

"Hal, I'm ashamed that you should be such a child" she said, a little smile hovering round her mouth. "Why should I love anyone but you?"

The boy appeared to be satisfied for he laughed and kissed her, but then he added, "I don't like the Spaniard, lass. I wish you wouldn't hark to his swaggerings."

Anny turned round.

"Hal, you wouldn't have me ill-tempered to the customers?" she said, as she picked up the half-cleaned candlestick and set to work on it again.

Hal thrust his hands into his pockets and shifted his weight from one foot to the other.

"Nay, lass, of course not. I would not bid you be uncivil, but truth, I thought you liked the foreigner's big talk and notice of you. I——"

"He is a pleasant gentleman," said the girl, "but, lord! I mark not half he says."

"You'd not let him kiss you, Anny?"

Hal spoke sharply and Anny looked up in amazement.

"Mother of Grace," she ejaculated, "for what do you take me?"

The boy was beside her in a moment.

"Forgive me, lass," he said, "I did but want ye to promise to have no dealings with the foreigner—I—love you so, see?"

"Oh!" said Anny laughing as she straightened her hair after his embrace. "No one would suspect you of kissing a lass before, Hal. You can't be knowing how strong you are."

"That's as may be, but will you promise to have no truck with the Spaniard?" the boy persisted.

"Ay, of course I promise," Anny sighed at his distrust as she spoke. Hal kissed her again, then walked over to the fireplace and stood for some moments, resting his head on the wooden ledge below the chimney-piece and staring down into the smoky, crackling fire.

He felt that he had appeared ridiculous in Anny's eyes and his young blood revolted at the thought. In vain he tried to comfort himself with the thought that it was only his love for her which made him so anxious, but the idea that she must think him merely jealous would force itself on his mind making him uncomfortable. However, he knew that the Captain might be a formidable rival so he said nothing else at the time.

Anny sat on the window-ledge, rubbing the candlestick with more energy than was necessary.

She was hurt that Hal should think her such a light-o'-love, but all the same she thrilled with pleasure to think that he was jealous of anybody because of her. It gave her such a pleasant feeling of ownership and, as she reflected happily, she was very fond of him.

Suddenly she paused to listen. Coming down the road she could hear the scrunching of heavy waggon wheels. She looked up at the old horologe on the chimney-piece.

"That won't be Master French yet awhile; will it?" she said.

"Eh?" Hal pushed his hand over his forehead and turned to her.

"I don't hear anyone," he said, "and it wouldn't be him yet; the roads ain't safe before dark nowadays."

Anny sat still for a moment.

"There is someone," she cried, as a tumbril drawn by a piebald gelding turned into the yard.

Hal stepped across to the window and looked out over the girl's head.

"Oh! 'tis Cip de Musset," he said, as the man in the tumbril climbed out and pushed back the oiled flaps of his head-covering from his face. "I warrant he brings the rum from the brig." He opened the door and went out bare-headed into the yard.

Anny watched him through the window, saw him greet the man heartily, and then look into the cart at the other's invitation.

"Right!" she heard him say. "Six of rum and three of canary. Here, John Patten."

A man came out of one of the stables. Hal said something to him which she could not catch. The man nodded and led the horse into a corner of the yard, where he proceeded to unload the cart.

The man of whom Hal had spoken as Cip de Musset was tall,

long-legged, and loosely built, with a black beard which curled down on to his chest. He stepped up to the inner door with Hal, and then stopped and went back to the cart as though he had forgotten something. After groping under the sacking coverings for a while he pulled out a fair-sized bundle tied up in a piece of sail-cloth, and with this under his arm, came back to the door where Hal was waiting for him. As he crossed the yard he caught sight of Anny peering through the window and smiled at her, showing a set of enormous yellow teeth.

Anny tossed her head and turned away from the window and picking up the two candlesticks carried them off to the first guest-chamber where they belonged.

When she returned, the sail-cloth bundle was lying on the table, and Hal and Cip de Musset were sitting together by the fire, the latter drinking hot rum.

"Good-morrow, fair one," grinned the visitor as he looked up, "there's somewhat on the table for thee."

His clothes proclaimed him a sailor, and his manners were free and easy.

"For me?" Anny looked first at the bundle and then over at Hal who was watching her covertly.

"And—er—and who will it be sent from, Master de Musset?" she said at last.

Cip de Musset laughed.

"Open it, lassie," he said, "open it and see."

Anny, nothing loath, pulled at the knots, and pushed back the sail-cloth; underneath was a white linen covering.

Hal rose to his feet and in spite of himself craned his neck to see.

The other man got up and stood beside the girl looking down at the bundle. The arrival of a parcel was an unusual occurrence at the Ship.

Anny fingered the linen for a moment, and then with a deft movement of her little brown hand switched it off. She gave a gasp of surprise, and putting out her hands held up a piece of Lyons silk. It was of a pale honey colour and of a texture not unlike taffeta. She shook out the glistening sheet and held the piece high up to her chin. The effect made even Hal gasp. Cip de Musset put his tankard down on the table and stepped back a few paces to look at her.

"That's right, lassie, just a bit nearer the window," he said.

Anny obeyed, as proud as a snake of its new skin, and stood so that the little remaining light might fall upon her.

Cip rested his huge hairy hands on his hips and leant back a little, his head on one side, and one eye shut.

"By the Lord! but you're as fair as a new figurehead, lass," he said approvingly.

Anny looked down and laughed with delight. She had never seen such stuff before, and the blood rushed to her face as she saw Hal's expression of amazed admiration as he stared at her. With a little sigh she folded up the silk, and returned to the bundle. It contained a letter, a piece of green frieze, and a little carved box. Anny laid aside the letter and the box, and looked at the frieze; there seemed to be a great deal of it.

Cip stepped forward to help her and taking one end walked over to the door, while she, holding her side, went to the fireplace, yet the strip sagged in the middle to the floor.

"Two new kirtles and a pair of galligaskins for Red," thought the girl, as she wound up the cloth, and turned her attention to the box.

Cip de Musset nudged Hal, and jerked his thumb in her direction.

"Look how the lassie plays with new toys," he whispered.

Hal turned away sharply, frowning angrily.

Cip stared at him in amazement and then, shrugging his shoulders, looked across at the girl.

Anny had not noticed Hal's expression, and Cip's face broke into smiles again as he watched her. She was trying to open the little wooden box, her face was flushed, and she was breathing quickly with childish excitement. At last she gave it up, and turning to Cip offered it for him to open. The sailor wiped his hands carefully on his green and yellow neckerchief before he took the box gingerly between his thumb and forefinger. After turning it over once or twice he tried his strength on the tightly-fitting lid and jerked it off, and held it out to the girl.

Anny took it eagerly and gave a little cry of delight as she examined the contents.

"Marry! Hal, I prithee, see!" she laughed as she pulled out a long string of polished amber beads and put them over her head. "And, oh, look you! look you!" she exclaimed, holding out a brooch about the size of a large oyster, which was of painted porcelain with a silver border studded with brilliants. "Oh, and see! Look, look, Hal! why don't you look?" she went on as she pulled first one trinket after another out of the little wooden box and held it up for their inspection. Suddenly she paused and putting in her hand very carefully brought out a little carved-wood elephant, brought no doubt from the East by some traveller.

"Oh, what a manikin," she exclaimed, fingering the exquisite workmanship in wonderment. "Look 'ee, Hal, whatever will it be?"

Hal looked down at the little figure as she stood before him, the carved bauble lying in the palm of her small brown hand, and sighed.

"Oh!" he said, as he picked up the elephant and looked at it quizzically. "I reckon 'tis some heathen image."

Anny snatched it away from him and held it tightly.

"Oh! nay," she said almost pleadingly, " 'tis not, indeed, or anyway 'tis marvellous dainty."

Cip stepped forward heavily and looked over her shoulder.

"Oh! nay," he said at last, " 'tis not a heathen image; 'tis a moulding of a beast."

Anny looked pleased.

"What fine little beasts they must be," she observed.

"Ah, yes," said Cip, nodding his head sagely, "wonderful fine little beasts."

Anny laughed happily, and turned to the silk and trinket-strewn table.

"Oh, won't I be fine," she exclaimed, flinging out her arms as though to embrace the table's load.

Hal grunted.

"Hadn't you better look at the sealed paper?" he said sulkily.

But Anny was too overjoyed to notice his tone.

"O marry! I forgot," she exclaimed with a little excited giggle as she picked up the square envelope and broke open the red seal.

"Ah!" said she as she studied the large flourishing script within.

Cip shot a covert glance at Hal and then hid his smile in his tankard.

"Ah!" said Anny again, turning the paper over.

Hal became impatient.

"Well, lass?" he said, rising.

Anny blushed, and then thrust the paper in his hand.

"Thou knowest I cannot read, Hal?" she said. "Wilt decipher it for me?"

Hal took it willingly although with some show of indifference and, holding the paper at arm's length, read it carefully through to himself.

"Plague upon it all!" he exclaimed.

Anny looked at him anxiously.

"What does it say?" she said, looking over his shoulder.

Hal flushed.

"I'll not tell thee," he said angrily.

"Oh!" Anny's tone expressed disappointment, and old Cip de Musset, who had been preparing himself to hear another man's letter, looked up.

"Oh! nay, lad, nay," he said solemnly, "tell the lass her own letter. Ay, marry, now you must to be honest."

Hal frowned.

"To be honest?" he said, puzzled.

"Ay, to be honest," Cip was emphatic. "For if you don't, lad, you alone will know the matter in the letter, which, look you, is not yours but the lass's. Taking is taking whether it be goods or fine phrases," he concluded, wagging his head sagely.

Hal shrugged his shoulders.

"Well then, harken," he said, and began to read sulkily and at a great pace.

"Into the lap of the fair lady who holdeth the whole heart of a great sailor in her sweet keeping, these fineries and divers other useful objects are munificently poured.

"Prithee deck thyself, wench, for the delight of thy noble and honourable admirer—DICK DELFAZIO, Captain of the *Coldlight.*"

"Did ever you hear such sithering foolishness?" he concluded.

But neither Anny nor Cip were looking at him; at the last

words of the letter they had turned to each other in mutual surprise and admiration.

"Ah!" said old Cip, leaning back on his bench. "Wonderful way he has wi' words and wenches. Damn me if they too don't go pretty well together," he added thoughtfully.

Anny sighed with delight and turned to Hal.

"Oh! isn't it a fine letter," she exclaimed happily. "Will I have to write one back?"

Hal looked up and the expression on his boyish face made her pause in her happiness, and turn to him anxiously.

"Anny Farran, what are you making of yourself?" he began slowly, his young imagination magnifying the occasion until he felt himself the injured lover leading his frail betrothed away from the pretty walks of folly.

Anny looked at him in wonderment and he went on:

"Anny, are you 'tending to accept these—these fripperies, like a common serving-wench, and worse?"

Anny blushed and started; then she looked from her lover to the table and back again.

"Not take them?" she said, her mouth drooping a little at the corners and her eyes growing larger and very bright.

"Of course not!"

Wrapped in the blanket of his youthful virtue the boy felt no sympathy for the despairing glance which the pathetic little girl in front of him cast at her shabby, much-stained kirtle and well-mended bodice.

Anny swallowed something in her throat and blinked her eyes once or twice, her long, dark lashes becoming spiky and blacker than before. Then she laughed a little unnaturally and rubbed her hand awkwardly down the sides of her skirt.

"Oh, of course not," she said, laughing still on a strange high pitch, as she gathered up the finery and put it carefully back into the sail-cloth covering. "Of course not," she repeated mechanically, never allowing her fingers to stray over the smooth soft surface of the silk or to play amongst the amber beads or ivory ornaments. "There," she said at last, as the last trinket was slipped into the little box, and she looked round, still the bright colour in her cheeks and the forced smile on her lips. "Oh! and the little beast?" she said half-questioningly, half-agreeing, as she picked up the little carved elephant and looked at it wistfully.

"And the little beast," said Hal firmly.

Anny sighed and slipped it in with the others, then tied up the sail-cloth with a firm hand.

"Master de Musset," she said a little unsteadily, "would you be kind enough to—to take this back to the Captain and say I can't accept it? Say—say of course not," she added.

Cip de Musset rose to his feet, bewilderment on his face as he looked from one to the other of the two young people.

"Say you sent it back?" he said at last, turning to the girl. "Nay, say he sent it back," he added, jerking his thumb in Hal's direction.

Anny stepped forward quickly and laid her hand on his arm, anxiety written in her very posture.

"Oh, nay! I pray you, Master de Musset, say I sent it back," she said eagerly. "I beg of you to tell my message rightly."

Cip looked into her earnest little face and smiled.

"All right, lassie," he said, "but," he added, his voice and face becoming suddenly grave, "you have a care how you anger Black-kerchief Dick. You young ones—you're sweethearts, too, ain't you?"

"Yes, but you won't say," Anny spoke quickly and Cip shook his head.

"Oh, no!" he said grinning. "I won't say. I be going."

He moved over to the window and looked out.

"Here be Ezekiel French just drove up," he remarked.

Anny looked up at the clock.

"Mother o' Grace!" she ejaculated, "I have forgot to call Mistress Sue," and she ran out of the door and up the stairs to the little room which she and Sue shared.

Hal picked up the sail-cloth bundle and handed it to Cip, who took it without a word and went out into the yard. He stood talking to French some minutes and then walked over to his cart.

"Poor little lassie," he muttered as he climbed into the tumbril and turned the piebald gelding out of the gate. "Poor little lassie," he repeated. "Lord, ain't we particular when we're young." He looked at the bundle on the floor behind him and shrugged his shoulders. "This here Blackkerchief Dick and all," he concluded sighing and whipping up his horse.

Big French stood in the Ship yard talking to Hal and old John Patten, the ostler. He leaned lazily against the shaft of his waggon, an arm stretched out over the back of one of the horses. The waggon was half-full of mysterious sacking-covered bales and little round casks, the first containing silk and the other tobacco.

"Have ye got them ten trusses straw I bespoke, Hal?" French was saying, the barley stalk he was chewing moving up and down in his mouth.

"Ay, in the barn; that on the right is yourn," Hal replied readily.

Big French looked at John Patten enquiringly. The old man grinned. "That'll be all right, sir," he said, pocketing the coin which the big man had given him.

"You'll cover the stuff well up?" French continued. "Undo the first five truss and spread it over the stuff and then put the rest, bound up, atop, you know how."

The man nodded.

"Ain't been on the Island for sixty-seven years for nothing," he said, winking one bright blue eye.

French laughed.

Maybe," he said, "but you never can tell when the roads will get dangerous again. What with footpads whom I fear not and excise folk whom I do—you never know," and he shrugged his shoulders, and soon added, a smile breaking over his handsome face, "but, Lord, it's all in the trade so what's the use of talking?"

He turned away with Hal, and John, touching his cap, went off to the barn—a long, low building on the left of the Ship.

"I'm taking that dog Blueneck and his mate Coot along wi' me," French remarked, as he and Hal neared the kitchen door. "You ain't seen them up here yet, I suppose?"

Hal shook his head as he lifted the latch.

"No," he said, "but they'll come, don't you fear, the sniffling Spanish rats."

French laughed and was about to reply, but as his eyes fell upon Mistress Sue who had stepped to the door to meet them, the words died on his lips, and he grinned sheepishly.

In the kitchen the dips had been lighted, the fire had got up, and all round the hearth was bright and cheerful.

Sue followed and stood in front of him.

Anny sat in her usual place at the window. She was sewing the buttons on an old coat of Gilbot's, and several times she pricked her fingers, and then hastily dashed the back of her hand across her eyes, but otherwise she was very still and no one else in the room noticed her.

Hal went to draw a noggin of rum for French, and while he was away, the door opened, and Blueneck and Habakkuk Coot came in.

French, who had just formed a complete sentence to open conversation with Sue, scowled at the intruders, turned his back on the astonished girl, and stared into the fire. Perhaps it was the wisest thing he could have done, for Sue as she bustled off to attend to the two sailors, began to think about him, a thing she had not done seriously since that evening when Blackkerchief Dick first came to the Ship.

It was strange, she thought. Usually Big French seemed so pleased to see her, so ready to laugh with her, so childishly shy when she spoke directly to him, and she found herself thinking with pleasure of that evening when Gilbot had interrupted him in a most important question. She laughed to herself. Ah! that was before the advent of the Spaniard. Ah! the Spaniard! she sighed, and then flushed hotly at her own thoughts. What was the Spaniard to her? A man who was not even interested in her. She tossed her head, but all the same she sighed again before she put the tankards down before the two shipmates of the *Coldlight,* and returned once more to the young giant at the fireside.

"Master French," she said, planting herself before him, "would you get me a thing or two at the market?"

French beamed at her.

"Anything," he said jerkily, as though the word had been released from captivity, "or everything," he added suddenly and earnestly.

Sue did not understand him and she looked down in surprise.

"Everything?" she repeated.

French blushed, opened his mouth, shut it again, then he cleared his throat noisily. "Everything you wish, Mistress," he said finally, inwardly cursing his shyness.

Sue perched herself on the table in front of him and enumerated the odds and ends that the Ship required.

Anny looked at the pair shyly from out her corner.

"Ah! but how much of the flannel, Mistress?" French was saying.

"Six ells an' it pleases you," Sue replied.

Anny gulped and applied herself industriously to her sewing.

Just then the door opened and John Patten put in his smiling head.

"Master French," he called.

French, who had just begun to enjoy himself, looked up with another scowl.

"All's ready," said John, "and, if you's going to get to Tiptree afore eleven, ye better start."

"Right!" French rose to his feet with a sigh and walked to the door. "Come on," he said to the two sailors who were looking round anxiously.

Habakkuk sniffed noisily and happily, his pale bilious little face positively shining with excitement as he got up hastily and trotted to the door, Blueneck following.

The rest of the company followed out into the yard to see the adventurers safely off the premises.

It was a sharply cold, clear frosty night, with a mist hanging low over the marshes. There was no wind and the place was very silent. The sky was clear and thickly sprinkled with stars, and the moon, nearly full, shed a white ghostly glow over the countryside.

Old John Patten, a large box lantern in his hand, hovered hither and thither like some old and bluff Will o' the Wisp.

French walked round the waggon to make sure that everything was in order. Then he climbed up on to the shaft and perched himself on the driving-seat, which consisted of a board nailed flat on the front of the waggon.

"Come on if you are coming at all," he called to Blueneck, who scrambled into the one remaining seat beside him.

"Hi, where shall I go?" said Habakkuk, sniffing and hopping about in his anxiety.

French shrugged his shoulders.

"Best get up on to the straw atop," he said.

Habakkuk climbed on to the hub of the wheel and with Hal's help got safely on to the straw where he lay quite still.

"Ready?" said French, and then turned the horses about without waiting for an answer, and drove out of the gate amidst the jests and farewells of the onlookers.

"You won't forget the flannel?" Sue called after him.

French's deep, pleasant voice rang back through the thin, cold air. "Rather would I forget the waggon, Mistress."

Sue laughed.

"There's a new gown on the way," she said with a sigh of satisfaction as she went back to the kitchen.

Anny gulped, and Hal, turning at that moment, saw her disappointed little face in the moonlight. She looked at him so sorrowfully without speaking, and then went into the inn.

He was about to follow her but checked himself; he began to realise a little how much she cared for pretty things, and what she had given up with the sail-cloth bundle. Pushing his hands into his pockets he walked out of the gate and down the road to the sea, his chin on his breast. He had not gone very far before he met old Gilbot stumping along alone.

The old man hailed him cheerily and bade him go down to fetch little Red who he averred was scooning stones on the clear sea. "No one obeys me," he concluded with a chuckle. "I can't make the young one come. Go fetch him, Hal."

He waddled off smiling and talking to himself.

Hal walked on in deep thought, kicking the stones in the road with his clogs.

Anny was fond of pretty fripperies and ornaments; she liked to be admired and looked at, and would have kept the sail-cloth bundle for its own worth, without a thought for the giver.

Hal kicked at a stone savagely, and swore loudly. He was eighteen and as bitter against the world as it is possible to be at that age.

He remembered Anny's little white face in the moonlight as Big French drove off, Sue's request in his ears, and her disappointed, sorrowful glance at him before she returned to the kitchen. He had reached the sea by this time and he stood for a moment peering out over the mist-ridden water. "If only I had money," he thought. "Lord!"

Staring out into the white moonlit vapour he saw Anny in her honey-coloured silk, her eyes bright and her lips a little parted, just as he had seen her that afternoon. Then he saw himself beside her, no longer a deputy landlord and everybody's errand boy, but a man of importance in a new blue cloth coat with silver buttons and a ruffle in the sleeves. He was holding her hand and they were married.

"Oh! if only I had money!" the words escaped from his mouth like a groan, and he shivered involuntarily, almost afraid of his own voice; everything around him was so shadowy and unreal.

"Hal Grame, is that you? Oh! how you frightened me," the voice seemed to start from the pebbles at his feet and he sprang back in alarm, crossing himself.

"Who's there?" he said sharply.

"Only me and Win," Red Farran got up from the bank of seaweed where he had been sitting and put a little wet hand into Hal's.

"Why do you want money?" he said. "Win an' me want money, too."

Hal looked down at the fantastic little figure before he answered.

"Why do I want money——?" he began, his voice rising with silly, sweet, half-theatrical boyish passion; then he checked himself and shrugged his shoulders. "Oh, nothing," he said.

Red looked at the sea.

"It's too dark to scoon stones," he remarked. "How many times can you make one hop? I made one go nine times once—in smooth water," he added modestly.

Hal vouchsafed no answer, and Red sat down again on a bank of seaweed.

"Here's Win," he said softly, as he fumbled in his ragged clothes and brought out the kitten, now quite dry but very sleepy, and hugged it up to his neck. "If we had money wouldn't we eat a lot and be happy?" He squeezed the kitten a little harder and the unhappy animal squealed sleepily. Red laughed. "Yes," he said, "I think so, too."

There was silence for a few minutes save for the gentle lapping of the water, and the scrape of moving pebbles as the waves rolled them up and down on the shore.

"Money's very useful, isn't it?" said Red at last.

"Ay," Hal replied fervently.

"Master Gilbot said that, too," went on the child as he pitched a stone and waited to hear the gentle "plop" which it made as it reached the water.

Hal looked up.

"What did he say?" he asked.

Red screwed up his face in thought.

"I forget," he said, "it was something about leaving the Ship to a man who had money." He tossed another stone, then turned his attention to the kitten.

"A man with money?" said Hal. "What man?"

"Oh! any man I suppose," said Red vaguely, stroking the cat's fur up the wrong way.

"Any man with money," repeated Hal to himself; then he began to laugh loudly, unnaturally, and very high.

Red clapped his hands over his ears and the kitten snuggled into his chest.

"Don't do that, Hal," he said imploringly, "it's just like Nan when she sees Pet Salt."

Hal stopped and pulled himself together.

"Best be getting back," he said, and started off along the lane.

The child got up without a word and trotted after him, the kitten wrapped safely in the folds of his kirtle-cloak.

Hal did not think about the boy; he strode along, his eyes on the ground.

"I will get money," he whispered to himself. "I've never had any. I've never had aught to give her, and women be capricious and whimsical. They care for that foolery. Before God I swear someday I'll own the Ship, and, oh, you holy Saints, let me keep her till then."

Chapter IX

About nine o'clock on the following morning, when the hoar-frost was still on the ragged grass and leafless trees, Anny hurried down the road which led to the Ship. She had been to see Nan Swayle, and was returning from her cabin with a large skip of onions which the old woman had insisted on sending to Gilbot in return for the half-keg of rum which he had given her.

It was bitterly cold, and Anny hugged the threadbare shawl very tightly about her shoulders as she hastened on, her head bent before the driving wind.

"Well met, Mistress," said a musical voice behind her. "Prithee, may I carry thy basket?"

Anny's heart sank as she turned her head.

Blackkerchief Dick came forward, a smile on his face, and stretched out a pair of dainty white hands for the skip.

Anny blushed and withheld it from him.

"Nay, I would not dream of letting you trouble, sir," she said. "I—I would rather carry it myself."

Dick laughed.

"And I would rather carry it myself," he said. "Faith, Mistress, I warrant me we'll have to bear it together."

So saying he gaily caught hold of the handle nearest him and they walked on, he chatting merrily and she alternately laughing at his sallies, blushing and smirking at his well-seasoned stories. They made strange contrast as they went, the skip swinging between them, the girl, her shabby green kirtle and torn black bodice, her heavy clogs sinking in the deep, slushy mud of the road, and the Spaniard, newly-clothed in shining brocaded satin, with pointlace collar and ruffled cuffs, his fashionable short surcoat displaying a tucked, embroidered shirt, marvellously laundered; his cloak of the finest Amsterdam cloth a little open in the front, showing the hilt of his famous knife as it hung in his gem-studded belt.

"Mistress, prithee why didst thou return my gifts yestere'en?" said Dick at last as they neared the Ship.

Anny, who had been waiting for this, took a deep breath.

"For what do you take me, sir?" she said, turning her big innocent eyes upon him.

Dick looked at her curiously. Was it possible that this little country drudge was different from all the other women he had met? He nearly dropped his side of the skip in his surprise.

"I crave thy pardon, Mistress," he said dazedly, and they walked on in silence till they reached the Ship.

Then Dick spoke again.

"I will come in for a stoup of mine host's sweet sack," he said, and then added softly, for the door was open, "and I would speak seriously with thee."

Anny went into the kitchen rather self-consciously and looked round. No one was there, and she went out to the scullery with the onions.

When she returned the Spaniard was sitting by the fireside, his daintily-shod feet resting on the hearthstone. He did not look up as she came in, so she tripped across to the shelves to get him a tankard, and then unearthed a flagon of sack from under the cask form.

"Prithee set it here to warm, child," said Dick, pointing to the hob.

Anny did as she was told. He touched her hand lightly as she passed him.

"And now, Mistress, will it please you to sit before me?" he said.

Anny sat down, and the Spaniard looked at her in admiration for a moment before he spoke.

"Hast heard much said of Dick Delfazio?" he continued, smiling at her, and leaning forward a little, his elbow on his knee, and one hand supporting his chin and shielding his face from the fire.

Anny dropped her eyes not quite certain what to say.

But as he waited for an answer, she stammered,

"Ay, a great deal an' it please you."

"Aught to my discredit?" the Spaniard spoke sharply and frowned.

"Oh, nay, sir, nay." Anny spoke hastily as she noted his displeasure. "Rather the other way."

A smile spread over the man's face for a moment, and he looked at her.

"Yet, Mistress, you refused my gifts," he said softly.

An expression of pain passed over the girl's face, but she said steadily:

"Ay, sir. And I would not have anyone think I would take them. Methinks you mistake me, sir," she added proudly.

The Spaniard did not speak; he sat looking at her steadfastly without moving his position, his glittering deep black eyes fixed on her face, and an inscrutable expression on his lips.

Anny did not look up and at last the Spaniard leaned back in his seat, new interest in his face, and a twinkle of pleasure in his eyes.

"Mistress, you mistake me," he said gently. "Believe me, I never thought you aught but a maiden as fair in reputation as in face. What villain can have read anything else but pure admiration in my small offerings to you?"

Anny looked up quickly, her face glowing with confusion. She thought angrily of Hal's outburst and opened her mouth to speak, but at that moment her eye caught the Spaniard's white hand playing with the hilt of his knife, and she looked at him again, as he sat smiling at her, his full red lips curled back a little, showing the white teeth within.

"I thought it myself," she said almost defiantly, as she rose to go about her work.

Dick put out a hand to restrain her.

"Prithee sit down, fair one, I would speak with thee," he said firmly, his eyes commanding her with their momentary fierceness, and continued as she reseated herself.

"Hast ever been off this Island, Mistress?"

"Nay, sir." Anny shook her head. "Not even to the West," she added.

Dick threw up his hands in mock surprise, and the girl could not help thinking how beautiful they looked rising so waxen-like from out the delicate lace ruffles which surrounded his wrists.

"The pity of it, Mistress, oh, the pity of it, that you should be wasted here on this desolate mud flat," Dick was saying, "which is only visited by a gentleman once in two or three months, and then only for a sennight. No, the jewel of your beauty is little suited to so drab a setting as the mud-beslimed shores of Mersea Marsh Island."

Anny looked at him uncertain if he was laughing at her or not, but she could get no hint of his mood from his face, which was nearly expressionless save for the eyes which regarded her almost mournfully.

"What would I find fairer than the marshes in another country?" she said at last.

The Spaniard laughed.

"The marshes?" he said. "Oh! Mistress, what have you known of beauty that you look on grey and purple marshes and call them fair!"

Anny frowned.

"Marry!" she said, tossing her head. "They're good enough for me."

"Nay, fair one, there you mistake, it's because they are not good enough for thee that I would quarrel with thee loving them."

The Spaniard leaned a little forward as he spoke.

Anny laughed uneasily and rose to her feet.

"Ah, well!" she said, " 'tis of no account what I think fair or ugly, see how late it is; I must be about my business."

Dick got up also.

"Look ye, Mistress," he said, "I had almost forgot what I came to see thee for. I sail again for France on Wednesday even," he paused, and looked at the girl for any hint of surprise or disappointment which she might show, but Anny did not look up and betrayed no other interest beyond polite attention.

The Spaniard smiled and his eyes began to sparkle again.

"And, little one," he went on, "when I sail it will not be on the *Coldlight,* but the *Anny* if you will permit me to rename the ship after thee."

Anny gasped. She knew a little about the importance which sailors in general, and smugglers in particular, attached to the names of their vessels, and was fully sensible of the honour which the Spaniard was conferring upon her. She began to feel flattered.

"You honour me too much, sir," she said, bobbing and smiling.

The Spaniard made a stately bow.

"Mistress, I thank you for deigning to accept so small a tribute," he said in his grand manner. "And may I beg of you two more favours, namely, that you will honour my ship with your presence, and will yourself bless the brig and proclaim thyself its guardian and patron?"

Anny blushed and laughed happily.

"Ay," she said, "and gladly if you can trust my blessings."

The Spaniard bowed again.

"What blessings might I trust in if not in yours?" he said gallantly. "I will come myself to bring thee there. Au revoir, fair one." He picked up his big-brimmed hat and, taking the little brown hand in his soft white one, respectfully raised it to his lips.

Anny smiled shyly as she drew it slowly away and put it behind her back.

Dick looked into her little face so very little lower than his own.

"Might I dare to salute your lips, Ann of the Island?" he said softly.

Anny's smile vanished and she drew back stiffly.

"Methinks you mistake me for some other wench, sir," she said.

"Pardon, I prithee, fairest of prudes."

Dick's tone was really penitent. "For but one moment I dreamed—shall I tell thee my dream?"

Anny looked at him in astonishment and in spite of her vexation drew a little nearer.

"Whatever——" she began.

Dick interrupted her.

"All in one moment I dreamt I was dead and in hell, and, as I trod on the burning stones, a sudden ease fell upon me and I looked up and beheld the fairest face in all the world before me, the lips put up to meet mine—and I—well, Mistress, then you woke me."

Anny looked at him in amazement wondering if the Spanish gentleman had suddenly become bewitched. Then she conjured up in her childish mind a picture which his words suggested to her of the fastidious little man hopping and dancing over hot paving bricks, and she began to laugh so heartily that she had to support herself by leaning against the door-post. Although this was hardly the way which he wished his excuse to be taken, the Spaniard was pleased to have the girl so completely mollified and began to laugh himself with her.

"Oh, go along with ye," said Anny at last, as she wiped away the tears of laughter with the back of her hand and held open the door for him.

Dick bowed again, and Anny smiled as she watched him out of the yard.

"Oh!" she said to herself, "he's a mighty pleasing gentleman, very fine to look upon, very bravely spoken, and I'll bless his ship for him gladly, but you can't love two lads at once."

Dick went off down the road towards the sea deep in thought. He had not gone very far before he was overtaken by Blueneck, who was just back from Tiptree. They fell into that easy kind of conversation which often takes place between master and his confidential inferior.

"We're renaming the brig to *Anny* on the evening of Wednesday," remarked Dick, as they went along.

Blueneck looked at his captain and opened his mouth to protest, but thought better of it and held his peace.

"What think you, Blueneck, the wench will have naught to do with me?" went on Delfazio.

The other man looked at him disbelievingly and laughed.

"Marry, 'tis so," Dick said laughing. "Faith, she sends back my presents and scorns my kisses."

Blueneck looked down at his master in surprise, then he shrugged his shoulders.

"You will not trouble with the lass further, sir, surely?" he said.

Dick smiled again.

"Hast ever known me denied aught I desired?" he said, his voice pleasant and smooth.

Blueneck shook his head.

"Nay," he said, "but, Lord, what's a silly wench, sir? She can have no interest for thee."

"Ah, thou hast hit it, dog, 'tis that exactly which the lass has for me—interest—interest greater than I ever felt for any other woman."

Blueneck laughed and turned the laugh into a cough.

Dick looked at him smiling shyly.

"Ah! you may laugh, friend of the unshaven neck," he said, "but as I told you this is so. Never have I been denied so much by any woman, and at last I find a game that makes the prize worth having. The end of a certainty will be the same, but the wooing is half the pleasure, eh, dog?"

Blueneck grinned as he fingered the ribbon which he had brought from Tiptree, and they went on together down to the brig, where Dick gave orders for the ceremony for renaming the *Coldlight.*

Meanwhile, up at the Ship everything was bustle; French had returned and was entertaining the company with the story of the night's adventures, and Anny and Sue were kept busy serving rums and preparing the midday meal.

It was then that Big French remembered the flannel he had bought and handed it to Sue with another little bundle which he had bought from a gipsy.

Sue hastened away to open it, and it being dinnertime the company slowly dwindled off until there was only the usual household and the young giant left to partake of lunch together. This was speedily served by Anny and Hal, who were now on the best of terms.

Sue came downstairs a few seconds later, blushing and smiling, with a string of blue beads round her neck, and French shuffled, reddened, and choked over his broth when he saw her so that everyone looked at him and then at her and smiled at one another knowingly.

Old Gilbot began to sing "Mary Loo," but soon gave it up and took to his rumkin.

After dinner, the delf being cleared away, Anny went up to her room, which was also Sue's, and sat down on her bed. She thought of Blackkerchief Dick and his brig and began to picture to herself the scene on board the *Coldlight* when she would change its name to her own. Then she sighed. She looked down at her shabby kirtle and passed her hand over its holes and stains. Downstairs she could hear Big French's deep voice raised as though pleadingly and could catch Sue's high, sweet, giggling replies. She turned over on the bed and lay face downwards for a few seconds, then she sat up and began hastily to re-arrange her hair. On Sue's bed she saw the flannel spread out, and she went over softly to have a look at it. It seemed very coarse and ugly when she mentally compared it to the honey-coloured silk or the wide, green frieze which she had sent back to Dick in the sail-cloth bundle. And she found herself wishing that Hal had money like French and Dick, but she checked herself and blushed at her own greediness, as she termed it. She sat down on her bed again sighing as she did so, and Sue, coming up some while later, finding her still there, took pity on her shabbiness and gave her the purple gown that Anny had wished for so long, and was then amazed to see the usually so grateful, peaceable little girl cast the old garment from her and, throwing herself on the bare boards, sob till the elder girl feared for her health.

Chapter X

After his conversation with Blackkerchief Dick, Blueneck found leisure to attend to his own amours. He first retired to the brig where, with the help of Habakkuk Coot, he arranged himself in his best clothes, tied the knee-latchets of his breeches with bright-coloured tapes, and borrowed a brilliant red and green kerchief from out poor Mat Turnby's bundle, and then, after carefully tying the length of cherry ribbon, which had cost him much time and trouble to procure, in a piece of muslin, he stowed the packet in one of his big side pockets and started out for Joe Pullen's house.

He had some little way to go, as the Pullens' cottage was situated slightly to the north of the church, and that was about a mile and a half from the point where the brig was moored. He walked along cheerfully, whistling a chanty, and mentally rehearsing the speech which he intended to make to Mistress Amy when presenting the ribbon.

In spite of the time of the year, the late afternoon sun shone brightly on the wet grass and there was a touch of spring in the air.

On nearing the cottage he stopped to see if he still had the little muslin packet, and, feeling it still there, strolled nonchalantly up to the door and knocked loudly.

Mistress Pullen opened it herself and seeing him put her finger to her lips.

Blueneck stood still looking at her, very disappointed and a little foolish. Inside the cottage he could hear deep rafter-shaking snores, and soon understood that the lady's husband was within. He opened his mouth to speak, but Amy shook her head violently and he shut it again with a snap; however, he did not move, and Mistress Pullen had to push him off the doorstep and whisper, "This evening," before he fully realised that he was not wanted. Fumbling in his pocket he hastily found the ribbon and snatching it out crammed it into her hand, then tiptoed off down the path feeling that he had been cheated.

Amy took the parcel without looking up and quickly slipped back, shutting the door carefully behind her.

Blueneck returned along the way he had come, in a much less cheerful frame of mind than when he started out. He no longer whistled, but lurched along his head bent and his hands thrust deep in his pockets.

On passing the Ship sounds of cheerfulness came out to him through the open door, and yielding to the impulse of the moment he went in.

As usual the scene in the Ship kitchen was cheering even to look at. The roaring fire in the open grate, the glinting lights on the pewter, and the shadowy, dusky corners in which faint outlines of casks and strings of drying onions could just be distinguished, all gave it a cosy, comforting appearance. At least Blueneck thought so as he joined the circle round the fire and called for hot rum to be served to him.

Old Gilbot was in a lively mood; he sat in his corner, his blue eyes twinkling from out huge creases of fat, singing, laughing, and drinking with the best will in the world, and keeping the company in a continual roar of laughter.

Big French sat on the other side of the fireplace, playing with little Red Farran and his kitten. The little boy was a favourite of the big man, and they chatted together with an equal share of enjoyment.

Sue leaned over the back of the seat, and from time to time joined in their conversation. At these times French smiled contentedly and almost as easily as he did on the days before the little dark-eyed, white-handed Spaniard landed East instead of West of Mersea Marsh Island.

Anny and Hal were talking together in the background as they polished up the tankards. She was telling him about the Spaniard's desire to rename the brig, and clearing away with her gentle cajolery all his little jealous fears and doubts.

Several other men were sitting round the fire. They were Habakkuk Coot, sniffing as usual and drinking spiced ale; Old Master Granger, guffawing at Gilbot, and sipping his neat rum with obvious relish; Cip de Musset, chewing a chunk of coarse, black tobacco, a habit much disapproved of by the Islanders, who thought the weed a dangerous newfangled drug, and of no use save to sell to other people; and one or two others. All very merry and cheerful and good company to each other.

Blueneck drank his rum and, beginning to feel more cheerful, he leaned forward a little to join in the talk.

"Ah! a wonderful funny thing that be," Granger was saying, as he shook his head sagely. "You're right, a wonderful funny thing."

"Ah! and what's more, it ain't the first time it's happened," put in another man casually.

"What?"

In an instant the company's attention was fixed on the new speaker, and he looked round as though he were going to say something very secret.

"Six months ago on Ray Island," he said.

"Oh, everyone knows that, Tom Fish. Go home with your old stories!"

There was a note of disappointment in their voices and they all laughed. The man muttered something about there being old and old, and subsided.

Blueneck came a little nearer.

"Might I ask what you are talking about?" he said.

Cip de Musset rolled his quid into his cheek and spat before he replied.

"A row-boat load o' rum and two men lost going from here to Bradwell," he said laconically.

"Ah," said Granger, "wonderful strange."

"What, ain't the boat been washed up?" said Blueneck, glad to enter into the conversation.

"No, nothing found at all," said Granger eagerly as he shifted his position slightly. "Nothing at all. But, ah well," he added, "I don't know what's come to them."

"Would the Preventative men have catched them, think you?" remarked Cip, chewing.

"Now that are likely," said Granger sarcastically. "Ain't it? There not being a sign of a Preventative man these nine months! Oh, yes, Master de Musset, it are likely they'd be spry enough to catch two chaps in a row-boat in the middle of the Blackwater without a soul on the Island or the mainland knowing aught. Lord, you ought to ha' been an excise man yourself, you ought."

"Maybe, Granger, maybe," said Cip de Musset placidly and without ceasing to chew.

"Maybe they drank the liquor and then pulled out the bung and sunk her theirselves," suggested Habakkuk, sniffing violently.

Granger turned slowly in his seat and let his gaze fall upon the nervous little man for a second or two before he spoke.

"Ah! Master Rheum-in-the-head, maybe they did," he said, "and maybe the devil come along and carried them off in a thunder-cloud, or maybe a sea-serpent swallowed them. Eh?"

Habakkuk looked into the others' unsmiling faces and sniffed, while a weak, ineffectual little smile spread over his bilious, pimply face, and then, as Granger betrayed no amusement, it struck him that he must have said something sensible, so he answered, "Ay, most likely," wagging his head sagely.

The company burst into a roar of laughter, and Habakkuk, feeling that this time he had been witty, joined with them happily.

"Ah, no, but it is unnatural," continued Granger thoughtfully after the laughter had subsided. "And ye know it ain't the first time a row-boat o' rum and two chaps have been lost," he went on. "Just in the same way, too, started off after dawn and never seen no more. Ah, unnatural, that's what it is."

"The currents be plaguy strong out i' the channel," said French, looking up for a moment.

Granger was up in arms at once.

"Currents!" he ejaculated. "Now tell me, just tell me, Master French, do you think either Clarry Kidley or Gustave Norton would be likely to run into anything like that, an' if they did to stay in it? Just tell me!"

French shrugged his shoulders and continued to explain to Red the kitten's natural objection to being stroked from tail to ears.

Granger looked round triumphantly. "Ah, I don't know, I don't know," he said at last.

"More do we," said Habakkuk with a sniff, and the talk drifted to other channels.

Blueneck was feeling that perhaps the world was not so dreary a place as he had imagined, when the door burst open, and young Tant Pullen rushed in without a hat and very breathless. He looked round the room for a moment as though searching for someone. At last his quick, bright eyes fell upon Blueneck and he darted over to him.

"Look out you, get out of here and hide quick," he gasped as well as he could for lack of breath.

The Spanish sailor looked at him in surprise, and the rest of the company seeing that something was afoot turned to listen.

Tant took the sailor by the collar when he saw that the man did not move.

"Quick, hurry, or he'll get you," he said.

Blueneck opened his mouth in astonishment.

"Why—what?" he ejaculated.

Tant took a deep breath.

"My mother's bin beatin' my father, because he said that she'd took presents from strangers," he volunteered. The company began to laugh and Blueneck still looked bewildered.

Tant gave one anxious look at the door.

"Mother says I was to come and tell you," he said.

Again the circle rocked and the mystified Blueneck looked up.

"Well?" he said.

Tant sighed.

"You best come," he said, "my father's wonderfully riled after he's been beat by my mother, an' he's coming up here, to beat you, now."

"Oh!" The company went off into another paroxysm of laughter, and Blueneck began to see a little more light in the matter. "Let him come," he said, shrugging his shoulders.

Hal stepped forward from the dresser where he had been arranging tankards.

"You better go, Master Blueneck," he said. "Joe's wonderfully strong, and after he's bin beat by his wife there's no holding him."

Blueneck hesitated. Then he shrugged his shoulders. Whatever he was, Dick Delfazio's mate was no coward and he stood his ground.

"I'm not feared," he said, "let him come."

Hal looked at Gilbot, who had been watching the scene attentively.

"Ohsh hesh all right," said the old man. "Let him come, Hal."

Hal shrugged his shoulders, and sent Anny upstairs to look at the guest's room. Then he quietly and unobtrusively moved everything movable to the sides of the room so leaving a clear space in the centre.

The company also shrugged their shoulders and edged a little away from Blueneck, so that the sailor found himself sitting alone on a bench. He looked round him uneasily, but did not move.

Suddenly Tant, who had been looking out of the window, remarked in a stage whisper, "Here he come," and then dived under a pile of sacking in a far corner.

Nobody spoke and the silence was almost uncomfortable. Little Red noticed it, and after looking about put his arms round French's neck and climbed on to his knee.

"Put Win into your pocket," he whispered, "she got hurt last time Nan and Pet fought."

French obeyed and, moving a little further into the chimney corner, he looked up shyly at Sue, who smiled and came round the high seat to sit beside him.

French made room for her on the inside of the bench, and she took Red from him and held the child herself.

By this time heavy footsteps could be heard coming across the yard, and the Ship waited in a silence only broken by Habakkuk's sniffs and the plaintive mews of Red's little kitten who was shut in the darkness of French's big pocket.

Then the door was kicked open with such a clatter that Habakkuk nearly fell off his seat with nervousness, and Joe stalked into the room. All his usual good-humour was gone and he seemed, to Blueneck at least, to have got quite six inches taller. He stood for a moment looking round, his face flushed and his eyes dark with fury; a long livid weal ran from his left eye to the corner of his mouth, and he trembled with anger as he stood there breathing heavily. Then, as he caught sight of Blueneck, he gave one whoop of exultation and leapt across the room landing on the top of the unfortunate man, whom he proceeded to punch with all his might.

Blueneck was no indifferent fighter himself, and, as Joe's first blow landed in his ribs, a dull light of anger kindled in his eyes and he forced his way to his feet, and then the greatest fight that the old Ship Tavern had ever witnessed began. They closed in, and Blueneck tried to take advantage of his superior strength by grasping his opponent round the body and swinging him over his head, but Joe was too wiry for that. Seizing his opportunity he dropped low, and throwing his arms round the sailor's knees he suddenly crouched so that the man fell over and stretched his body full length on the floor. Before he could again regain his feet Joe was upon him and they rolled over and over together kicking, the Spaniard swearing softly. Joe said nothing but grit his teeth and fought steadily and swiftly, always making for the man's throat. At last he got there; the Spaniard lay on his back and Joe, making a desperate dive between his clawing hands, grasped at the hairy throat and held on tightly.

Blueneck's mouth opened, and his eyes bulged; slowly his movements grew less effectual, and more convulsive. Joe held on grimly and without a word; finally he stood up.

"Give him a rum," he said. "I've not done with him yet by a long way."

Nobody spoke, but Hal stepped forward with the rum. He had drawn it in readiness, and between them he and Joe raised the half-strangled man to his feet and forced the spirit down his throat. Then, as he grew stronger, Joe took him firmly by the collar and dragged him out of the inn, without a word or a glance behind him.

Sue was on her feet in an instant.

"Will he kill him?" she cried.

Hal shrugged his shoulders.

"No," he said, "I don't reckon so—and if he does, what's a Spaniard, anyway?"

"Yesh," said Gilbot, holding out his rumkin to be refilled. "What's a Spaniard, anyway? Letsh have a shong."

And as Joe, his wrath hardly one whit abated, dragged the half-suffocated Blueneck down the road to the sea, he heard the jovial strains of "Pretty Poll" roared out in lively chorus from the Ship's kitchen:

"Pretty Poll she loved a sailor
And well she loved he,
But he sailed to the mouth
Of a stream in the South,
And was lost in the rolling sea,
Lost in the rolling sea!"

"Ah, ha," said Joe between his teeth as he shook his unfortunate captive by the collar. "And that's what you're goin' to be, my lad, 'lost in the rolling sea.' "

Blueneck opened his mouth to expostulate, but Joe swung him round like a meal sack and tightened his neckerchief, so that it was all he could do to breathe, and they hurried on.

Joe strode over the ground at a tremendous pace dragging the Spaniard after him. And not one other word did he speak till they came to the water-side, where Joe's little row-boat, the *Amy*, flopped and see-sawed on the rising tide.

Still keeping one hand on Blueneck's collar, Joe stopped, caught at the riding-line, and pulled it in.

"Get in," he commanded.

Blueneck obeyed as meekly as a lamb, and Joe stepped in after him, and pushed off. He rowed steadily for some seconds and, as the water was very calm, made good progress. About twenty-five yards from the shore he pulled in the oars and sat looking at the other man a full minute. Then he spoke sharply.

"Change places and row a bit," he said.

Blueneck shrugged his shoulders and did not move.

Joe's eyes began to sparkle and a dull flush suffused his neck and face.

"Do as I say," he said quietly.

The fresh air and the rum had revived Blueneck and he began to feel angry again. Still he did not move. Joe seized an oar; holding it in both hands, he wielded it above his head; it was a clumsy weapon, however, and the boat rocked dangerously. Instinctively Blueneck drew back and before he knew what he was doing raised himself to a sitting position on the gunwale; this was Joe's opportunity, and he grasped it. Lowering the oar as swiftly as possible he hove it sharply into the Spaniard's stomach, who immediately doubled up and fell backwards into the water.

Joe crawled along the boat and looked over the side. Blueneck came up a little to the left and seized hold of the side; Joe pushed him off, and he sank again and tried to strike out for the shore, but his wind was gone and he floundered, gasping.

Joe looked at him critically.

"You won't come near my wife no more," he observed, as he threw the helpless man a line. "Oh, no, you can't come in my boat dripping as ye are," he said cheerily as the other, wild-eyed and half-drowned, clawed at the boat. "You hang on that there line and I'll tow ye in," Joe continued, and suiting the action to the word picked up both oars and struck out.

When at last the keel grated on the soft shingle, Joe got out and after first dropping his anchor looked round for Blueneck. The man lay still in the water, both hands tightly grasping the line, the ripple of the waves tossing him to and fro.

Joe dragged him in, threw him down on a bank of dry seaweed, and stood looking at him for a minute or two.

"Ah, I wonder if he be dead now," he said to himself, and he bent down to lift the sailor's eyelids. He tore open the wet remains of Blueneck's best surcoat and put his hand in the left side.

Then he stood up and shrugged his shoulders.

"Ah, well!" he said, addressing the unconscious body, "seeing that you ain't dead, you may as well live, but you won't come round my house in a hurry again, or there won't be any not quite dead about it—see?"

Blueneck opened his eyes for a second and then fell back again into unconsciousness.

Joe looked round him, heaved a sigh of relief and, as he strolled off up to the Ship, his face assumed once more its wonted good-humour, his heavy sandy lashes fell half-over his eyes as usual, and, thrusting his thumbs in his belt, he whistled as clearly, happily, and tunefully as a linnet in May.

Chapter XI

Everything on the shore was very dark and very silent when Blueneck regained consciousness and sat up. His head ached and his body was stiff and cold while his clothes, still wet and sticky with brine, clung to him uncomfortably.

He peered round in the darkness striving to remember where he was and what had happened to him. There was no moon, or at least if there was it was so hidden behind the clouds as to be of no use to anyone, and he could only faintly distinguish a kind of haze some quarter of a mile in front of him which he supposed was the sea. Behind him he could see nothing at all, only blackness. He put out a cold, trembling hand and felt cautiously about; the first thing he touched was the dry crumbly seaweed. Not sure what it was he grasped a handful of it and pulled it up. Immediately the sickening stench of stale salt water arose and he spat and swore aloud. Then he reached out his other hand and touched still more seaweed. He groaned with stiffness and pain and threw himself back on the heap. As he did so his shoulders encountered something hard and he almost screamed aloud so much did it jar him. Changing to a sitting posture again he felt for the obstacle and found that whatever it was lay beneath the seaweed. Wearily he pushed the stuff aside and thrust his hand into the clammy depths beneath. The hard thing was lower down still and he burrowed feverishly in a tired thoughtless way, hardly knowing what he did or why he did it.

Suddenly he paused, and felt more gingerly—yes, surely he could not be mistaken, he was running his hand over the hard round belly of a rum keg. He twisted round quickly and winced as his stiffened muscles twinged at the movement. Beside the first keg he felt another; and yet another at the side of that. He lay back exhausted by the effort and wondered at his find. He had no doubt it was some smuggler's private store, but was surprised that on such a lawless coast such secrecy should be resorted to. He knew that in Mersea everyone was more or less his own master and thought that it was therefore a rather unnecessary precaution.

When he had arrived thus far in his thoughts, however, he felt a return of the giddiness which he had before experienced and lay back, his eyes open, staring in front of him.

He had not lain so many minutes before he caught the glimmer of a light in the distance and he stared at it in surprise. It was not coming from the sea and was therefore not the riding light of a boat, neither was it coming from the direction of the brig or the Ship Inn, but from the West, from the lonely strip of coast between the little villages of East Mersea and West Mersea.

Nearer and nearer it came, till he could see how it jogged and danced along the beach, swaying from side to side, pausing a minute here, and then darting off again, sometimes vanishing completely only to reappear considerably nearer.

Blueneck watched it fascinated, a strange uncanny fear creeping over him; everywhere was so dark and lonely, and he strained his eyes peering at the light fancying that he saw sometimes a man behind it, sometimes a beast, or a fiend. This fear grew upon him every moment, and he tried to struggle to his feet, but his legs were too benumbed to bear him and he sank back again.

The light came nearer and nearer, dancing and swaying more than ever. In a flash the story of the lost row-boat ran through his mind and his flesh began to creep.

Like most sailors, and Spaniards especially, Blueneck was very superstitious; he shuddered and his teeth chattered as he imagined the thing that was holding the lantern to be first a blue swollen corpse with dead sightless eyes, then a rampaging devil with swinging tail and ram's horns, and then a mermaid whose white teeth were adder's fangs, and whose lips were the nightshade's berries.

His hand crept up to his neck where a little wooden crucifix usually hung, but it was gone; he must have lost it in the fight with Joe. He trembled and mouthed a prayer.

The light seemed to be making straight for him, and as it came nearer wild unearthly crooning noises came from it.

Blueneck gulped, and his eyes started from his head and the blood tingled and danced in his veins.

The noise, it was certainly not a song nor yet the cry of an animal, but a sort of long-drawn-out sighing on a high quavering note, came nearer and grew louder. Now the light was within fifteen paces of him and he held his breath. Nearer it came.

"Donna Maria, let it pass," he prayed. Now it was within five yards of him, and came nearer still. Straining his eyes he could make out a fearful bundlelike figure behind the lantern. The noise grew louder; nearer it came till the light stopped three feet away from him, and fell on the most evil and half-human face the terrified sailor had ever seen.

This was the last straw and Blueneck screamed. The sound rang out high and short as he dropped back on the weed, half-insensible. However much the thing with the lantern had frightened him, he certainly frightened it with his yell, for it sprang back and emitted a howl which started the echoes and woke the sea-birds, who screamed also as they flapped sleepily away.

Blueneck shut his eyes and waited three seconds of horrible suspense. Then he felt the light beating on his eyelids, and heard a cracked human voice very near him say:

"Oh! ye would be spying on me, would ye, ye hell-traitor?"

The words reassured Blueneck more than perhaps anything else would have done and he opened his eyes. The terrible old face was very near his own, and hot spirit-tainted breath blew into his nostrils, but what fixed his attention was the glitter of steel above the figure's head.

Blueneck rose to the situation now that he was assured of the old woman's mortality (he decided that it must be an old woman). He was not the man to be frightened of a knife other than his captain's.

"Pity a poor sailor; so stiff with the cold that his legs will not bear him," he moaned, in a pitiful pleading whine.

The old woman laughed horribly.

"You don't catch birds like Pet Salt with chaff, hell-rat," she said.

"Pet Salt!" Blueneck began to understand.

"Mistress," he said, "what are you about?"

"Killing a spying knave," was the reply, and the blade descended until its point pricked his throat.

Things were turning out more seriously than Blueneck had expected and he spoke quickly.

"Is it rum you want, lady?" he said as steadily as he could, the blade pricking deeper as the words moved the muscle of his throat.

"It is, hell-rat—it is," Pet Salt bent nearer, "and no spying dog shall stop me from getting it. Ye waited out here till you were too stiff to move, did you? Ah, you blue-livered pike, the devil looks after his own."

"Then I'm the man to get it for thee. I'm the mate of the *Coldlight.*"

Blueneck had just time to get out the words or she would have killed him.

"How do I know you be not?" she said shrewdly, though visibly shaken at his words, as she withdrew the knife.

"I swear," began the sailor.

Pet Salt stopped him.

"Swear!" she screamed. "What's a seaman's oath to me?"

"Look at my garments," said the anxious Blueneck. "Are they those of a comman man or one befitting my station?"

Pet, like many other women before and since, was moved at the sight of the bright colours and good stuffs.

"They be ruined with salt water," she remarked. "What happened to you, hell-rat?"

Blueneck paused before he spoke. His pride forbade him to tell the truth, and his prudence warned him against a lie. Finally he made a compromise between the two and told a fairly plausible story of two men setting upon him, of a fearful fight, and finished up with a faithful account of the ducking which he had received.

Pet seemed satisfied. How much she believed is another matter but, as she often told Ben Farran, she understood sea-folk and all their tricks.

She put up the knife somewhere in her rags and set down the lantern.

"Try and stand," she commanded.

Blueneck obeyed as one in a dream; slowly and painfully he staggered to his feet, only to drop again almost immediately.

Pet waddled after him.

"Rub your legs," she said, "and hurry. You've got to work for me before the cocks crow."

Wearily Blueneck did as he was bid, and the old woman hobbled off to the bank of seaweed where she set to work unearthing the kegs. With a grunt of satisfaction she set the last one beside the others and turned to Blueneck.

"Come on," she said.

Blueneck staggered to his feet; he was still very unsteady, but the rubbing had partially restored his circulation and he was just able to stumble along.

Pet pointed to the three kegs.

"Carry two," she said shortly.

Blueneck looked around him hopelessly. It was still dark and lonely and some of the horror he had felt when he first saw Pet Salt returned to him. He shuddered; the bent old figure in front of him clad in dirty evil-smelling rags seemed again to take on some of the fear-inspiring qualities of a fiend or marsh-goblin. He struggled on to where the kegs were lying and with great difficulty hoisted one on to his shoulder.

Pet lifted up another.

"Put this under your other arm," she said, "and mind your stepping; it's heavy."

Blueneck took it without a word.

Pet took up the last keg and turned to him, her ugly bulbous face showing red with exertion in the lantern's flickering light.

"Now follow after me," she said, and hobbled off.

Long afterwards Blueneck described this journey from the bank of seaweed to Ben Farran's boat as a walk through hell itself.

Time after time the keg under his arm slipped and fell in the soft powdery shingle, and he had to bend his stiffened and aching body to pick it up again, while the terrible cracked voice of Pet Salt railing in the most fearful language rang in his ears.

But he went on. Once he fell and cut his head on a breakwater stone, and the old woman kicked him with her wooden-shod foot and bade him rise in a tone that had fear in it as well as command.

Once they saw a lantern in the far distance and Pet made him crouch and wait silent till it passed on. Again and again he felt that he must break away and regain his lost courage, but always the fear of the dark desolateness and the awful old woman prevented him, and he went on meekly.

How at last he managed to climb up the rope-ladder and scramble on to the deck of the *Pet* and then down the hatchway to the stifling cabin and bunk-room below he did not know. However, he did it and fell through the doorway into Ben Farran's presence in a fainting condition.

When he recovered himself the air was full of a strange sickening odour, mixed with the fumes of steaming rum.

He looked round him curiously. The room was very small even for a boat and marvellously dirty and untidy.

A few rags were bundled together in a corner forming a rude sort of bed, and an old iron stove smoked and spat in another. On the top of this stood an iron bowl, and it was from this Blueneck decided that the strange smell came.

In a corner by the stove lay Ben Farran snoring loudly with his mouth open.

Blueneck looked at him curiously. He had been a fine big man he judged, and had some strength and comeliness, but much rum had changed him, and he sprawled there a most ungainly, loathsome figure. His shoulders were bent till he lost any pretension to height, his jaw was weak and drooping, and great blue pouches of flesh hung under his eyes. This, combined with an enormous stomach and bent podgy legs, gave him a great resemblance to a fat toad.

Blueneck looked away and turned his attentions to himself. He found that his outer garments had been removed and that his arms and legs were covered with a black-greenish paste. He looked at them in surprise and disgust and began to rub off the caked mixture as fast as he could. But he noticed that his stiffness had left him and that he felt as well and strong as he had done the night before he had his fight with Joe Pullen.

Pet came in presently and he saw that she was growing fast like Ben, rum-sodden and old. She smiled when she saw him, and he thought how horribly pale her toothless gums showed across the flaming purple redness of her face.

"Now, master mate of the *Coldlight,* I would bargain with thee," she began, as she handed him his clothes newly dried and motioned him to dress.

Blueneck said nothing, but took his garments and began to put them on.

"Methinks your Captain the Spanish Dick has set eyes on a pretty wench," she said slowly.

The sailor did not look up; he was mournfully regarding his best doublet coat stained and faded with salt water.

"Oh, there be many pretty wenches who have had his eyes upon them," he said carelessly.

Pet swore roundly and with such vehemence that he glanced at her.

"But one particular wench?" she went on, relapsing again into quietness. "I have long ears."

Blueneck, who was slow of comprehension, looked at her in surprise; her remark struck him as being strangely irrelevant.

"I hear what is said on the Island," the old woman continued. "I know your Captain hath a great liking for Ann Farran, Ben's gran'daughter."

Blueneck looked even more puzzled.

"Ay, and if it be so, what then?" he said.

Pet smiled again.

"Your Captain carries much rum," she observed.

Blueneck nodded and pulled on his boots.

"This Ann Farran hath but one kinsman in the world save her

bastard half-brother," Pet went on crooningly.

Blueneck stood up, he began to see to what she was leading up.

"There would be none to look for the wench, or hark to the wench if one were quieted," she went on suggestively.

"And that one loves rum!" observed Blueneck.

Pet smiled again.

"And that one loves rum!" she repeated.

Blueneck stood thinking for a moment or two, his hands clasped in his pockets.

"For this news, Mistress, I will say naught of what has passed this evening, nor of the three rum kegs," he said.

Pet nodded; the man seemed intelligent.

"Nor will I say aught of a lost boat," continued the sailor, darting his bright black eyes upon her.

Pet blinked. This man was too intelligent, she told herself.

"I will tell the Captain of your bargain," Blueneck went on. "It may be he will hear. Meanwhile," he looked at the array of little kegs on the floor, "you will not die of thirst, Mistress."

Pet shrugged her shoulders and looked across at the slovenly figure by the stove.

"We both drink well," she said.

Blueneck looked from one to the other.

"Of that I have no doubt," he sneered, and walked out up the hatchway. "I will tell the Captain," he called back, as he climbed down the rope-ladder and on to the now sunlit wall.

He walked along talking to himself in a whisper. Now and again he paused and made as though to go back. Then he recovered himself and went on still muttering. Finally he shrugged his shoulders.

"Well, it won't be the first time rum has bought a fair lass anyway," he said aloud, "and it ain't a right thing in a man to go against old habits."

And lifting his head he began to whistle blithely.

Chapter XII

It was seven o'clock on the following Wednesday evening and there was an air of expectation in the Ship's kitchen.

The *Coldlight* was due to sail under a new name at the late tide.

Anny was upstairs preparing herself for Dick's coming, while in the room below the talk ran high and many conjectures as to the Captain's intentions were put forward and withdrawn, as the company drank round the fire.

"Osh, where's the man as can withstand a pretty lass?" said Gilbot, smiling and hiccoughing over his sack.

"Ah, maybe, maybe, but 'tis a wonderful risky thing, this changing names o' crafts," put in Granger, wagging his head. "I don't hold with it myself."

"Ah, I reckon the Captain knows what he's about; there ain't many like him to a mile," remarked another man.

"You're right there," said old Cip de Musset, who had been sitting silently in a corner for some time. "He ain't no crab, but I'd not let a lass o' mine have much to do with him."

"What do you mean?" said Hal, firing up and coming over from the doorway where he had been standing.

Old Gilbot began to laugh.

"Hark to th' lad," he gurgled. "One would think he loved her hisself."

Hal turned away from the light before he spoke and no one saw the deep flush which crept up over his features even to the roots of his hair, making his scalp tingle uncomfortably.

"We look after our wenches at the Ship, Master Gilbot," he said hastily.

Gilbot nodded happily.

"Ay," he said, "wesh do, wesh do!" and the talk continued.

Just as the clock by the chimney-piece struck the quarter, steps were heard coming across the yard, and Blackkerchief Dick, flanked by Blueneck and Habakkuk Coot, and backed by some nine or ten hardy ruffians, marched in at the door.

In an instant the little Spaniard was the centre of an enthusiastic group, for, since his first coming to the ship, Dick had done much to make himself popular, and now his deep musical voice was raised good-naturedly above the din calling for rum all round and sack for those who wished for it.

Hal and Sue darted about in obedience to his order and soon the company stood silent, mugs in hand, waiting for the toast. At this moment the inner door opened and Anny, dressed in the purple gown that Sue had given her, stepped into the kitchen.

Dick was at her side in a moment and respectfully taking her hand led her into the centre of the room.

"Ann of the Island, her health and beauty for ever!" he shouted, his tankard high above his head. The toast was given boisterously, and Anny blushed and smiled shyly.

Old Gilbot was enjoying himself thoroughly and took advantage of a lull in the conversation to exclaim:

"Letsh have a shong!" and then without any more ado began to quaver "Pretty Poll "at the top of his voice.

The company took up the burden and the final "Lost in the rolling sea" was bellowed till the rafters shook.

"More rum," called Dick, and then, as though obeying an impulse of the moment, he sprang upon one of the forms and resting one foot on the trestled table exclaimed:

"Hark ye, dogs! here is a new song, mine own song, a song of Dick Delfazio's own composing."

And then throwing back his head he began to sing in a remarkably true tenor voice, swaying his body in tune to his own music:

> "Fair as a seagull and proud as the sea,
> As naught in the world is fair Anny to me,
> So gentle, so tender, so wise without guile,
> Oh! where is another like Ann of the Isle?
> Ann! oh! Ann of the Island,
> Where is another like Ann of the Isle?"

By this time the rumkins were all replenished and the chorus of the song was taken up and repeated to the accompaniment of jingling pewter.

Dick still kept his position and took up the song again, his dark eyes flashing and smiling at the girl who watched him fascinated.

> "Avaunt ye fine ladies of France and of Spain,
> So wayward, so wanton, so proud, and so vain.
> No sweet pleading look, no trick, or no wile,
> Shall ever more tempt me from Ann of the Isle.
> Ann! oh! Ann of the Island,
> Where is another like Ann of the Isle?"

And then he added before anyone could speak, "To the brig, boys," and skipping lightly off the table he offered his hand to Anny and led the way out into the yard, the whole company following, roaring as they went:

> "Ann! oh! Ann of the Island,
> Where is another like Ann of the Isle?"

Anny looked up shyly at the Spaniard, her heart beating quickly with excitement. He was strolling jauntily along her hand tightly held in his own; the starlight touched the jewelled hilt of his knife, and his big mournful black eyes winked and smiled happily.

He loved display, pageant, parade; she could see that by the way his men marched around him in regulated order, and by his gorgeous clothes, and she herself became a little intoxicated by the air of excitement, and the singing of the laughing, jostling crowd.

Glancing at him under her lashes she slipped her hand through his arm and laughed a little self-consciously.

A curious self-satisfied but half-regretful smile passed over his face and he bent towards her.

"Give me a kiss, little one," he said softly.

A wave of cold water seemed to dash over Anny's pleasure and she drew her arm away stiffly, saying: "Prithee, sir, I would return to the Ship."

Again the curious smile spread over Dick's lips, but this time there was no regret.

"Pardon, Mistress, methinks thy beauty and mine own singing hath made my brain whirl. Prithee, prithee, fair one, give me thy hand again."

Anny looked at him and held out her hand without a word. He seemed so debonair, so gracious, such a fine gentleman, and his soft eyes sought hers almost beseechingly, she thought.

"Ann! oh! Ann of the Island,
Where is another like Ann of the Isle?"

sang the company as the little procession neared the water-side.

Sue, who walked between French and Cip de Musset, looked at the two small figures in front and sighed involuntarily. She also thought that the Spaniard was a fine gentleman and she also had seen his dark eyes fixed mournfully on the other girl's face, and she began to laugh and talk noisily to hide her vexation.

Gallantly Blackkerchief Dick led the little serving-wench down over the planked way to the row-boat, helped her in, and then stepped lightly after her. Several of the company crowded in behind them and they pushed off. The rest of the band seized other boats that were anchored near the shore and followed as best they could.

Once on board the brig, Anny looked about her with delight; the shrouded sails and spider-web-like rigging pleased her immensely; the swinging lanterns overhead showed the clean boards and newly-painted sides, and she laughed with satisfaction as she noted first one thing and then another.

Dick was no less pleased; he loved his boat and derived more pleasure from showing it off than from anything else in the world. He took her from end to end, telling her tales of hairbreadth escapes and secret cargoes of papers and documents. Indeed, carried away by his own enthusiasm, he even hinted that good King Charles owed more to Dick Delfazio's courage than His Majesty was aware of.

Anny listened to him open-mouthed, as he talked on, embroidering his tales with a network of fine and polished phrases, and interrupting them here and there to shout an order or swear at an unhandy seaman, as the man hurried to obey him.

When at last the greater part of the company which had followed Dick from the Ship stood on the deck of the *Coldlight,* he opened the proceedings after the custom of the Island by calling for rum all round.

After the toast, the whole crowd, which was by this time very boisterous, congregated in the forepart of the ship to inspect the figure-head, which was at the moment covered with a piece of sailcloth.

Dick, with his inborn love of dramatic effect, had seen to this, and now stepping forward he whipped it off with a flourish and stepped back, observing with delight the impression it was making.

Old Ned Hutton, the ship's carpenter, was certainly not an artist, but he had done his best, and all that paint and a chunk of rough-hewn wood could do had been done. The figure was undoubtedly meant to represent Anny and that was enough for Mersea folk. Everybody cheered loudly, and Dick called for more rum. Then he and the girl went forward to examine the figure-head more closely.

The ugly awkward thing was profusely decorated with gold paint; so much Anny could see by the light of the lantern which Dick gallantly held for her, and her name, *Anny,* was painted on the bright blue band that went round the figure's black head.

" 'Tis lovely," she whispered half to herself as she ran her fingers over the great arms and breasts on which the paint was hardly dry.

Dick smiled and made her the obvious compliment, and they went down to the bows and leaned over the gunwale so as to see the four great white letters, *Anny*, painted on the smooth brown sides.

The girl was delighted, and her infectious gurgling laugh rang out clearly several times on the cold air as she listened to Dick's sparkling conversation.

"Tide's full and wind fair," sang out a voice suddenly from the watch-tower.

Instantly there was confusion: Dick shouted orders here and there, but did not take his hand from Anny's arm. Everyone made for the boats shouting farewells to the crew which responded cheerfully.

Dick bent nearer to the girl.

"I will come again," he said softly.

Anny smiled and nodded.

"We are ever pleased to see company at the Ship," she said demurely, slipping her arm out of his grasp and moving over to the side where French, Sue, and Hal waited for her.

Dick followed her.

"Give us your blessing, Mistress," he said loudly. There was silence at once; the sailors attached much importance to a blessing and they stood quietly.

Anny looked round desperately; she had never had a blessing in her life, much less given one, and for a moment she was entirely at a loss. No one spoke, however, so at last she crossed herself devoutly and said as clearly as her nervousness would permit, "I pray God bless this ship, Amen."

"Amen," repeated the crew solemnly, and then dashed off on their business and the bustle recommenced.

Sue climbed over the side of the boat, French followed her, and then Hal.

"Farewell, Ann of the Island," said the Spaniard softly. "I will return to thee."

Anny looked at him and he seemed to her very comely. She held out her hand and he raised it to his lips.

"Farewell, sir," she said, and then followed her lover into the little boat.

"Farewell!" came the deep and almost beautiful voice again; there was the clink of chains and the anchor was weighed, and then the brig, her sails all set, glided out into the Channel.

Hal bent his back to the oar he was plying and spoke to the other three in the little row-boat without looking up.

"There goes a damned nuisance off the Isle for a bit," he said.

French grunted and pulled hard. Sue sighed and looked out to sea, while Anny laughed a little ruefully, and patted Hal's broad shoulders with her little brown hand, upon which the Spaniard's kiss still burnt.

Chapter XIII

"Anny, are you gone to sleep yet?" Sue sat up in her bed and peered through the darkness to where the other girl lay in a far corner. Her hair was unbound and fell over her coarse night-garment like a soft black shawl, as she leant forward speaking almost in a whisper.

It was nearly a month since Dick had sailed away from the Island, and the quiet country life had flowed peacefully on at the Ship without interruption. But Sue had not forgotten the little Spaniard. It was a continual source of amazement to her that she could have entertained a liking for him or ever a thought when big handsome Ezekiel French was by, but she was not sure about Anny.

Sue had an observant eye and she noticed that Hal and the girl were not as often together as they had used to be, and she drew her own conclusions. She had a kind heart, and she felt herself Anny's guardian in a sense.

Poor, quaint, foolish little Anny, she thought, so fond of admiration, so willing to love and be loved, so pretty and so gentle, and then she thought of the Spaniard, with his bright, devil-may-care eyes, and full red lips, and she nodded her head into the darkness and leaned forward again.

"Anny," she said distinctly.

"Ay," Anny's voice came clearly out of the dark corner.

"Have you been asleep yet?" whispered Sue.

"Nay." Anny turned over on her side.

"Did you not hear me speak before?" the other girl persisted.

Anny sighed and turned back again.

"Nay, I have lain long a thinking," she said.

Sue drew her knees up to her chin and clasped them with her arms before she spoke again.

"Do you ever think of the Spaniard?" she said at last, and then added, as Anny vouchsafed no answer:

"Blackkerchief Dick?"

Anny moved in her bed.

"Oh, him!" she said, with a note of contempt in her pretty child-like voice. "Oh, nay!"

Sue sighed again, and when she spoke her tone had a certain tenderness in it.

"Why do you lie to me, Anny Farran?" she said.

Anny sighed softly.

"Oh! Mistress Sue," she said, "what would you have me tell you? How many times he begged a kiss of me, or held my hand, or bore my onions with his fair white hands?"

Sue flushed.

"Sure he never carried onions for thee!" she said.

"Marry! did he not?" said Anny quickly. "Ay, with his thin white fingers cracking under their weight, and the muddied side o' the skip rubbing on his silken hose did he carry onions for me, and I stumbling along at his side for all the world like a Hythe oyster wench: oh, Lord! the tales he did tell," and she broke off into a little chuckle, and Sue frowned.

"I would speak seriously with you, Anny," she began.

Anny sighed and tossed like a naughty child and then resigned herself to the lecture she felt was coming.

"I am listening," she said.

Sue spoke earnestly and sincerely.

"Methinks you care too much for the Spaniard, lass," she said.

Anny gasped audibly but said nothing, and Sue mistaking the sound for a sigh of confession went on:

"He is a dangerous man for a young wench to think on," she said. "I would not trust a man who looked so boldly at every smirking lass who chanced to stand in his way as he walked from the yard to the brig. Ah! you may laugh, but I know. I served in this inn long before you came, and I've seen men and wenches, time and again. Remember what befell Maria Turnby when her husband left for the Indies. There's a thing for him to hear when he comes back again, poor fellow—his own children left to starve that sweetbreads may be served for another man's brats. Oh, Anny, lass," Sue's voice shook in its earnestness, "have a care, have a care. Men be eels wi' maids. And this Delfazio, as he is pleased to call himself, is a deal more eel-like than many other menfish. What with his soft laughter, and hands like white and polished bone, together with black, wanton eyes! Oh! have a care, I know tales of him; they say no one ever dares to come between him and his wishes, and that never since he was a squalling brat has he been stayed from getting what he wants. Oh! Anny, perchance he wants you, and perchance you will be bewitched into letting him get his way."

Anny sat up on her straw mattress, her bright eyes glittering in the ray of starlight which shone in through the uncurtained window, and her little white teeth clenched.

"Methinks you wrong me, Mistress," she said, restraining her voice with difficulty. "I have no love for any crawling foreigner. What if he do eat and talk like the quality; I tell thee there are thirty other men I would rather marry than a brown-skinned Spaniard."

"Marry?" Sue laughed and Anny flushed.

"Methinks," she went on, her voice becoming colder at every word, "that not to me so much as to thee, Mistress Sue, should such talk be addressed. Is your heart so free from thoughts of this same Dick that you can hold him up to me as dangerous? What was it made thee lose thy taste for Master French's talk so suddenly? Oh! truth! you make me sick to see you take me for so senseless a wench that you think I do not see your cleverness. Mistress, beware of jealousy."

Sue gasped. She had never considered the possibility of her words being taken in this way, and she could think of no adequate reply at that moment, save a reproachful, "Anny!"

There was silence for a moment or two and then Anny spoke again over her shoulder.

"Rest assured," she said, "'tis not thoughts of thy pesky little cheap-jack that keeps me awake o' nights. There be many here better than he, and one amongst them whom I love."

Then she buried her head under the blankets and did not speak again, in spite of Sue's protestations of dislike for Dick, and the elder girl getting tired of talking to seemingly deaf ears lay down also and beguiled herself to sleep with thoughts of her own lover.

The next day broke fine and fresh after the heavy rainfall of the preceding three weeks, but Sue went about her work with a certain nervous fidgetiness, which irritated Anny and sent her out over the fields with Hal.

Several times when they were out, Sue went up to her room and there peered into the cracked mirror, putting a curl back here, another forward there, smoothing down her eyelashes with a moistened thumb and forefinger, and biting her lips till the red blood suffused them glowingly. More often did she go to the window, however, and stand there for minutes on end, staring out into the new begreened landscape, where the young leaves danced like lambkins in the cool, strong, sea breeze, the sun on their wet surfaces lending them some of the splendour of jewels.

Sue had made up her mind. Nobody came to the Ship all the morning, and by three o'clock she was in no pleasant humour so old Gilbot found when he asked her to sing for him, for she was up and off in a moment with the sharp remark "that there was more to do in the world than sing and get deep in liquor."

Gilbot was amazed; his little blue eyes stared surprisedly in front of him and he absent-mindedly put his rumkin upside down on the stove, and it was some minutes before he discovered that the kitchen was reeking with burnt rum dregs.

This made Sue angrier still and she bustled about throwing open the doors, muttering the while that she was ashamed to let visitors into a room that smelt like Pet Salt's boat and looked like a sty.

Little Red Farran, however, found her in a very different mood for, when he came creeping into the scullery with his kitten (now wellnigh a cat) tucked under his arm, she caught him up in her arms and kissed him, and then to his astonishment gave him a large slice of oat-meal cake high-heaped with quince jelly and sent him off on his way rejoicing.

Her charity was well-rewarded, for some two minutes later the kitchen door was kicked open, and Red and French came in together.

Sue began at once to bustle about with unnatural gaiety, and Gilbot regarded her with still greater astonishment, until he suddenly looked round and saw French. Then he nodded his head sagely once or twice, and, getting up with difficulty, tottered to get his coat which hung behind the door.

"Redsh an' Ish goin' foa walk," he announced.

Red gave a whoop of delight and ran after him happily.

French looked after them in surprise.

"Whatever made him go off like that, now?" he said, as he sat down at the table.

Sue blushed and clanged the pots together noisily.

"I'm sure I don't know," she said almost sharply.

French turned to her, his handsome boyish face blank with astonishment.

"Why, what's the matter with you?" he said.

Sue shrugged her shoulders and bit her lips. Why was he so different to-day, she wondered?

"Me—oh, nothing. Is there aught in my face that should make you ask that?"

Sue turned a fiery cheek towards the young giant, and then moved away.

French got up.

"I don't know what's taken you all," he said, puzzled. "When I first comes in, Master Gilbot flies out wi' the young lad, and now you look at me as though I'd done some mortal wrong. What is it?"

"Oh! go to with ye." Sue's back was towards him and he could not see her face, but her voice sounded sharply. "I'm getting your rum as fast as may be."

"What need you be worrying about rum?"

French looked round him miserably.

"I'm sorry," he said, changing his weight from one foot to the other, and his hands becoming noticeable and awkward.

Sue only sighed impatiently and busied herself with the rum.

French turned on his heel.

"All's well then," he said finally. "I'll be getting down West. I reckon I knows when I'm welcome or not, Mistress—Mistress Susan Gilbot," and he strode to the door. "There's other inns," he said meaningly.

Sue turned about in a moment.

"Oh, wait for your rum, Master French," she said.

French did not move, but stood straddle-legged in the doorway looking out into the yard.

"Rum? Oh, that don't matter; an inn's got more uses than just to sell rum, Mistress," he said.

"Indeed, to provide wenches for any man to insult, I reckon," said Sue, tossing her head and dashing her hand across her eyes.

French turned round quickly.

"Why, who's been insulting you, lass?" he said sharply.

Sue laughed and turned her head away.

"What's that to you?" she said.

French shrugged his shoulders.

"I'm going," he remarked and stepped down the stone stair into the yard.

Sue swallowed once and then ran after him.

"Prithee wait while I hot your rum, sir," she said.

French turned willingly.

"I'd do aught for you when you ask me like that, Sue," he said gently, as he followed her back into the kitchen and sat down while she bustled around with a tankard hardly knowing what she did.

French watched her critically.

"Aught been upsetting you, Mistress?" he asked.

"Nay." Sue blushed again and stumbled over a form.

The big man sighed and looked into the fire.

"Been thinking of the Spaniard?" he asked half between his teeth.

"No," said Sue so vehemently that he jumped. "I have not, nor am like to."

French smiled on her.

"Well, that's all right then, ain't it?" he said cheerfully.

"I don't know what you're talking about," she said stiffly,.

French's smile faded.

"No, that's right," he said, almost mournfully, "that's right."

And there was silence for a few moments. He drank his rum and after opening and shutting his mouth once or twice rose to go.

Sue watched him to the door, and then in spite of herself the tears began to trickle down the side of her nose, and she sobbed once audibly.

French was at her side in a moment.

"What is the matter, lassie?" he said kindly, all his shyness vanishing as he whipped out a large yellow handkerchief and began to wipe her eyes hastily. "Are you ill?"

Sue sobbed violently.

"No," she said angrily, and then, snatching the handkerchief out of his hand, buried her face in it.

French put a big hand on each of her shoulders and shook her gently.

"If I asked you for something would you give it to me?" he said.

Sue still covered her face with her hands.

"Oh! why don't you ask me?" she sobbed.

French lifted her up in his arms to kiss her, and she stopped crying and began to blush as he carried her over to the chimney corner where they sat, laughing and whispering, till Gilbot and Red, driven in by the rain, which had restarted with as much violence as ever, came for their tea.

"I thought you watched that damned Spaniard a deal too much, sweetheart," said French, as he and Sue walked to the end of the lane together, although the rain came down in torrents.

"Oh! go along with you. Would I rather not have a man to love, than a live knife?" said Sue, as she stood on tiptoe to kiss him.

Chapter XIV

Master Francis Myddleton leaned back in his chair and gently stuffed a wad of coarse Virginia into the slightly blackened bowl of his stubby clay pipe, and lifted his gouty foot on to one of the bronzed firedogs which ornamented his spacious hearth, and then after pulling once or twice at the short stem, he took out a bundle of letters from one of his capacious pockets and began to read them. They were from his son who held a fairly responsible place at the court of his Gracious Majesty King Charles II., and from time to time a low wheezing chuckle broke from the old man's lips, and he coughed and spat, the tears of laughter starting to his eyes as he read.

"The sly devil," he muttered, laughing, "bribed her serving-wench with a kiss, did he? Oh! dearie, dearie me—Good King Jamie was more particular. What a thing it is to be young and to have a king to serve," and he laughed again, this time quite loudly.

A female voice called shrilly from the room above.

"What's ailing you, Francis?"

Master Myddleton put the letters hastily into his pocket.

"'Tis naught, Eliza, my foot doth trouble me somewhat."

"Marry," came the high, strident voice from the other room, "'tis strange that a gouty foot should make you laugh like a moonstruck lunatic."

Master Myddleton made no reply, and, after a moment's pause, the voice went on again:

"'Tis a wonder you can laugh when we have a man coming to take the very bread out of our mouths. You should be praying the Lord to succour your wife and daughter, not laughing yourself daft by the fireside."

The old man sighed and shook the ashes from his pipe and began to slowly refill it.

"What's o'clock?" he called out after a minute or so's silence.

"Half after eight; he should be here by now if the river ain't high over the bridle path by Tenpenny Heath."

"Ay," said Master Myddleton reflectively.

There was the sound of a chair being pushed back and of heavy steps on the stairs, and Mistress Eliza Myddleton entered the dining-room where her husband sat.

She was a big fair woman who still preserved a remnant of the great beauty which had once been hers, but as she often told her neighbours when she was in confidential mood, what with having a rapscallion stepson and a pretty daughter to look after, an exciseman for a husband, and also being a staunch, God-fearing woman and a puritan at that, lines and wrinkles would come, and they had—as indeed anyone might note for himself.

Now as she came into the room, her thin face pale with worry, Francis looked at her and old villain that he was he wondered why he had ever married her.

"What are you going to say to him?" began the lady, planting herself before him, her bony arms akimbo.

Master Francis shrugged his shoulders.

"Say?" he said. "Why, naught!"

Mistress Eliza threw her hands above her head in a gesture of despair.

"You would," she said. "I don't believe you realise the state we are in. I don't believe you care if your wife and child are thrown into the streets. I don't believe you could say a word to save yourself hanging. In God's truth I don't believe you have your wits about you, Master Myddleton."

Francis sat still, puffing at his pipe, and his wife went on:

"Had you only done your duty, and gone out after the Mersea smugglers, I might be a fine lady this day or at least——"

"A widow!" put in Francis, without removing the pipe from his mouth.

"Oh!" Mistress Eliza gasped. "For shame, Master Myddleton, are you a coward?"

"Not more 'an others, but, Lord, Eliza, you wouldn't have me trapesing about i' the dusk hunting rum kegs?"

Francis took the pipe from his mouth and looked at his wife, a quizzical expression in his little grey eyes.

" 'Tis what you're paid for," said Mistress Myddleton, lifting her eyes to the low-raftered ceiling.

Master Myddleton coughed explosively and his face grew red with anger.

"God's body! Isn't that just like a woman," he shouted, dashing his hand so violently on the arm of his chair that his pipe flew into shivers, whereupon he swore an oath which made his wife shudder. "Just like a woman, sweet as honey till aught goes wrong," he continued, getting more and more angry at every word. "Did you ever talk of hunting smugglers before the Mayor of Colchester must needs appoint an assistant to me? Lord! woman, you drink smuggled tea every day of your life so as to be i' the fashion—don't talk to me!"

"It's very well for you to call this Thomas Playle an assistant, Master Myddleton," observed his wife with asperity. " 'Tis you are to be his assistant I'm thinking. That will be a nice thing for the neighbours to hear—now if only our Matilda and he could——"

Francis Myddleton fairly roared with fury.

"Peace with ye, designing woman," he shouted, "Will I have my only daughter disposed of before my eyes? Unfeeling mother! Elizabeth, I am amazed at ye."

Mistress Myddleton gulped with indignation.

"Francis, I am surprised at you. I disposing of your daughter! Oh, you scandalous man! Why ever was I married to such a lump of lying perfidy."

"God knows!" said Master Myddleton bitterly.

Mistress Elizabeth's answering outbreak was checked by the

sound of horse's hoofs in the cobbled yard outside.

"There he is—God help us!" she had time to whisper, and then composing her features into an amiable smile went out to meet their unwelcome guest.

Master Myddleton sat looking down at the fragments of his pipe: then he felt in his pocket and drew out a twist of tobacco which he smelt and rolled lovingly round his fingers.

He sighed.

"Drat women and work," he said to the roaring fire which blazed, crackled, and spat as though it quite agreed with him.

Master Thomas Playle sprang out of his saddle and threw his bridle rein to the grinning ostler who ran out to meet him, and then marched up to the front door and pulled the bell sharply.

Mistress Myddleton was before him in an instant and so overwhelmed him with welcome and motherly concern for his wet muddy condition that he had nothing to say for himself for a minute or so.

The candle-light in the stone-flagged hall showed the newcomer to be a tall, rather handsome man, some seven and twenty years of age.

Mistress Myddleton regarded him with approval and mentally summed up her daughter Matilda's attractive qualities: the result seemed to please her, for she smiled and conducted him to the dining-room.

"My husband hath a troubled foot," she was at some pains to explain, "and prays you to pardon him for not being on the steps to meet you."

Playle bowed coldly and followed his voluble hostess in silence.

Master Myddleton looked up casually as they entered, and after returning the younger man's bow without rising he bade his wife hasten the supper, and, after waiting until she was out of the room, motioned his guest to a comfortable chair on the opposite side of the hearth.

"His worship, the Mayor and his——" began the young man sententiously, as he sat down and stretched out his high mud-caked boots to the friendly fire.

Master Myddleton waved his hand.

"After we have eaten, I pray you. The morning will do," he said. "Until then I would like to speak of this heinous crime of smuggling as carried on in this town and on the Island over the Fleet."

Playle felt disquieted. Here he was in this old gentleman's house, drying himself at his fire, and making himself generally comfortable. How could he boldly announce that these affairs would be his care in the future, and that Master Myddleton need trouble himself no further? He decided to put it off till supper was over. After all he considered the old man must know something of use to him in his future work.

Master Playle was a very conscientious young man and one who had ambitions. He had fought for this appointment and meant to show his ability. He had served for a time in one of his Majesty's own regiments and still held a commission.

Master Myddleton began to speak.

"We have a very difficult task before us, Master Playle," he began in the deep pompous voice which he used on all official occasions. "I think I can truthfully say that on no other part of the coast is King Charles' law—God bless him—more persistently, and I might almost say, courageously violated."

He paused, and his little grey eyes sought a flicker of surprise on the young man's face, but they were disappointed. Playle's easy smile still played round his thin lips, as he listened with polite attention.

Master Myddleton began again.

"With such a violent, all-daring, cut-throat gang against me, I have—er—yes, to be plain with you, Master Playle—I have—er—felt it unwise—not to say foolhardy—to take more than preliminary measures against these unruly vagabonds, until I received assistance from headquarters."

Playle's smile deepened and Francis, looking up suddenly, saw it. Instantly his manner changed.

"Ah, I see you know something of their customs, Master Playle," he said, laughing wheezily.

Playle looked up a little disconcerted, but he laughed with the old man and nodded his head.

"I can see I can be quite plain with you," went on Francis, his eyes scanning the other's face.

Playle was a simple straightforward soldier, and he felt rather at a disadvantage with this quickwitted old villain with the gouty foot. However, he deemed it prudent to make some remark.

"Oh, yes, of a certainty, of a certainty!" he said as intelligently as possible. "I am determined to abolish this illegal trading."

Master Myddleton sighed. He began to see a little more clearly how the land lay.

"Very right, an excellent spirit in youth," he said heartily. "Go in and conquer—sweep all before you. That's how I like to hear young people talk. It is for the old, with our gouty feet and long experience, to sit at home and think out campaigns, and for you, the young and healthful in body, to carry them out gloriously."

He slapped his knee in applause at his own words, and then, as the young man said nothing, but sat still smiling into the fire, he continued, his voice resuming the pompous note:

"But believe me you have a difficult task, as I said before—a difficult task indeed. Now let me advise you first to attack the smuggling here on the mainland. Had you half a troop of infantry it would be madness to attempt to quieten Mersea Island."

Playle sat up and became interested.

"The Island," he said. "Yes, I've heard of the smuggling there; the block-house there was well guarded in the war I know."

Master Myddleton waved him silent, and continued to talk. "There are two principal smuggling vessels," he said casually. "The first, the *Dark Blood,* belongs to a man called de Witt, and then the *Coldlight,* which belongs to a mysterious Spaniard."

Young Playle gasped. That the old man should know all this and yet take no measures to stop it, amazed him, and his youthful imagination began to play round his old ambitions until he saw himself lord of the customs and his Majesty's right-hand man.

"Why not stop all vessels that enter the river?" he said.

"I had thought of it—I had thought of it," said Myddleton, wagging his head sagely.

"Well, I'm going to do it," replied Playle quickly.

Old Francis laughed deprecatingly and was about to answer him when Mistress Eliza, her daughter, a tall girl, fair like her mother and buxomly beautiful, with their little maid, Betsey, entered with the supper.

During the meal, Mistress Eliza talked almost incessantly and her husband filled up the few pauses in her streams of conversation with lurid stories of the smugglers' cruelty. Once, after a more vivid one than usual, Mistress Matilda looked archly at the young soldier.

"If only it could be stopped!" she said, while her mother made some remark about poor little Matty's childishness.

Thomas Playle looked up from the lump of boiled fish he was eating.

"It shall be stopped, Mistress," he said. "Such flagrant crime is a disgrace to the glorious court of his Gracious Majesty."

While Francis felt the bundle of letters in his pocket and grinned wickedly to himself.

"You have some men in your pay and arms for them, I suppose, Master Myddleton?" observed Playle a little later on in the evening.

"About five," said Francis, and then, noting the other's surprise, he added: "But some twenty more trustworthy men can be called out at a moment's notice, if you find it necessary."

Playle could hardly repress a smile of pleasure; life seemed suddenly to have opened up to him. Twenty-five men at his orders, a gang of ferocious smugglers to attack, and a pretty girl to stand by and admire at the proper time. His smile broadened.

His ambitions flew away with him and he sat staring at his plate, his brown eyes twinkling with pleasure, until Mistress Myddleton had to touch him on the shoulder and give him a candle, before he realised that Betsey, the little maid, waited to show him his room.

Once in their room Mistress Eliza and her husband argued over the situation until both were exhausted.

"He's a handsome man, anyway," said the lady at last, as she brushed her little wisp of grey-yellow hair before the oval mirror. "I wonder if Matilda——?"

Francis, who was already tucked in his side of the huge four-poster bed, growled through the curtains, and Mistress Eliza bit her lip.

"He'll make a difference to the price of tea hereabouts, I'll warrant," she said, after a minute's silence, as she blew out the candles and shut the casement.

Francis grunted.

"Methinks he'll be a deal of nuisance to the trade," he said bitterly. "No more cheap tabac—God help us!"

Mistress Eliza echoed his sigh, and they settled themselves to sleep.

Chapter XV

"There, look, there now, will that be the *Coldlight—Anny,* I mean?"

Anny paused in her walk and stared out across the bay. Hal followed the direction of her hand and then shook his head.

"Nay," he said, " 'tis too small."

Anny sighed and moved on, but the boy still stared out at the white-sailed boat on the horizon.

"Last time I saw a craft like that," he began reflectively, "was when the Preventative folk chased Fen de Witt half-way up the Pyfleet and then got stuck."

Anny stopped quickly.

"Lord! It won't be them, will it?" she said, a note of fear creeping into her voice.

Hal shrugged his shoulders.

"Like as not," he said carelessly.

The girl stared fascinated at the white speck in the distance.

"And the Captain coming back this very day!" she said.

Hal reddened at her words, and wheeled round fiercely, but she was not looking at him and he turned away again.

"Hal, what if the Preventative folk got anyone?" she asked.

"They'd die, that's all," he replied laconically.

The girl looked round at the early summer landscape and shuddered.

"Look again, are you sure about the boat?" she commanded anxiously.

Hal threw a casual glance over his shoulder.

"Sure? Sure of what?" he asked gruffly.

"That it's the Preventative folk!" Anny shook his sleeve as she spoke.

Hal wrenched his arm out of her grasp, and replied irritably:

"No, of course I'm not sure; don't be stupid, girl; I only said 'twas like one."

Anny looked at him in surprise.

"What's the matter?" she laughed; they had come to a part where the wall melts into the high-lying fields and the path is very wide, and Hal stepped back a pace or two and turned a red and angry face towards the girl.

"Look here, Anny," he said, his voice shaking with anger. "I'm tired of this hankering and whining after that dirty little Spaniard. You know we're going to be married as soon as I can get some money; then I'll be able to give you things—better things than him—aren't you going to wait for me? See here, I won't have this carrying on with the foreigner."

Anny's blood was up and she turned to her lover as fierce as a tiger-cat.

"Indeed and will you not, Master Hal Grame?" she said bitingly. "I'll have you know that you have no authority over me, you—you tapster!"

Hal blinked; he had never seen Anny like this before, and he stood staring at her in amazement, his mouth half open.

"I have not hankered after the Spaniard, as you call it."

Anny's eyes were bright with tears at his injustice, but she spoke firmly, and with great intensity.

"And as for you being tired, master Lord of the Island, so is Anny Farran, your servant—very, very tired of this fooling. Lord! you child—is it me that hankers," the word seemed to have stuck in her mind, for she repeated it, "hankers for the Captain? Is it me? Oh, Hal Grame—I—I hate you."

Hal stepped back another pace or two and looked round him vaguely. This was a new departure of Anny's. He had never seen her so indignant, and he thrust his hands in his pockets and turned on his heel.

"I hope that is the Preventative folk then," he remarked, jerking his thumb over his shoulder, "then they'll catch the little dog."

Anny reddened.

"Hal Grame, you're a jealous coward," she said clearly, and then her tears began to fall and she sat down on the grass, looking out over the cloud-shadowed water.

Hal did not speak, but stood idly kicking the dust with his foot.

"You're not saying that you don't love me?" he said confidently.

Anny bit her lip.

"I've told you I hate you," she said clearly; she was still very angry for the boy's mistrust had hurt her.

He turned round slowly.

"Don't be silly, Anny," he said not unkindly. Anny furtively wiped her eyes; his confident attitude annoyed her, and she spoke clearly.

"Go away, Hal Grame; I won't ever marry you."

Hal gasped. "Anny, you're bewitched," he exclaimed. He couldn't have chosen a more unfortunate remark for Anny was more irritated than ever.

"Nay, not now, but I was, ever to think at all on the likes of you," she snapped. "Oh, go away."

Hal wavered; his little sweetheart sat on the grass, her face turned away from him, but he felt that she was crying, so came a little nearer.

"Give me a kiss," he said laughing. "You're a smart little wench," and kneeling down behind her he bent to kiss her cheek.

Before he realised what had happened he felt a smart blow across the mouth, and Anny sprang to her feet and walked off quickly.

Hal sat back on his heels and passed his hand across his lips.

"You little vixen," he gasped.

Anny laughed, a bitter, angry little laugh, and went on.

Hal looked after her anxiously for a moment or two, and then as she did not turn back he scrambled to his feet and followed her.

"Anny, you're not angry?" he said, as soon as he was near enough to speak softly. The words came shamefacedly from his mouth and he slurred them one into another.

Anny gulped; she was very angry and Hal's attitude annoyed her.

"Indeed I am," she said, "and turning a slobbering calf won't make me any better. Oh! go home, Hal Grame."

Hal was amazed.

"Anny!" he ejaculated.

Anny repressed a howl of disappointment and contented herself with saying wearily:

"Oh, go home—go home!"

The boy looked at her for a moment or two.

"Anny," he said at last, "are you trying to leave me for the Spaniard?"

This was more than she could stand, and turning to him she broke out into a stream of angry incoherent abuse and denial.

"Why are you for ever plaguing me about the Spaniard? Why does everyone talk of him? I'm sick of hearing his name—if you're jealous of him go to him, not to me."

Hal shrugged his shoulders and said with irritating calmness:

"Then there is that for me to go to him about, eh?"

Anny raised her little clenched fists above her head and cried aloud:

"You make me mad, Hal Grame. Of course there isn't," and then, as she saw that he didn't believe her, she went on, "of course not, of course! Oh, Hal! if you were a man you'd do other things than worry a poor lass dead with your foolishness."

Hal flushed.

"Ah, that's like a wench!" he said. "What if I haven't a golden jacobus to my name! I shouldn't think you'd throw that at me if you loved me."

Anny did not speak and he went on, "If I were a man—yes, that's it, if I were a dirty, sneaking, knife-throwing Spaniard, with a fleet of rat-ridden cockle-boats, and a crew of mangy dogs behind me, you'd be content—then I could do other things—bring you gauds and laced petticoats. Faugh! I'm glad I've seen you thus; I wouldn't wed a cormorant and a shrew."

His anger had carried him away with it, for like most Norsemen he had a strain of bitterness under his usually sunny, peaceful disposition.

Anny winced at his words.

"It's not that—you know it's not that, Hal," she said piteously. "But why worry me? If you're jealous of him, fight him."

Hal looked at her in astonishment; he was no coward, but neither was he a hot-head, and he knew some things of Dick's reputation as a swordsman and a knife-fighter.

Anny shrugged her shoulders.

"Fight him," she repeated mechanically.

A sneer played round the boy's mouth when he next spoke, and his eyes had grown cold.

"Marry, Anny Farran, I did not think you capable of it," he said. "You would have me die on the Spaniard's knife and so rid of for ever."

Anny began to cry hopelessly. She felt there was no use in saying anything to him while he was in this mood, but she was very fond of him and he hurt her much more than he knew.

Hal turned on his heel, and as he strode off began to realise how much he loved the wayward beauty. A great wave of self-pity swept over him. He was very young, barely nineteen, and once or twice he bit his lip convulsively, as he imagined the future loneliness, the constraint at the Ship, old Gilbot's sallies, and then, as he stayed to look out over the glancing, shimmering water, he noticed that the little white-sailed ship was still hovering about the mouth of the Mersea river, and he laughed wildly.

"May you sink the Spanish weasel!" he exclaimed aloud, and then went on, and every step he took he became more miserable and angry with himself and the girl.

"Oh! I'll go and see Joe," he thought, as he turned into the lane. "It's a fine thing to have a mate, so it is, when your lass leaves you for a yellow heathen," and he turned down towards Pullen's cottage.

Anny sat on the bank where he had left her. She was very sorry for herself, too, and she looked round her through tearful eyes.

No one was in sight. Behind her the bright sun lit up the countryside with beautiful green and yellow light, while in front, the sea, clear and smooth as glass, sparkled and glittered peacefully. She got up slowly, and started back for the Ship, and for the first time a sense of insecurity came upon her, and she realised rather fearfully that she was very much alone. Hitherto, she had always relied on Hal to take care of her, but now he was angry, very angry, she could see that; perhaps he would never forgive her. She shivered involuntarily. Old Ben was her only relative, and the thought of him and Pet Salt frightened her. Sue and Gilbot were very kind, but would they trouble themselves to protect a little serving-wench from a wealthy customer?

All these questions ran through her head, and the image of the dark, wanton-eyed debonair little Captain rose up in her mind like a spectre. She knew now that she did not like him, and she began to be afraid. She remembered the times he had tried to kiss her; and how each time at the thought of Hal she had repulsed him successfully. Now Hal would be indifferent. A sob stuck in her throat, and she swallowed painfully.

Then an idea struck her. There was always Nan Swayle—poor, disappointed Mother Swayle had always a soft spot in her hard-crusted heart for little Anny Farran, her old lover's grandchild. She would go to Nan—but then the picture of the lonely old woman living with her cats in a tumble-down shed on one of the many small dike-surrounded islands in the marshes presented itself to her, and she began to cry afresh, as she walked wearily up to the Ship.

Meanwhile, out in the river's mouth, alone between sea and sky, the little white-sailed craft patrolled steadily to and fro, as Master Thomas Playle, a telescope to his eye, swept the horizon anxiously and impatiently.

Chapter XVI

The sun was just about to set over the Island in a blaze of glorious colour when the *Anny*, sailing peacefully under half-canvas, came in sight of Bradwell Point.

Blueneck and Habakkuk Coot were below deck in the latter's little bunk-hole which he had fitted up as a sort of wash-house. It was one of Blackkerchief Dick's fads to have his linen always spotless, and marvellously laundered, and, as this was a luxury hardly dreamed of on the Island, during his visits to England, the valiant Captain had to have his washing done aboard. The job of laundryman had almost naturally fallen to Habakkuk, who had accepted the office joyfully, and he now stood, clad in nothing but his breeches, in front of an old emptied canary tub, immersed up to his elbows in soapy water.

Blueneck leaned against the doorway watching him.

"Santa Maria! what an occupation," he remarked contemptuously.

Habakkuk sniffed.

"It's very nice when you're used to it," he said, without looking up from the garment he was pounding and squeezing with a kind of vicious delight.

Blueneck shrugged his shoulders.

"Maybe," he said, "anyway, I'm going on deck; this here rathole's too stinking for me."

Habakkuk sniffed again but took no other notice of his friend, who presently lumbered off up the hatchway.

The water was very green and the waves rolled lazily after one another as though it were hot even for them, while the *Anny* dipped and rolled gently among them at about one-third her usual speed.

They were early, and, careless though he was, Dick did not like landing until it was at least dusk.

Blueneck strode across the deck and stood staring towards the Island, now just a streak on the flaming horizon.

Suddenly he started and speaking sharply ordered one of the sailors who was sprawling on the deck to bring him a telescope.

The man went off at once and returned in a second bringing a long brass spy-glass with him.

As the mate of the *Anny* clapped it to his eye an exclamation of surprise escaped him.

"Mother of Heaven! what will that be?" he murmured, and putting the glass under his arm went down the deck in search of the Captain.

As usual the little Spaniard was standing against the main-mast, his arms folded across his chest, and his heavy-lidded eyes half-closed.

Blueneck approached him deferentially and reported: "Ship ahead, Capt'n."

The deeply sunken eyes opened at once and Dick put out one delicately scented hand for the glass.

"She's sighted us, dogs," he remarked calmly a second or so later.

Blueneck gasped.

"I'll go and head her round, Capt'n," he said at once.

Dick lowered the telescope and looked over it in quiet surprise.

"That you will not, son of a snipe," he said, his soft voice playing musically with the words.

Blueneck began to expostulate.

"The Preventative folk?" he said fearfully.

Dick swore.

"And since when have you been feared of the Preventative folk, dog?" he asked, and his fingers played round the hilt of his knife.

Blueneck flushed.

"I'm not feared," he said stoutly, "but 'tis madness to go on."

Dick laughed happily, putting the glass up again. Suddenly his whole manner changed. His bright black eyes lost their sleepy indifference and became alight with interest and excitement, his slender white hand ceased to play with his knife, and his voice, no longer caressing, now adopted a note of command, as he wheeled round and strode off down the deck shouting orders here and there.

"Put on full canvas and keep her straight," Blueneck heard him say, and he groaned inwardly.

Under the extra load of canvas the *Anny* plunged and righted herself, cutting through the water at her full speed.

The other brig was well in sight now, and she hailed the smugglers several times.

Dick took the wheel himself and shouted an order for the cannon to be looked to.

The other brig had turned her head straight for the *Anny* as soon as she saw that her salute was ignored, and now a ball from one of her several brass cannon fell some two yards short of the smuggler's bows.

"Fire!" shouted Dick, and Noah Goody, the *Anny's* old gunner, lit the match; the shot cleared the pursuing brig and Noah loaded again.

Nearer and nearer came the brig until Blueneck could read the name on her bows, the *Royal Charles.*

Faster and faster went the *Anny,* but the *Charles* gained on her every second. They were well inside the bay by this time, but escape seemed impossible for the tide was barely past the turn, and between them and the Island lay a great grey field of soft slushing mud. Any moment they might strike a bank of it and be compelled to stay there an easy prey to the Preventative men.

Dick looked behind; the *Charles* was very near. For a moment he hesitated. He knew the Western creeks like the back of his hand, but in order to reach that side of the Island he would have to cross in front of the enemy, and although he was a daring little man Blackkerchief Dick was no fool. The only course left open to him then was to make for the East. He knew there were two creeks that were deep enough to take the brig, but they were no more than thirty feet in their widest part and that was dangerous going. Besides he was not nearly so familiar with these as with those on the Western side.

At this moment a ball from the *Charles* dropped through the little deck-house and then rolled off the deck harmlessly.

Dick made up his mind.

"Send Habakkuk Coot hither," he shouted, for he remembered that the man had spent his boyhood in the East of the Island.

Everyone had forgotten Habakkuk in the excitement of the moment, and now he was nowhere to be found.

Dick cursed him for a skulking rat and in other terms.

Blueneck went down the hatchway to look for him; the smell of steaming soap and water still came from the dirty little hole where he had left him.

Blueneck looked in; Habakkuk was there, his arms still in the soapy water. He was singing in a high nasal voice and sniffing at frequent intervals.

He listened to Blueneck's incoherent account of the chase in profound astonishment, but nevertheless went steadily on with his washing, and refused to leave it until Blueneck in desperation took him by the scruff of the neck and the seat of the breeches and carried him before the Captain, his arms still wet and soapy, and a dripping shirt clutched in his hand.

But the situation was too serious for Dick, or, indeed, anyone else, to notice any little irregularities of this sort.

The *Royal Charles* was within a musket shot of the *Anny's* bows and every second the mud flat in front grew nearer.

Habakkuk, however, had a very good memory, and under his guidance the *Anny* shot down a wide, river-like stream of water, the mud forming banks on either side.

Dick looked at it in surprise.

"I did not know there were any creeks as wide as this on the East," he said.

"Ah," said Habakkuk wisely, "this ain't no more 'an twenty foot wide—it's very deceiving. Look over the side, Captain, there's about six inches of water on the starboard—an'—they don't know that, do they?" he chuckled, jerking his thumb over his shoulder to where the *Royal Charles* had just turned after them. "It's only about fifteen wide a bit further along," he announced cheerfully a little later. "I hopes I ain't forgot where."

Dick stood watching the *Charles* as she followed them down the treacherous creek. "She must have a pilot who knows the place," he thought, for she still gained on them.

At last, when they were within five hundred yards of the shore, Habakkuk gave a short exclamation.

"We're stuck," he cried.

"What?" Dick sprang round on his heel.

Habakkuk grinned foolishly.

"Little tiny channel's silted up, I reckon," he said. "We're aground."

Dick struck him off his feet with an oath.

"Out with your knives," he shouted.

It was beginning to get dusk and the *Charles* bore down upon the *Anny* like a great grey tower; nearer she came and nearer until they could plainly hear the voices of the men on her deck.

And then it happened. In his excitement the man at her tiller let it swerve a little, a very little, but enough; there was a soft swishing sound and the *Charles's* nose cut deep into the soft cheesy mud—she also was aground.

Exciseman Thomas Playle swore with disappointment as he ran forward and saw the very little distance between the two brigs, but he loosened the broad-bladed cutlass at his hip and, shouting to his men to follow, swung himself into one of the boats.

"Maria! they're trying to board us," shouted Blueneck, whipping out his knife and running to the side.

Instantly there was confusion, the greater portion of the crew running after their mate to the still floating side of the brig.

This sudden change of weight saved the situation. With a lurch, a roll, and a quiver, the *Anny* jerked off the mud, Habakkuk seized the tiller just in time, and the brig slid on down the creek.

A yell of disappointment rang out from the first boat-load of Preventative men and echoed over the fast-darkening mud flats. The tide was coming in like a mill-stream and any moment the *Charles* might also swing clear, but Playle would not wait; springing into a second boat he urged his men to row faster in a vain attempt to catch the *Anny.*

Old Noah Goody did his best with the cannon, but the progress of the little row-boats was so irregular that he could never get the exact range.

The *Anny* shot away from the boats at first, but as she came nearer into the shore the channel grew narrower and narrower and she was forced to take in most of her canvas.

Dick stood on the bows looking at the fast gaining boats, and thinking. If on reaching the shore he abandoned the brig and he and his men ran to hide on the Island, the Preventative men would scuttle the *Anny* and confiscate her cargo, which was an extra valuable one of Jamaica rum and fine Brussels lace. His only alternative was to fight.

By this time the brig was within twenty yards of the beach, and in another moment her keel grated on the muddy shingle.

The excise men were not far behind.

Dick seemed suddenly to come to life; leaping out into the centre deck he shouted:

"To the shore, lads, and fight the liverish dogs on land!" Then, agile as a monkey, he slid down the hawser and pulled in a boat—the crew followed, some wading through the shallow water and others in the boats.

Once on shore they ranged themselves in a double line along the beach, waiting, with drawn knives, for the boats. It had grown almost dark by now, and one by one the stars had come out in the fast-deepening sky, but there was a big moon and the line of rugged, rum-stamped faces on the shore showed clearly in the yellow light. Their brutal expressions and the flicker of steel about their belts might have frightened many a man older and more tried than Master Playle, but the little boats came on undaunted, and just as the first keel touched the shingle a musket shot rang out and the man next to Blueneck dropped silently.

Dick swore in Spanish and, raising his pistol, the one he had taken from Mat Turnby—fired at the man nearest him, a fat elderly servant of Master Francis Myddleton's. The man was almost out of range, but the shot wounded him, for he screamed and dropped into the water. For half a second there was no sound, and then with a yell the crew of the *Charles* charged over the soft slithering mud at the solid line of grim, taut figures who awaited them.

"Pick out your men!" Dick rapped out the order, and as he spoke the handle of his knife slipped into the hollow of his soft white palm as if it had suddenly grown there, and the slender hand and delicate weapon quivered as one living thing.

There were full ten more excise men than smugglers and they came on with such a rush that the crew of the *Anny* were forced to give way a little, but they rallied immediately, and although the Preventative folk had the advantage of numbers Dick's people had the priceless knowledge of the ground they were fighting on. The wiry grass which covered the unlevel saltings that lay the other side of the narrow beach was very slippery, and in the pale light the ridges and dikes were almost invisible.

Dick soon realised that if the fight was to be fought to a finish the sooner they got to level ground the better, as his own people found the light deceptive. So he worked his way round to Blueneck, slashing right and left as he went.

Blueneck was apparently enjoying himself for, although the moonlight showed a gash across his temples about six inches long, from which blood poured freely, it also showed a smile on his ragged mouth and a dripping cutlass in his sinewy hand.

Dick spoke to him quickly, just a few muttered words, and almost immediately the smugglers began to give way. Back, back they went until they were flying across the saltings, over the meadows, and straight for the Ship, with the Preventative men in full pursuit.

Once the mocking voice of Playle called out to the *Anny's* crew to surrender, and the flying smugglers paused and half-turned with many oaths, but Dick's voice dragged them on again with "On, dogs, on, for your damned lives," and the chase continued.

Suddenly, as they reached the Ship yard, Dick vanished: Blueneck, looking round for further orders, could not see him, and his heart sank. Was it possible that a knife-thrust from behind had killed the Captain? He dismissed that idea almost as soon as it came to him. The Spaniard was too wary to be the victim of such a mishap. The only other alternative was that he had deserted his crew.

Blueneck feared Dick, but he had no love for him, and this last seemed to be the only possible explanation. He spat on the ground contemptuously.

But by this time the Preventative folk were well upon them and Blueneck realised that it was a case of each man for himself, so calling a halt he turned on the oncoming force.

The smugglers were only too glad to obey, and with a redoubled force they turned on their enemy and hewed their way into them.

The Preventative men were not sorry to fight, however, and young Playle threw himself into the thick of the scrap with something very like pleasure.

The smugglers fought like wild beasts, preferring to close in and kill, but the others liked to thrust and parry, pricking and wounding, giving way here and pressing there, and as they had longer weapons than the smugglers they found their method an excellent one.

Back went the smugglers down the Ship yard, Blueneck slashing wildly, Noah Goody defending himself only, and little Habakkuk, his bare chest and shoulders a perfect network of cuts, darting here and there like a robin.

Onward pressed young Playle until he had the smugglers with their backs against the kitchen door, which opened suddenly from the inside.

Blueneck put himself on the step in the way of the excise men and shouted to his mates to get into the kitchen and form a guard. When the last man was in he retired also, but the excise men pressed on; first one of their men fell on attempting to enter the kitchen, then a second, and a third, but before the fourth was struck down, in response to a great crush behind him he broke through the smugglers' guard and the Preventative men swarmed in.

Hal Grame suddenly darted forward out of the darkness. He carried an old sword which had hung over the kitchen shelf for years, and he now laid about him with great strokes, but a certain recklessness distinguished his fighting, and his red shirt was soon dyed a still deeper shade.

In spite of his help, however, the excise men drove on.

"God! if the Captain were only here!" groaned Blueneck aloud.

The man next him caught his words and looked round, so did his neighbour, and in a moment all that was left of the *Anny's* crew realised that their Captain had deserted them, and a certain hopelessness crept into the fighting from that time on, and in a minute or two the smugglers retreated in a body, knocking over the barrels and benches as they went. They scuttled into the inner room and then slammed the heavy oak door behind them.

Habakkuk alone was left behind and he, finding the door shut upon him, turned to fly through the other door into the yard, but a Preventative man's sword ran him through just as he reached the threshold, and with one last sniff the brave little laundry-man fell prone in a pool of his own blood.

The kitchen was very dark, there being no fire, as it was summer-time, and the only light was the moonlight which showed in through the windows and fell on the floor in two bright patches.

So when the door slammed on them, Thomas Playle took the opportunity of counting his forces. He found to his deep disappointment that he had lost a great many more men than he had dreamed, and those around him in the kitchen numbered at the most no more than six or seven.

"We must get them yet," he said, speaking to his few remaining followers in a low tone. "An you two stay here and I and Jacques go round to the other door we——" Suddenly he caught his breath, his voice trailed away into silence, and he started back, his drawn sword put up to shield his body.

The man to whom he had been principally speaking had quietly dropped without a cry, and as he touched the ground his head and shoulders rolled into the patch of moonlight, and his horrified comrades saw a thin spurt of blood shooting out from a clean, small wound in his neck just over the collarbone.

Before they could collect their wits after this shock there was a faint patter of feet behind them and another man staggered, tried to speak, reeled, and fell.

Instantly there was confusion; men slashed about in the darkness striking anything and anyone, shouting, and screaming. A terrible fear of something unknown and horrible possessed them and each man made for the yard, but one by one as they approached the doorway the unseen terror caught them and they fell. At last there were but three left, young Playle himself, his mate Jacques, and the *Charles's* gunner, a tall, powerful man called Rilp.

These three stood back to back in the centre of the kitchen, making a triangle, their swords drawn before them, so that it was practically impossible for anything to harm them from behind.

They stood there for some moments holding their breath; everything was silent. Then there was a light patter of feet again and a small bent shape darted through the patch of moonlight. It seemed to Playle's terrified eyes to be an evil spirit not three feet high from the ground and to have its head almost level with its waist while its back was bent into a monstrous hump. Instinctively he put up his sword to shield his head and at that moment something brushed past him; he slashed at it and fancied that he had wounded it, but the next moment he felt Jacques grunt and stumble. He was just going to spring away when he felt the man right himself, and once again a man's back was firm against his own.

Then there was silence again for a second.

Suddenly Rilp staggered, shivered, and dropped.

Playle immediately darted forward, when to his amazement and horror the man whom he thought was Jacques darted after him; something sprang on his shoulders from behind, a streak of silver light darted before his eyes and plunged down into his neck; he felt the blood well up in his throat, his breath failed him, a dark cloud passed over his eyes, and he died, crashing face downwards into the little patch of moonlight.

In the scullery, Blueneck, his shoulders against the door, turned to his comrades and urged them to pull themselves together; put forward every excuse for Blackkerchief Dick's extraordinary behaviour, and he besought them to get ready to fight again.

Inside the kitchen they could hear the Preventative men talking together, and by their low tones came to the conclusion that they were planning the next attack.

Suddenly Blueneck started.

"Marry! they're fighting among themselves," he whispered. "Hark!"

From inside the kitchen came the sounds of clashing steel and angry oaths and ejaculations, followed by screams and groans. Then there was silence for a while immediately followed by footsteps, mutterings, and one terrible yell.

Then all was silent again.

"Shall we go in?" whispered Hal.

"Nay, 'tis a trap," said another man, whose hand and cutlass were one red mass.

"Nay, I'll go," said Hal stubbornly.

"I shouldn't, lad," said Blueneck, stanching the bleeding wound on his forehead as best he could.

Hal put his hand to a dark patch at his side and brought it away wet and sticky.

"Oh, what does it matter?" he said; taking a candle from the table he opened the door, holding the light above his head. Then he gasped and threw the door wide.

"Mother o' God!" he exclaimed weakly. "Look!"

Blueneck and the others crowded behind him and they, too, gasped and fell back in astonishment.

In the centre of the room, the flickering light showed a terrible bent little figure; it was a man, but the crouching attitude in which he stood suggested rather a beast of prey. He was literally surrounded with bodies, and he looked down at them with an almost ghoulish delight, which was terrible to see. But only for a second; as soon as he became conscious of the little group in the doorway he straightened himself and stood smiling at them.

He was clothed only in his breeches and immaculate white shirt; his black kerchief was half off showing the black curls beneath, while his white hands were clean and undyed.

Dick Delfazio smiled again, and then began to clean his knife on a dainty lace-edged handkerchief.

Then his crew entered, and he looked up casually as they filed in, and turning to the least wounded man he pointed to a chair over the back of which his black silk coat was hung.

"Prithee, friend, help me into my surcoat," he said, his voice caressing and honey-like as ever. "For see," he added, turning round, "I am much hampered."

The crew started.

The sleeve of the white shirt was split from the shoulder to the elbow, displaying a terrible ragged wound which at one place had laid bare the bone, and from the bend in the elbow the warm blood trickled on to the floor.

This was the last act of Thomas Playle's hand and he had done his best.

Dick slipped into his coat and then surveyed the crew.

"Wash thyselves, friends," he admonished, "the wenches will come down now and may be feared at the sight of blood." He staggered a little and his face grew ashy pale, but he rallied himself and with some of his usual jauntiness said loudly, "Bring me some wine." Already the black silk sleeve of his coat was sodden and sticky, and the arm inside it hung limply from its socket; once again he staggered, tried to recover himself and failed, and then, very faint from loss of blood, Blackkerchief Dick rolled over on his side unconscious.

Blueneck picked him up like a child and, stripping off the coat, called loudly for Anny.

"Surely the girl knows somewhat of physicing. The Captain may bleed to death," he said sharply, in answer to Hal's suggestion that they didn't want wenches about the place.

Hal put his hand over his own wound and, shrugging his shoulders, a gesture which cost him a great deal of blood, went off to find Anny and beseech her to attend to his rival's arm.

Late the same evening a tumbril borrowed from a neighbouring farmer carried a gruesome burden from the Ship door down to the beach, and along the road it stopped from time to time to collect additions to its load.

A little later a party of men in three rowing-boats loaded a terrible cargo into a lonely ship which rode at anchor not far from the shore where a brig lay aground, and then that same lonely ship sailed off out of the bay, and later, after three boats had left her side, broke into flames.

And later still, widows and children in Brightlingsea wept to see charred spars and planks cast up on the beach outside their homes.

Chapter XVII

"There, there, Master Dick, don't fluster yourself so; 'twill only smart your arm the more."

Anny spoke timidly and shrank behind one of the high-backed seats in the old Ship's kitchen, as Blackkerchief Dick, his eyes dark with anger, raved up and down the room. It was some three weeks after the affair with the Preventative folk, and the Island had once more regained its usual serenity.

"You are bewitched, girl; what are you to refuse the love of a man like me?" Dick said angrily, and then as she did not answer, he continued more softly, "Why not come with me, beautiful Ann of the Island? We will leave this God-forsaken mud heap and sail away to Spain, cross the great river to the beautiful country beyond, where all the grass is green and all the plants have bright flowers. What is there about this rum-sodden drinking hut that you will not leave it for Utopia?"

"I never heard of Utopia and Mersea is good enough for me," said Anny stolidly. "Besides, if you want to marry me, why not tell everybody and have a proper wedding by the parson from the West? but even then I wouldn't marry you; I don't love you, sir."

The Spaniard paused suddenly in his walk up and down and looked at her.

"Never has a woman said so much to me before," he said slowly, his voice soft and smooth as ever.

Anny shrugged her shoulders.

"'Tis time then one should," she laughed. "Rest your arm, sir, and leave worrying a poor girl that has work and enough to do, now that Mistress Sue be for ever out along the beach with Big French." She turned away.

The Spaniard was beside her in a second and his slim white fingers fastened round her chapped little wrist like a vice.

"Oh, you silly little wench," he said, with a laugh in his voice, "do you think you can turn off Dick Delfazio easily like that? Mistress, I am of some account on the Island. Is a man who kills six Preventative folk single-handed to be stayed in his heart's desire by a little serving-maid, think you?"

"What would you do?" Anny, her big green eyes wide with apprehension, and her back against the wall, jerked out the question fearfully.

Blackkerchief Dick looked at her in admiration, and, swinging her towards him, he put his arm round her waist, and Hal, passing the window at that moment, suddenly changed his mind about entering the kitchen and marched off down the garden coughing and swearing to himself.

Anny freed herself in a moment and stood with her arms akimbo.

"An you were not wounded and a customer, I should smack you across the mouth," she said, her eyes filling with tears.

Dick laughed.

"Come, we should not quarrel, sweetheart," he said. "When you are aboard the *Anny*——"

"I pray God I shall be dead before," the girl interrupted angrily, her tears overflowing and rolling down her cheeks.

Dick caught her hand again and looked at her fiercely.

"I have played enough, lass," he said. "You must come off secretly with me or——"

Anny laughed.

"Must?" she said. "Must, indeed! and why-fore? I tell you, sir, I hate you, and if you pursue me more I'll have the landlord at you."

"The landlord!" Dick sneered.

Anny was desperate.

"Or Hal Grame," she said.

Dick threw back his head and laughed aloud.

"A tapster! Oh, pretty, pretty little wench, you are very amusing!"

The girl wrenched her hand away.

"Master Blackkerchief Dick," she said slowly, her little face very white and grave, "will you understand please that I do not love you, I do not even like you, and I will never go anywhere with you of my own will?"

The Spaniard stepped back a pace or two. He seemed to have realised at last that she was speaking the truth, for he looked at the earnest little face in front of him with a mixture of amazement and anger.

"You do not like me?" he said, his voice losing all its music and becoming almost childish in its extreme surprise.

Anny nodded.

"No, I don't like you. Will you please go away and leave me to my work, sir?"

Dick's anger rose up and boiled over in a moment.

"I tell you you shall come, you pretty little fool," he swore. "Or——" he paused suddenly. "Is there some other man you love? Tell me, tell me!"

Anny cowered before his angry, distorted face.

"No, sir, of course not, no, sir!" she lied vehemently. "Let go my wrist, sir. Marry, how you hurt me!"

"This great hulking French, now, have you set your heart on him? Speak out, girl!"

"No, sir, of course not!" Anny's amazement was too genuine to be mistaken.

"Yet you will not marry me?" Dick spoke sharply.

"No—no—no, sir! Go away!"

Dick turned on his heel and went to the door.

"By this knife," he said, turning on the threshold, "you shall come with me. I wish it, and never yet have I been prevented from my desires."

"Lord! you're mad!" Anny flung after him.

"Ay, mad for you, Mistress."

Dick's voice had grown soft again and he laughed unpleasantly as he strolled off down the yard. Anny watched him go and then turned back to her work.

"Now I wonder will I ever be married at all?" she said to herself, as she picked up a broom from the chimney corner and began to sweep away the dirty sand which lay all over the floor.

Blueneck was sitting on the sea-wall, thinking regretfully of Habakkuk Coot, when Blackkerchief Dick strode up, and without speaking, dropped down beside him.

Blueneck looked at his Captain slyly and without turning his head.

Dick was smiling sardonically and his knife slid in and out the slim white fingers of his right hand.

Blueneck considered it prudent to sit still and say nothing.

Dick did not speak for some time, and Blueneck began to get uneasy. Finally he rose to his feet as nonchalantly as he was able and started to stroll off down the beach.

Dick raised his eyes.

"Sit where you are, dog!" he said sharply.

Blueneck slid back to his place without a murmur.

The silence continued. At last, however, Dick put the knife back in his belt and turned his sharp eyes on his mate.

"The lass refuses me," he said.

Blueneck shrugged his shoulders.

"These country wenches be mighty particular about marrying their husbands and so forth," he observed.

Dick raised his eyebrows.

"I have said I will wed her," he said stiffly.

Blueneck's jaw dropped.

"Wed her?" he ejaculated. "Why, Capt'n, you must——" he broke off lamely.

Dick snapped out the question, "Must what?"

Blueneck did not vouchsafe an answer, and they sat in silence for a minute or two.

Dick began to speak, slowly and carefully, as though he was thinking out each word separately.

"There is a thing on this earth, my friend, called love. And a very vile and evil thing it is. It descends upon a man unawares like a shower of rain, and soaks through to his very marrow. It takes away his energy, his pride in his work and person," he looked down at the lace ruffles at his cuff and stroked them lovingly, and then added, "and I have reason to think that great men feel it more sharply than others."

Blueneck glanced quickly at the dapper little figure by his side, and shrugged his shoulders.

The Captain was showing signs of strain, he thought.

"Must the wench be willing?" he asked. "Why not carry her off?"

Dick shrugged his shoulders.

"I would rather she were willing," he said.

Blueneck looked at him exasperated.

"Well, if you can't persuade her I don't know who can," he muttered, but Dick did not hear him. He was smiling, his eyes half shut.

Blueneck spat.

"Bewitched!" he commented silently to himself. Then an idea struck him and he turned to the Captain.

"There's Pet Salt," he said. "She might do much."

"Pet Salt?" Dick turned to him quickly. "Who's she?"

Blueneck told the story of his night on Ben Farran's boat, with as much credit to himself as was possible.

Dick listened in silence until he had finished; then he rose to his feet.

"I will go to see this crone," he said grandiloquently. "Lead me, dog!"

Pet Salt sat on the deck of her boat mending a net. She was mumbling to herself, and her old knotted finger-joints cracked as she fumbled about with the rough twine she was using. Beneath the hatches she could hear old Ben swearing loudly as he hunted among the empty rum kegs for one that still contained a little of the precious stuff. To judge from his language he had been so far unsuccessful, and the woman shifted uneasily as she sat thinking of the beating he would give her if he found nothing.

It was then that she heard a voice calling her from the beach.

"Pet Salt! Pet Salt!"

Noisily she scrambled to her feet and hobbled over to the side of the hull, and looked down.

Dick and his mate stood together staring up at her.

"Good-morning, Mistress," Dick began in his best manner.

Pet stared at him open-mouthed, her yellow teeth looking like fangs. She had never seen such finery.

Dick, although himself rather taken aback at Pet's appearance, could not but feel flattered at her evident approval of his own.

Pet's bleared eyes now fell on Blueneck and a shade of recognition passed over her wrinkled, spirit-sodden face.

"Oh! it's you again, ronyon, hey?" she cried, in her cracked crooning voice into which an eager note had crept. "You have no rum kegs slung about you, eh?"

Blueneck waved his hand impatiently.

"Throw down the ladder, that we may come up and talk with thee, hag," he ordered peremptorily.

Pet hobbled off to obey him without a word, and Dick turned to his mate in something like admiration.

"You have been well schooled, friend," he said approvingly. "Yours is an excellent way of dealing with crones."

"Have a care!" called Pet from above as she threw the rope-ladder over the side. The end passed within an inch of Blueneck's shoulders and he looked up angrily.

Pet was leering at him from the deck.

"Come up, ronyon," she said coaxingly.

Blueneck scaled the ladder in a minute and clambered on to the rolling deck beside her.

Dick followed, more dignified but not a wit less agile.

Once on deck he looked about him in disgust. The worm-eaten boards, the empty kegs and other lumber, and the general filthiness of the place disgusted the little Spaniard. His own brig was always kept neat and fastidiously clean.

He shrugged his shoulders.

"A very vile place in truth," he observed, and then, turning to Pet, he raised his hat as gallantly as if she had been a duenna.

"I would descend and talk with thee on the shore, if you please, Mistress," he said. "This ship distresses me."

He went again to the ladder, picking his way daintily across the dirty deck. Slowly he climbed down again; Pet and Blueneck followed him without a word.

"Prithee, Mistress, be seated," said Dick, indicating a bank of seaweed and seating himself on a breakwater some four feet away.

Pet sat down heavily and looked from Dick to Blueneck in a half-witted, puzzled way, her big loose mouth sagging open on one side, showing the large yellow teeth which so irritated Blueneck.

Suddenly she stretched out a bony hand towards Blackkerchief Dick and began in a droning whine:

"May the Lord bless ye, fine gentleman; could ye spare a drop o' rum for a poor woman to take to her man who is dying of cold? Old Pet Salt knows you, pretty sir. Old Pet don't forget a generous face when she sees one. Pet remembers when she came to the Ship and you gave her a keg. Could you spare a little, fine gentleman?"

Dick stared at her; he remembered her now, and instinctively drew a little further away.

"Hold thy peace, hag, and hark to me," he said sharply, "and much rum may come of it—nay," he continued, as the old woman struggled to get to her feet and come towards him, "keep thy distance and let thy dull wit take in as much of this as it can. You have a grand-daughter?"

A cunning light crept into the old bleared eyes.

"Ah!" she said, putting on a pathetic whine. "I have, God bless her pure heart and body. One my man loves dearly! What would you have with her, fine gentleman?"

Dick waved his hand.

"Woman," he said softly, his voice taking on that musical quality which his enemies knew so well, "it would be well if thou and I knew each other's mind a little more clearly—rum is a precious thing to you, eh?"

Pet's eyes glistened and her lips moved without sound.

"I have much rum," Dick went on, looking at the old woman steadily, "and I would wed your granddaughter."

"Wed?" the exclamation escaped her before she could stop it.

Dick went on as though he had not heard her.

"At your boat and by a priest that I shall bring with me, I would wed her."

"Oh!" Pet said, and smiled knowingly.

"But so far the lass will have none of me," Dick continued, noting Pet's amazement, "and so, Mistress, I would wish you to persuade her to wed me here secretly."

"Ay, and if I do?" Pet broke in.

"If you do—you earn enough rum to keep you and your husband in liquor for the rest of your life."

Dick put his hands on his belt and looked at the old wretch quizzically.

Pet began to laugh. It was a terrible sound, half a wheeze and half a choke.

"I'll persuade her," she muttered.

Dick quickly put up one white beringed hand.

"Nay, Mistress, you must use no violence on her," he said, "neither must you harm her with spirit charms or other bedevilments; I would not have her hurt."

Pet Salt looked at him out of the corner of her eyes.

"I'll not hurt your love, Master," she laughed—"she shall marry thee—and by a priest you bring—ha—ha!"

Blueneck had never seen his Captain blush before and he now regarded the little Spaniard with great interest.

The usually sallow skin was stained with a vermilion, as he turned on the woman in anger.

"Keep to your promise then and be silent," he said softly, "or by Heaven I'll blow your pig-sty of a rat-ridden hulk off the Island."

The woman looked at him frightened for a moment, but soon she began to laugh.

"She shall wed thee, my pretty, fine gentleman, she shall wed thee—I'll see to that," she said, scrambling to her feet—"and the rum shall be paid, you promise, master?"

Dick nodded.

"I swear it," he said. Then he got up and beckoned to Blueneck to follow him.

"Good-morrow, Mistress," he said, taking off his hat.

Pet stood looking after them.

"I'll coax her," the woman called. "I'll coax her," And all the way as they went down the beach they could hear her cracked, horrible laughter.

Chapter XVIII

"Rum! rum! ru-u-m-m!"

Nan Swayle sat in her miserable little cabin with her knees drawn up to her chin; her cat was perched on a rum keg beside her and there was no light save for the cold gleam of stars coming in from the open door. She sat there, a tall, gaunt figure, steadily rocking herself to and fro as though keeping time to some monotonous rhyme. She was talking to herself in a deep, weary voice, and the words she uttered were always the same, "Rum—rum—ru-u-m-m!"

Outside on the marshes everything was very quiet, and she rocked on, undisturbed for a while. Then from the direction of the Stroud she heard the squeak of a frightened gull as it flew up disturbed from its rest, and then another a little nearer, and again nearer still.

The woman did not cease her rocking; she knew someone was coming over the dykes to see her, but what mattered that?

Suddenly she stopped, however, leaned her head forward to listen, and then sprang from her chair with surprising agility and hurried to the door.

"Nan—Nan, where are you?" called a girlish voice out of the darkness.

"Stay where ye are, Anny lass, till I get ye a light."

Nan's stentorian tones boomed over the flat bogs. Hurriedly she crossed to the darkest corner of the little hut, where she fumbled for a minute or two. There was the sound of soft scraping of flint on steel, then the tinder caught fire and Nan lit a tallow dip and carried it to the door, holding it high above her head.

There was no breath of wind in the cloudless night and the flame burned steadily.

"Oh! Nan, I'm so glad ye're here," came the same voice out of the darkness, this time a good deal nearer.

"Why, lass, wherever else would I be? What's ailing ye, my girl?"

Anny scrambled over the last dyke and staggered breathless into the circle of light thrown by the little flame of the dip.

"Let me come in and talk with ye, mother," she said, clutching hold of the elder woman's ragged kirtle.

Nan put a strong, bony arm round the girl's shoulders, and when she spoke her deep voice had a softer quality in it than before.

"Sit down, lass, sit down, and get your breath, and then I'll listen to ye as long as my eyes will keep open," she said kindly.

Anny sat down on the upturned rum keg, after first displacing the cat, who spat at her viciously.

Nan snatched a leather thong from the wall and lashed at it savagely, whereupon it slunk into a corner and lay down on a heap of onions, keeping one baleful eye fixed on its mistress's visitor.

Nan sat down on a three-legged stool, the only other article in the room save for a huge iron bowl which hung on chains over the now empty grate and several bunches of dried herbs hanging from the roof, and looked at the girl critically.

Anny's face was very white and drawn, and she looked about her with a hunted expression in her wild green eyes. She had evidently been crying as she came along, for there were tear marks on her white cheeks.

Nan said nothing, but sat looking at her, her strong, rugged face absolutely expressionless.

"I've got to marry Blackkerchief Dick, Nan," Anny said at last. "What will I do?"

Nan's eyes flickered.

"Got to? Who says Anny Farran's got to do aught she don't want to?"

"Pet Salt said——"

"What!" Nan's face blazed with fury. "That blue-livered, mange-struck ronyon! Truth, lass, you're mad to think on her! The louse-ridden, thieving, man-stealing, spirit-sodden devil," she muttered to herself.

Anny shook her head.

"She says I'll be took to the Castle if I don't do as she bids," she said hurriedly.

Nan lashed the earthen floor with her strip of leather.

"The woman's a lying fiend," she said quickly and intensely.

The girl laid her hand on the other woman's trembling arm.

"I know she is, mother, I know she is, but what will I do?" she said softly.

Nan looked up impatiently.

"Do? why, do naught, the old hell-kite, the sithering——"

"Ay, but listen, mother! Listen!" the girl's voice was so insistent that the older woman allowed her voice to die away to a muttering.

Anny went on.

"If I don't wed Master Dick, Nan, Pet Salt"—Nan began to mumble again, but Anny took no notice—"saith that he will carry me off without him marrying me—and, mother, I would be wed."

Nan paused in her muttered imprecations to look at the girl. This was a new side of the affair, and she realised the importance to the girl's mind. She began to consider it carefully, while Anny watched her face with almost painful eagerness.

But Nan's hatred for Pet Salt was too great to allow her to think clearly on any subject connected with her old enemy for more than two minutes at a time, and she soon broke forth into low, tense reviling.

"Look!" she said, suddenly springing up and standing between Anny and the open doorway, a tall, black figure against a background of stars. "Look at me, child—do you know how old I am?—forty-three! You're surprised? Of course, I look sixty, don't I? Tell me—tell me."

Anny looked at the rugged face that had evidently once been so beautiful; the light from the dip flickered over it and accentuated each wrinkle and hollow. She nodded.

"Ah!" Nan lifted her clenched fist above her head. "That is her work, the woman of hell. Once my cabin was the sweetest, cleanest, and neatest on the Island, my lips were the reddest, my hair the blackest, my smile the most prized——Oh, that crawling filcher, would I might feel these hands about her scabby neck!"

Anny sighed. She knew it was no use to attempt to stop Mistress Swayle in this mood so she crouched back in her corner, while the cat, which had at first objected to her, now came to hide in the folds of her kirtle. He also knew his mistress's vagaries.

Nan went on, her voice rising higher and higher, and her words coming faster and faster until she seemed to be repeating some frenzied chant.

"She took my man—your grandsire—she stole him from me with promises of rum to rot his soul with—God curse her. I, a sweet milk lass working all day in my dairy with a flowered kirtle to my back and shoes to my feet—and she, a dirty, mange-eaten quean. Oh! may the red-plague fall on her and her rat-eaten boat. And he, a simple, kind-hearted lad with a liking for the spirit! Oh! that kite shall go through torments in her time! But he loved me—not her, devil baste her."

Anny rose to her feet and the cat ran away squealing.

"Mother Swayle," she said pleadingly, "what will I say to her?"

Nan seemed to come to herself again for she patted the girl kindly on the shoulder.

"You run back to the Ship, lass. I'll see the ronyon," she said.

Anny took her hand.

"You're good to me, mother," she said.

Nan pulled her hand away sharply.

"Go off with you, child," she ordered harshly, and, as Anny sped over the marshes, she heard the deep voice behind her getting fainter and fainter, calling, "Rum—rum—rum!"

Early on the next morning Mistress Swayle set out for Pet Salt's boat. The sun, rising red out of the sea, tinged her black gown and flying elf-locks with a certain rustiness as she bent her head before the salt morning wind and strode down the ill-made road. She walked along with sweeping strides a five-foot bramble stick in her hand. On either side of her stretched the grey-green, dyke-patterned saltings, while ahead gleamed the fields of ripening wheat and blue vetches.

She was murmuring to herself as she went along and often paused to shake her stick at some unseen adversary.

Her cat followed her at a respectful distance, always keeping one eye on the bramble stick.

As it was some way to Pet Salt's boat, Nan was tired by the time she reached the Ship and would have gone in and rested there had she not been beset by a pack of young urchins, Tant Pullen and little Red among them, who danced round her in a ring, calling "Witch!" and "Devil's Aunt!" and so forth.

The old woman—for she looked old—laid about her vigorously with her stick and as she was very strong soon prevented them from barring her way, but they followed her for a long distance along the wall.

Pet Salt lifted a tousled head above the hatchway, sniffed the cool clean salt air, and shivered. Then, hastily wrapping a piece of old sail-cloth round her mouth and nose, she scrambled on to the dirty deck and hurried across to a heap of kegs piled up high. Under these she at last unearthed a partially full one, and hugging it to her bosom, ran back to the hatchway, her bare feet sounding oddly on the rotten boards.

It was at this moment that Nan tapped on the side of the boat with her stick and shouted in tones loud enough to awaken the seven sleepers:

"Ho, there, you dirty ronyon, come out, come out, Pet Salt, Heaven blast ye!"

At the sound of her voice Pet dropped the keg she was carrying, and tearing the sail-cloth from her face, hobbled over to the side and looked down.

"What! you round here, you hell-cat, sneaking a look at your love, I suppose, you old——"

A stream of unprintable language broke from her ragged lips.

Nan, leaning heavily on her long stick, gazed upwards and when Pet paused for breath she began to talk in her big, booming voice.

"What have ye been doing with my god-daughter, you stealer of loves?" she shouted.

Pet began to laugh.

"Your god-daughter!" she shrieked, "and who is she, you mother of witches? You're not talking of my grand-daughter, are you—you tike?"

Nan shook her stick at her fiercely.

"Your grand-daughter! You mange-struck man-stealer," she ejaculated.

"Man-stealer!" Pet shrieked in her fury. "You jade, you miserable, jealous jade—still whining about your lover as you call him, you old she-goat. My Ben never loved you—your lover! You're as old as the Island. What do you want with lovers?"

Nan stood there, a tall, imposing figure, her black rags gently stirring in the wind.

"You lie, Pet Salt! In your rotting throat you lie," she said calmly. "I am not so old as you say, not so old as Ben—and he loved me well—and would have wed me had not you stolen him——"

"I stole? Marry, hell-kite, I stole in truth! I stole, when he came begging to my door and beseeching me to save him from you? I stole, you vile devil?"

"He did not!" Nan spoke hotly.

"Indeed, did he not, ronyon?" Pet was foaming at the mouth in her anger. "Ay, he did, he crawled to my boat and said on his knees: 'Oh, save me, my own Pet o' the saltings, save me from yon scabby wanton who waits for me!'"

"May the green grass turn to ashes in your way for that lie, Pet Salt," said Nan slowly.

Pet put up her hands.

"Ye're not to curse me, Nan Swayle," she shrieked, "ye witch of darkness, ye're not to curse me, or by Heaven I'll call Ben up to ye."

Nan laughed a hard crackling laugh in her throat.

"You daren't, you slut," she said. "Ben may not have forgotten his old love!"

Pet grew purple with rage.

"I dare not let him see you!" she screamed. "What! you ronyon—I dare not let him——Oh, you're mad!"

Nan laughed again.

"Still I say you dare not," she said.

Pet choked with anger; then a crafty look came into her eyes.

"Oh, I see your mind, Mistress Nancy Swayle," she said with a scornful laugh. "I did not think you would be so cunning. Do you then long so much for a sight of your old love that you walk five miles in the early dawning to beg for a look?"

Nan's rugged features twitched convulsively, but in a moment she was laughing again.

"Still I say you dare not, slut," she said.

Without another word Pet turned away from the side and called down the hatchway.

Nan waited on the beach below quite still and leaning on her stick, a proud smile playing round her wide, humorous mouth.

Two or three minutes later Pet reappeared supporting Ben, who in spite of the early hour was very unsteady on his feet.

He lurched forward and sprawled over the side of the hull looking down at Nan. She was evidently much surprised at the change in him, for she started back a little.

Pet laughed derisively.

"Ain't he a pretty one?" she said.

Nan gulped and came forward.

"Hail to ye, Benny," she said softly.

Ben looked at her vaguely.

"Hail!" he said, and then after a moment added abruptly, "Whosh you?"

Pet shrieked with laughter, and settled herself down beside him.

"Who are you, old one?" she screamed.

Nan went nearer.

"Do you not remember Nan Swayle, Ben?" she said pleadingly.

"Ah, yesh! I remembers Nan Shwayle," said Ben cheerfully.

"That's her, ducky," said Pet, her face red with laughter.

Ben leant further over the side to look at Nan, then he drew himself up and turned to Pet.

"Slut, you lie," he said, as clearly as he could. "That's"—he pointed to Nan—"an old hag—but Nan Shwayle—no, Nan Shwayle was a shweet lash—a shweet milk lash—an'," he went on very seriously, "a very pretty lash."

He leaned over the side and had one more look at Nan, who stood beneath him, her arms outstretched and her bright eyes brighter than usual.

"No," he said, "no, no, nosh—that ish not a bit like Nan Swayle.

Nan Swayle is a pretty lash, a shweet, pretty lash."

Pet rocked herself to and fro in a paroxysm of laughter.

Ben stood looking at Nan.

"Go away, hag," he said, "find Nan Shwayle and send her to me and I'll go with her, but yoush not Nan Shwayle, or, anywaysh," he went on, "not Nan Shwayle I knowsh, you ugly old hagsh." And he began to laugh. "That's not Nan Shwayle?" he giggled, poking Pet's fat side with his fingers.

Pet rolled over on the gunwale in a fit of laughter.

"No, ducky," she roared, "that's not Nan Swayle. That's a witch telling us she's her."

"Ah! she couldn't cheat me!" Ben chuckled. "I knowsh Nan Shwayle, a pretty lash."

"Pet Salt, the time will come when you shall pay!"

Nan's voice drowned their laughter for a moment. She stood there on the shingle, the waves lapping up to her feet and the newly risen sun lighting her wrinkled face, where two tears sparkled on her yellow cheeks, but her eyes were bright and hard.

Then she turned away and strode off, holding her head high, and as she went the wind carried after her the sound of their derisive laughter.

And it was not until she reached her cabin that she remembered she had said no word to Pet on the business on which she had set out, Anny's marriage.

Chapter XIX

"Pet Salt, are you sure all this is so? I wouldn't wed with him if I could help it."

Anny spoke anxiously, her little face white with apprehension.

She and Pet Salt were alone together on the deck of Ben's old boat. The tide was well up and the waves leaped against the stern with a gurgling sound.

It was late in the evening, the wind was rising, and the sun was setting over the Island in a blaze of red and green light.

On board the *Pet* there was the customary muddle; empty kegs, rotting sail-cloth, torn fishing-nets, and derelict baskets lay strewn about the decaying deck in endless confusion.

Pet was leaning against the stump of the mainmast, her red arms akimbo, and her tousled grey head cocked on one side, while Anny stood looking on to the darkening water with her back to the old woman.

"Sure? Why, girl, certain I'm sure. As sure as this boat's a vile hell, Master Blackkerchief Dick will have you one way or another—wed or unwed, which way lies with you."

Pet's harsh voice broke the warm quietness of the summer evening unpleasantly.

Anny caught her breath, and, shrugging her shoulders, turned towards the old woman. Then she laughed.

"Lord! you must be mad, Pet Salt. How could Master Dick carry me off from the Ship, the whole village there to stay him?" she said brightening.

Pet laughed unpleasantly.

"You think too much of yourself, lass," she said. "To stay him? And why should anyone stay him?"

Anny's eyes grew big with surprise and fear.

"What do you mean?" she said as slowly as she could. "Why, Gilbot——"

Pet began to laugh.

"You, lass, have less wit than most girls, if you think anyone would turn away a moneyed captain because of a little serving slut," she said.

Anny looked round her helplessly.

"Did you see Mother Nan yesterday?" she asked suddenly.

Pet began to swear.

"I did," she said viciously, "the old ronyon. Come prowling round here for a look at your grand-sire, like an old hen clucking for its chick."

"Did—did she not speak with you of me?" Anny's voice trembled.

Pet laughed again.

"Lord, girl! the whole Island don't spend its time thinking and talking o' you," she said. "I heard naught of you from her."

Anny looked round her hopelessly, the tears welling into her eyes. The sun had sunk out of sight behind the belt of oaks on the mainland, and everything around had grown grey and cool.

Suddenly she turned and threw herself before the old woman.

"Grandam—what will I do? What will I do?" she sobbed.

Pet kicked her away hastily and spat on the deck.

"Get up and behave yerself, Anny Farran," she said sharply. "What should ye do but marry the handsome Spaniard and sail off with him? Such a chance don't come to every dirty serving maid."

Anny sprang to her feet.

"I'll not wed him," she said, her voice clear and loud. "I'll not if he kills me."

Pet Salt's smile vanished and a crafty, anxious light crept into her watery eyes. She crossed over to the girl with a peculiar smooth movement and stood very close to her, her villainous face very near to the young girl's frightened one.

"Anny Farran," she said, her harsh, high voice growing more and more uncanny, "there be some as say Pet Salt is a witch."

Anny started involuntarily. The light was fading and faint shadows were creeping fast all round the boat.

Away over the fields a corncrake called plaintively once or twice, and then quite near an owl screamed loudly.

Pet's face grew distorted in the shade.

Anny shuddered; she shared in all the superstitions of the day, and witches and the evil eye were well known to her.

"Ay, they do," she faltered, "but what say you?"

"I say—naught!"

Pet came a little nearer and her voice sank to a whisper.

Anny shrieked and started back.

"Holy Mother of God, defend me!" she muttered.

Pet laughed weirdly.

"Prayers don't frighten Pet Salt," she whispered, coming still nearer to the terrified Anny, who clung to the gunwale.

"What will you do?" The girl's voice was so low that Pet could hardly hear it.

"Nay! What will you do, ronyon? Shall the handsome Captain lie by thee or no?"

Anny clenched her little brown hands so that the nails cut into her palms. The vision of Hal's hurt and angry face kept rising before her.

"And if I do not wed him what will you do?" she said at last.

"Bewitch you, girl, so that even your young slave Hal may loathe you," Pet began in a slow, sing-song voice. "So that your beautiful black hair may fall off on the sand like seaweed leaving you old and hairless—so that your eyes may burn up and grow dim and the sight of the sea never more be seen in them—so that your teeth may grow black and ache with the pain of ten thousand devils tearing at their roots—so that your nails may drop off and lie on the floor like shells, and your fingers wither and grow black, and their knuckles decay and the joints drop off, and——"

Anny covered her eyes.

"Oh, peace—peace, I pray you," she screamed, "I will do anything. Oh, peace——"

Pet began to laugh.

"Have a care, Anny, how you tell this," she said, "or I will bewitch thee certainly."

Anny looked at the old woman curiously.

"Yet I will not wed," she announced suddenly. "I mind me when you vowed that Master Patten should have a blister grow on his skin to the size of an egg, and I mind me that he had no such thing at all."

Pet began to swear heartily.

"The hell-kite went to the priest at West," she explained.

Anny's eyes lighted.

"Then so will I," she said promptly.

"That you shall not," Pet laughed raucously. "Look you, Ann Farran," she said, "if you do so there's other things that Pet can do. Send Hal Grame and you to Colchester to the Castle to rot your lives out in the foul dungeons they have there."

This was the last. Anny, who was by this time thoroughly frightened, had been brought up along with the other Island children to fear Colchester Castle worse than death, and, indeed, the stories of the dungeons current at that time were very terrible, the Civil War being only just over. She began to cry.

"I will wed with him," she said.

"Secretly on this boat to-morrow night?"

Anny gasped. Nevertheless she shrugged her shoulders and nodded.

"Yes."

"Good! The Captain comes to-night to hear of it, will you wait to see him?"

"Nay," the word broke from her lips like a sob, and she ran over to the rope-ladder.

"If you fail——" Pet's voice grew threatening.

Anny's voice trembled.

"I will not fail," she said, and then added beneath her breath, "Oh, Hal, what will I say to you?"

As she ran back to the Ship across the fast-darkening saltings,

Anny began to realise the situation a little more clearly. She had bound herself to marry Dick on the morrow; that was terrible enough in itself, but after she was married, what then? The girl stopped in her stride to think on it.

"After I am wed I can go back to the Ship," she said, half-aloud, "but why be wed first? Oh! whatever will I do?"

Two weeks ago she would have gone to Hal naturally, now she swallowed uneasily in her throat.

Hal had hardly spoken to her of late; he had grown strangely sullen and taciturn, and spent all his spare time in a fishing-boat with Joe Pullen. She knew that they took the fish they caught up the Colne and sold it in the little inland villages. She had tried to speak to him several times, but he had always looked at her so fiercely that she had abandoned the attempt.

Alone on the wild, wind-swept marshes, the girl sank down on her knees on the damp, spiky grass, and covered her face with her hands. She remained quite still for several seconds and then sprang up with a little cry. Hastily she passed her hands over her shining plaits as though to make sure that they were still there, and examined her nails anxiously. Then she sighed with relief and, with one fearful backward glance at the *Pet,* set off to the Ship, her skirts flying out behind her as she ran.

Chapter XX

The same evening, Hal Grame and Joe Pullen walked up the Ship lane together in silence. They had just returned from one of their fishing expeditions, and Joe carried the catch in a dripping basket on his shoulder.

Hal strode along beside him, his hands in his pockets and his eyes fixed moodily on the ground.

No word of Anny had passed between them since the night a fortnight before, when Hal had stumbled into Joe's cottage and told the story of his quarrel with her. Ever since with natural delicacy Joe had carefully avoided the subject, and had carried his mate off fishing as often as he could, thinking that this would take his mind off the girl.

Suddenly Hal stopped.

"How much had we from the sale of yesterday's fishing?" he asked abruptly.

"Four groats," replied Joe promptly.

"Wilt thou give me two, mate?"

Joe looked at his friend in surprise; Hal was not wont to want money, but he answered readily enough:

"Certes, lad, certes," and setting his basket down, he brought out the two coins almost reverently from his pocket and held them to Hal, who took them thoughtfully, weighed them in his hand, and then looked up at his mate questioningly.

"How much silk can I buy with these at Tiptree?" he asked slowly.

Joe looked at him in astonishment.

"Silk? Why, Hal Grame, what in Heaven and earth do you want with——?" he broke off abruptly, a wave of understanding passing over his face. "She's not worth your troubling, mate," he said at last.

A dull flush of anger spread over the younger man's face and he broke out impetuously:

"Not worth my troubling! Lord save you, Joe Pullen, if it was any other man who said as much, I'd——"

Joe put a huge paw on the boy's shoulder.

"That's right, lad, that's right," he said kindly. "The lass is your love when all's said an' done—pray Heaven you may not be as fooled as I was, though," he added mournfully, the thought of Mistress Amy flashing through his mind.

Hal smiled in spite of himself at his friend's lugubrious expression, but he soon became serious again.

"Joe," he said hesitatingly.

"Ay!"

"You have had a deal of truck with women?"

Joe grunted. "Wi' one woman, you mean," he said savagely.

Hal looked at him curiously before he spoke.

"What will I do about Anny?" he said at last.

Joe cleared his throat; he had very strong views on this subject.

"You make too much ado about her," he said.

"But for these last two weeks I have said naught to her," Hal objected.

Joe knew this was true and he shrugged his shoulders.

"I should be sharp with her, lad," he said at last. "Tell her there be other lasses you could love, and she'll come round in no time."

Hal nodded.

"I had thought as much myself," he said.

"Depend on it I'm right," said Joe, shaking his head sagely, and reshouldering the basket he continued thoughtfully up the dusty road.

On turning into the Ship yard they saw the usual company seated on benches before the kitchen door, drinking beer and rum, each man to his fancy.

Old Gilbot's chair had been moved out into the porch, and he sat in it, drunk and happy, singing to his heart's content.

The two mates were greeted cheerily; Joe sat down and called for rum, but Hal, seeing Blueneck and one or two others of the *Anny's* crew among the company, walked into the kitchen, put his cap and coat by, and looked about for Anny.

She was not in the kitchen or the scullery, so presently he wandered out into the garden where the evening shadows lay deep over the plants and shrubs. He sat down on an upturned barrel, his elbows resting on his knees and his chin on his hands.

Hardly had he been there a moment when there was a rustling in the shrubbery at the end of the garden and Anny, her plaits flying out behind her, sped up the path towards him. She did not notice him, and would have passed had not he put out an arm to stay her.

At his touch the girl gave a little terrified scream and started back like a frightened animal. When she saw who it was, however, she gave a little sigh of relief and a smile crept into her face, while her heart beat faster.

Hal was going to make friends with her at last, she thought, and as she smiled up at him she felt that here was the solution of her difficulties.

Hal on his side felt a glow of pleasure at her obvious friendliness and a warm impulse to take her in his arms. However, he remembered Joe's advice, and the smile died on his lips as he said sharply:

"Where have you been, Ann Farran? and why come you in so quickly by the back way?"

The eager, happy light died out of the girl's eyes in a moment, and a flush of anger spread over her cheeks.

"And what will that matter to you, Master Hal Grame?" she said pertly, tossing her head.

Hal's young face grew hard and he laid a hand on her arm.

"Indeed, it has a great deal to do with me, Ann Farran. What duty am I paying to Master Gilbot if I let his serving wenches go flying about the Island at all hours of the day, and besides, Anny, don't forget that you—you——" his voice had grown much softer and even trembled a little, but Anny was too angry to notice it.

"Indeed, I think you take too much on your shoulders, master—master tapster," she burst out.

Hal gasped, and then as his anger rose his grip on her arm tightened and he shook her violently.

"Take care, Anny, take care," he said between his teeth, "don't forget that you were to wed me?"

Anny tried to wrench her hand away.

"Were? Ay, you're right, Hal Grame," she said proudly. "Marry! I would not wed you now if you and I were the last to be on earth."

Hal blinked and let go his grip on her arm; then a smile broke over his boyish features, and he said, half-laughing:

"Lord, you're daft, Anny, you know you love me. Come, say I lie, you can't!"

Anny's black brows came down on her white forehead until they made one straight line across her brow and her big green eyes blazed.

"I say you lie, Hal Grame," she said very quietly and distinctly. "I say you lie and that you are an overweening puppy and think yourself too fine."

Hal was stung into replying sharply:

"Lord preserve you, silly wench! Who do you think would marry you, a little serving slut, without a portion, or even a father, for that matter?"

Anny tossed her head and looked at him disdainfully.

"I could be wed to-morrow to a finer man than you," she said, forgetting prudence in her irritation.

Hal laughed savagely.

"Oh you fool, you fool, Anny," he said bitterly. "Do you think your little sea-rat will wed you?"

Anny looked at him with child-like surprise.

"I do not think at all," she said, and added under her breath, "I know."

Hal looked at her hopelessly. He felt that Joe's advice had not been altogether helpful, and as she stood there, a wild, free-looking little creature in the dim light, he could not help feeling that if he had coaxed her instead of attempting to drive her into his arms things might have gone better with him, and Anny, as she stood looking at him, felt a pang in her heart when she thought of the old Hal, the Hal whom she had loved, who had been so different from this new Hal who seemed to be deliberately trying to make her hate him.

For two seconds they stood looking at one another, each hoping against hope that all would yet come right; yet neither of them spoke. At last Anny turned away and went slowly into the house, her mind made up about her marriage, and her thoughts on Blackkerchief Dick.

Hal watched her go and then sat down again, his head on his hands. Presently he put his hand into his pocket and brought out the two groats, and looked at them as they lay shining in his palm, and then made a gesture as though to fling them from him away into the bushes, but thought better of it and repocketed them.

"The lass may love me still," he muttered to himself. "I'll get the present for her. Lasses are slippery catches. I would I knew the way of them."

Then thrusting his hands deep into his pockets he got up heavily and strolled slowly up the path, kicking savagely at the loose gravel as he went.

Chapter XXI

"Ho, there, you mange-struck dogs, broach a keg and drink to your Captain's lady!"

Blackkerchief Dick, his eyes flashing, and his face showing bright and triumphant in the flickering lantern light, shouted the words over the side of Ben's boat, to a little knot of picked men of the *Anny's* crew, who were ranged on the sand below.

They were present to witness their Captain's marriage to Anny Farran, and incidentally to carry the rum which was the price of his bride.

The worn deck of the *Pet* had been cleaned and partially cleared for the occasion. Dick had insisted on this, and, in spite of the protestations of the two old people, Ben and Pet, the work had been done and the place presented a fairly tidy aspect.

The empty kegs were ranged in neat rows round the gunwale, the clothes' line had been removed, and the rest of the litter swept down the hatchway.

It was almost dark, and the cloudless sky was a pale blue, shading off to rose and green in the west, where the first two or three stars shone faintly.

On deck a big ship's lantern stood on the stump of the mainmast, while two smaller ones hung on each side of it; they showed sick and yellow in the half-light.

Standing before this improvised altar stood a man dressed as a priest. He held a book in his hand and was mumbling to himself nervously in a foreign tongue. On either side of him were Blueneck and Noah Goody; their knives were drawn and their faces set like wooden masks.

Before them, in a gorgeous ill-fitting gown of yellow Lyons silk which Dick had brought and insisted on her wearing, stood Anny. Her cheeks were flushed and her eyes dancing with excitement. Round her neck hung a great silver pendant studded with garnets, and every now and then her hand would stray up to this and her fingers caress it lovingly, half-wonderingly. On the little brown hand shone a ring; it was an extraordinary jewel, consisting of a little gold hoop supporting a large flower, each petal of which was a different kind of stone, diamond, ruby, emerald, onyx, pearl, and sapphire, with a little piece of amber for the centre.

Dick had told her that it was very old when he had put it on her finger, and she looked at it with something very like awe.

Behind her stood Ben and Pet; the old man swayed to and fro drunkenly, taking little or no interest in the proceedings, but the old woman watched eagerly, half-enviously, her bleared eyes following Anny's every movement and each gleam of the jewels, her quick ears catching every word that was spoken. Nothing escaped her, and she noticed that the priest's garments were made for a much larger man, and that his book was upside down, but she said nothing and merely smiled wickedly to herself as the ceremony went on.

The men on the beach below were not long in obeying their Captain's order, and in a minute the toast was given.

"Health and good fortune to the Captain's lady!" Everybody drank heartily, the priest more than anyone, and Dick, his brocaded coat and soft lace ruffles shining in the dim light, and his black curls showing a little more than usual from under his black kerchief, raised his glass above his head and taking Anny by the hand threw back his head and laughed joyously. He had once again got his own way in spite of difficulties. He drained off his liquor, and throwing the empty cup over his head, began to sing:

"Fair as the Island, and proud as the sea,
As naught in the world is sweet Anny to me."

The rich musical voice echoed round the old boat and floated out over the marshes.

Anny caught her breath and her grip on the Spaniard's pulsing white hand tightened. She was carried out of herself by the excitement of the moment, the wonderful frock, the jewels, and above all the singing.

Dick felt her emotion and his arm slid round her waist much like a snake slips round a tree-stem, and, as her pretty head fell back on his shoulder, the song grew louder, sweeter, and a triumphant note crept into it:

> "So gentle, so tender, so wise without guile,
> Oh, where is another like Ann of the Isle?"

Anny sighed deliriously and she shivered with pure excitement; the Spaniard's full red lips brushed her hair, before the wonderful voice rang out again, in the chorus:

> "Ann! oh! Ann of the Island,
> Where is another like Ann of the Isle?"

The crew took up the strain, and Dick and Anny stood together in a circle of singing men each with his rumkin held high above his head and his foot keeping time to the rhythm.

Old Pet spat on the deck and an envious light came into her evil old face. All her life she had longed to be the centre of a scene like this, the magnet of an admiring crowd of hard-drinking, hard-fighting, hard-loving men. All her youth had been spent in dreams of a night like this. Now in her age it was bitter to see it come to another woman.

As for Anny, she was intoxicated with it all; any sense of prudence had left her. She was supremely happy. Now and again a faint regret that she could not marry Hal rose in her mind, but she dismissed it promptly.

The future had no being for her, and the past was a dream; the thing that counted was the present, the laughing, pulsing, living present.

And as the *Anny's* crew roared out their Captain's own love-song, and Dick, his Spanish blood on fire with love triumphant, kissed her hair, her eyes, her mouth, she laughed as freely and as joyously as he had done.

The shadows were deepening by this time and the deep blue sky was studded with stars, and Anny, looking up from the Captain's shoulder, said suddenly:

"It is late, sir; I must go back to the Ship now."

Dick looked at her in astonishment for a moment, and a contemptuous crackling laugh broke from between Pet Salt's thin, blackened lips.

At the sound of it Anny shuddered involuntarily and drew a little closer to the Spaniard, who noting her agitation turned on the old woman angrily, his eyes suddenly losing their dreamy love-heaviness, and becoming hard and bright.

"Peace, hag!" he rapped out, "get thee down thy rat-hole, and take thy sodden man with thee, or nothing shall you see of me or my cargoes from this night on."

Pet began to mumble and curse under her breath, but nevertheless she obediently hobbled across the deck towards the hatchway, half-carrying, half-dragging the drunken Ben along with her. The company watched them in silence and Anny, as with fascinated eyes she followed them to the dark hole, down which they disappeared, could not help being reminded of one big muddy crab dragging its prey after it into its noisome hole there to feast.

Dick, too, watched them and shrugged his shoulders.

"So may all evil creatures drag themselves out of thy path, my Ann of the Island," he said, and then as-though a new idea had struck him, "Thou art right, dear heart, get thee back to the Ship. That will be the best way, and then I will come for thee. Until then say nothing of this."

Anny smiled happily and ran to the hatchway to change her frock again, and as she laid by the soft silk she felt in her childish, happy-go-lucky way that she had laid by the whole evening's business with it.

She had been half afraid that Dick would not let her go back to the Ship. Now it seemed that he wanted her to. She had some sort of vague idea that she was to be his wife on the Island only, when she would see him in the ordinary way at the Ship.

She sighed relievedly; the matter did not seem to be as important as she had imagined.

When she came on the deck again dressed in her usual kirtle and bodice, the crew were rolling several unopened kegs on to the deck, and the priest was helping them, but Anny did not notice this for Dick was waiting for her.

"I will go with thee along the way," he said gallantly, his soft eyes seeking hers, and his slim, white hand closing on her little brown one.

Anny smiled at him as he helped her down the rope-ladder and on to the beach. Once again his silk-sleeved arm slid round her, and she laid her head on his shoulder. They walked on in silence.

Suddenly the Spaniard stopped and his other arm encircled her, pulling back her head and raising her little white face to his.

Anny could see him earnest and grave in the moonlight.

"You are my first love, Ann of the Island, though there be many others I have sported with," he said in a strangely quiet even voice, "and I am a strange man; take care how you use me."

Anny looked at him with frank, innocent eyes; he was very handsome she thought.

"I pray you kiss me, sir," she said softly.

They did not move for a second or so, and the wind rose over the sea, whistled through the long grass at the sides of the path, and rustled the seaweed at their feet. Suddenly they became aware that someone was coming towards them.

Anny grew suddenly rigid; it was a step she knew.

Dick looked up quickly, and they began to walk on.

The figure came nearer and nearer. Dick strained his eyes to see who it was, but the man was in the shadow, and he passed without speaking.

When they had gone on a little way Dick paused.

"Didst see who 'twas passed us, Ann?" he asked.

Anny swallowed, and then said as carelessly as she could:

"Oh! 'twas no one of any account; 'twas the tapster from the Ship."

Chapter XXII

"Nan, are you within? I've come to beg a thing of ye, mother."

Anny stood outside Nan Swayle's little cabin and knocked at the door. It was early afternoon and the hot sun poured down on the grey purplish saltings, but in spite of the heat the hut was shut up.

Anny began to be afraid that the old woman had gone away, and a sudden feeling of terrible loneliness seized her; she knocked again frantically.

There was silence for a moment or so and then Nan's great booming voice came out to the waiting girl like a welcome peal of thunder after a lightning flash.

"Good swine, peace to ye, whoever you are. What do you want wi' old Mother Swayle?"

"'Tis I, mother—Anny Farran, and in great need," the girl spoke eagerly and her voice shook unsteadily.

There was the sound of someone moving hastily across the hut; the door flung open and Nan's great gaunt form appeared in the opening.

"Come in, child, in," she said kindly, her shrewd, keen eyes taking in the girl's white haggard face and miserable expression.

Anny looked up at her for a moment, and then her mouth twitched convulsively at the corners, her eyes filled with tears, and she flung herself in the old woman's arms sobbing hysterically.

Nan led her into the little dark hut and sat on an empty keg, gently pulling the girl down beside her. Then she began to rock herself gently to and fro. She said nothing for some minutes, during which Anny's sobs grew less and less violent.

"Now what's the matter, my daughter?" said Nan, after the girl's grief had somewhat abated.

Anny began to cry afresh.

"Oh, Nan, what will I do?" she sobbed, "what will I do?"

The older woman put her hands on the girl's shoulders and held her firm.

"Cry till ye can cry no more, lass, and then tell your story; 'tis the best way; crying eases the heart. The Lord gave women tears that their hearts might not break every day," she said, her great kindly voice echoing round and about the little shanty.

Anny lifted up her tear-stained face from the old woman's knee, and carefully avoiding her piercing brown eyes, began to speak in a half-whisper, stopping here and there to wipe her eyes.

"When I came home from the wedding wi' Master Dick," she began—Nan started at her words and carefully suppressed an exclamation of horrified surprise—"we passed—Hal—on the way—and, when I got to the Ship, no one was in the kitchen, so I sat down on the long seat and thought on the Captain, and after a while Hal comes in, and——" she paused.

Nan said nothing but sat staring in front of her.

Anny looked up quickly.

"You knew that we had quarrelled, mother?" she said.

Nan nodded.

The girl paused and when she spoke again her voice had sunk into a murmur.

"He did not see me at first for the kitchen was dark and I in the corner. I watched him, Nan, I watched him come in, sit down before the counting-table, and take down the slate, and I saw him push it away, and then draw it to him again, and I saw him put his hand through his hair, and I heard him breathe loudly and slowly, and as though somewhat hurt him, and I—oh, mother—I heard him call me; 'Anny, Anny, Anny,' he said as though he was speaking from a long way off; then he laid his head on his arms there on the counting-table and I heard him breathing again, loud and fast."

Her voice died away and there was no sound in the coolness of the little hut; then she began to cry again.

Suddenly Nan spoke and her voice sounded sharp after Anny's impassioned murmuring.

"And you were married to the Spanish Captain?" she asked.

Anny sat up, her beautiful green eyes brimming with tears.

"Yes," she said pitifully, "and I love him."

"Who? Blackkerchief Dick?"

"Nay, oh nay, mother; nay; Hal, Hal Grame—my love!" A sob rose in her throat, but she swallowed it down and continued almost eagerly, "And as he sat there, and I watching, I knew 'twas he I loved, for all his foolings, and I wondered would I creep behind and put my arms about his neck, and put my face to his hair, but I minded I was married to the Spaniard, and I knew I could not wed with Hal, and I wondered what would I do, and then, as I was watching him, he looked up and saw me. His face was very pale; I have never seen anyone but the dead so pale. I thought he would have cried out, for his mouth opened and his lips moved, but he said naught; then he stood up and came towards me, slowly, as though I had been a spirit, and his eyes were so dark and full of something, I know not what—that I put up my hands to hide my face."

She broke off abruptly and looked round her, and brushed the hair off her forehead before she spoke again. All the time Nan rocked silently to and fro.

"Then I heard him speaking below his breath, and his voice hurt me, Nan, his voice hurt me. 'Anny,' he said, 'Anny, are you come back to me, my love?' and I heard him fall on his knees at my feet, and I felt his head in my lap and his arms about my waist—and I loved him. Oh, Nan! I loved him so!"

Her hands clutched at the older woman's gown convulsively.

"Mother, will you tell him? Will you tell him?" she broke out suddenly. "I couldn't, I couldn't, not when he was kneeling there more like a young lad than a man."

Nan stopped rocking and faced the pleading, frantic little girl before her:

"You did not tell him?" she said slowly.

Anny shook her head.

"Nay, I could not tell him—I love him so," she said. "I got up and ran away to bed, leaving him there, his head on the seat I had left, and, oh, Nan! all night long I dreamed I could still hear him breathing heavily like that and calling 'Anny, Anny, Anny.' Oh, Nan! tell him for me, tell him for me! I could not stay in the Ship and he there not knowing. Both our hearts would break."

Nan looked at her curiously.

"I will tell him," she said.

A sigh of relief broke from Anny's lips and Nan went on: "I did not know you had wedded with the Spaniard, lass; why did you so? You must have been mad; what will ye do now?"

Anny looked at her in astonishment.

"I had no choice," she said. "Pet——"

A light of understanding swept over Nan's expressive face and she sprang to her feet.

"Miserable hell-cat that I am," she exclaimed, her great voice shaking with fury, "to be turned aside by Pet's damned witchcraft, and sent home without having done aught—oh, why did ye do it, lass, why did ye do it?"

Anny shrugged her shoulders.

" 'Tis nothing, mother, nothing," she said wearily. "I shall not be known as his wife. There will be no difference, save that I cannot wed with Hal." Once again her voice broke on the name.

Nan stared at the girl incredulously.

"Did he say so?" she gasped.

Anny shrugged again. "Nay, not in words," she said carelessly, "but he said, 'Go back to the Ship and I will come,' so you see nothing will change."

The elder woman seized the girl by the shoulders.

"You're mad, Anny," she said fiercely. "Don't you see he'll take you away? When the Spaniard comes to the Ship, he comes for you."

Anny sprang to her feet, her eyes wide with fear and amazement. This view of the affair had not presented itself to her before.

"Take me away?" she repeated wonderingly, and then, as the full meaning of the words came to her, a little terrified scream escaped her. “I won’t go,” she said quickly, “I won’t go—leave this Island? leave the Ship? leave Hal? No, I won’t go—I——” She stopped suddenly and turned to the old woman, an expression of horror on her face.

“There was none who could stay him wedding me,” she said slowly, her eyes growing larger and more frightened at every word. “There was none who could stay him wedding me; there will be none to stay him taking me away—oh!——”

She dropped down on the beaten earth floor shuddering violently.

Nan looked down at her for a few seconds, and then out of the door over the flat marshes to the hilly wooded island beyond.

“The witchcraft of Pet Salt—blast her—stayed me once, Anny,” she said, “but none shall stay me the second time, my daughter.”

Chapter XXIII

As Anny ran back to the Ship, her mind was full of one thing only—fear of leaving the Island.

Nan's few words had thrown an entirely new light on the situation. Before hearing them she had thought of the future as simply a continuation of her present life. She could hardly imagine a world in which the Ship, the Island, and Hal had no part. They had become necessary to her; and the thought of losing them terrified her. She had been somewhat reassured by Nan's promise to prevent her from going with the Spaniard, but, as she thought of Dick, with his determined air and ready knife, her heart sank again, and she hurried on, her head full of troubles.

That evening the usual company gathered together in the old kitchen of the Ship, and Anny was kept busy serving liquor; she had no one to help her. Sue was down walking on the beach with Big French, and Anny felt half envious when she thought of the other girl's smooth love affair compared with her own. Hal, too, was away; he had gone off to a mysterious summons which had been brought to him some two hours ago and had not yet returned.

Old Gilbot was very merry, and as the time drew on he called for the candles to be lighted and then, leaning back in his chair, treated the company to one of his favourite songs—"Pretty Poll, she loved a sailor," and soon had the rafters shaking with his music and their laughter.

No one noticed Anny, and the girl went about her duties quietly, almost dreamily. Often she would pause to listen, and stand waiting, her eyes on the door for some seconds, before she went on with her work again, her face set and white.

Just when the chorus of "Pretty Poll" was at its height, however, there was the sound of footsteps on the cobbles outside and the door opened suddenly. No one noticed it save Anny, and she stood rooted to the spot, her eyes fixed.

Hal came into the kitchen slowly, screwing up his eyes until they should have got used to the light. The girl watched him fascinated. His face seemed to have suddenly grown very grave and quiet. A man's face, she thought, and she looked at him wonderingly.

Suddenly he turned and saw her.

Anny met his eyes with difficulty, and then dropped them before his gaze, so reproachful and yet so kind. She shivered a little.

Nan had kept her promise.

For the next two days Anny saw nothing of the Spaniard and her spirits began to revive. Like all the Island folk, she took life very casually, and, as the days slipped on uneventfully, the event of her marriage, although barely a week passed, grew more and more like a rather exciting dream.

She was thinking like this as she sat alone in the kitchen's open doorway, stitching a seam in one of Sue's new kirtles, when she saw Blueneck coming across the yard towards her. Instantly all her fears returned and her fingers trembled as she pushed the needle to and fro through the coarse flannel.

He came up and saluted her courteously, as became one addressing the Captain's lady.

"Mistress, I have a message for thee," he said, looking round him cautiously.

Anny glanced up quickly.

"There is none with us," she said, jerking her head towards the kitchen.

Blueneck looked round the yard hastily, and then bent a little nearer to the girl.

"Mistress, the Captain bids me tell you that we sail to-morrow night," he said softly.

Anny caught her breath and the sailor went on:

"And, Mistress, he bids me tell you to be ready to go with him when he comes for you."

Anny's sewing slid off her lap on to the ground unheeded.

Blueneck noticed her confusion and dropping his voice to a whisper, said kindly:

"Take heart, lass, if ever the Captain kissed a woman, he loves you," and then, recovering his respectful manner, he added, "and the Captain prays you to be secret for a while."

Then with a smile and cheerful wave of his hand he turned and left her.

Anny sat spellbound.

It had come.

Immediately her thoughts flew to Nan. She must tell Nan at once for, whether the old woman could help her or not, the girl realised that she was the only person on the Island who was willing to do so.

She got up to get her shawl and then remembered that she dare not leave the Ship.

Sue and Hal were out in the fields and Gilbot had walked down to the sea. The inn could not be left unattended; suddenly she remembered Red.

The child was playing happily in the garden; he came rather unwillingly when she called him and stood before her, a quaint, bedraggled little figure biting his nails, but he was fond of his sister and listened to her instructions with great attention.

"Red, will ye run along to Nan for me?" she said, as calmly as she could.

The child's face fell, but he nodded all the same.

"And will ye tell her this? Now do keep it in your head, Reddy," she was trembling in her agitation. "Tell her this—he wants Anny to go to-morrow, and none can stay him."

She spoke very distinctly, as though she was trying to imprint each word on the child's mind.

Red screwed up his eyes in a great mental effort.

" 'He wants Anny to go to-morrow, and none can stay him,' " he repeated at last. Then he turned to his sister. "Who wants you, Anny?" he asked curiously.

Anny frowned.

"Oh, go along, dear, go along, hurry!" she almost sobbed.

Red looked at her in mild surprise, and then trotted off obediently, muttering to himself as he ran and letting the words keep tune to the soft pad of his feet. "He—wants—An—ny—to—go—to—mor—row, and no—one—will—stay—him."

He was very hot and breathless by the time he reached Nan's hut, and he stammered out the words to the old woman, who listened eagerly, a strange light in her eyes.

"To-morrow?" she said, as the boy sank down on the floor, panting and gasping.

Red looked up.

"Yes," he said, and added: "And no one will stay him." He repeated the words as though they held no meaning for him.

A fierce expression grew on Nan's rugged face and she bent down to the little fellow and shook him half-angrily.

"You lie, boy, you lie," she said, her face very close to his. "Do you hear?—you lie—for there is one who will stay him, nay, who shall. Get back to your sister—tell her not to fear."

Chapter XXIV

"Ah, Master Gilbot, 'twill be a deal quieter than this to-morrow night, I reckon."

Master Granger leaned across from his seat in the chimney corner and jerked his head in the direction of the body of the room where everything was in commotion.

The *Anny* was due to sail on the night-tide, and her crew were celebrating its departure with rum and song.

One of the long tables had been pulled out and round this some ten or twelve men sprawled in more or less comfortable attitudes. Behind these were others sitting on rum kegs or leaning against the walls. They were all very merry, and from time to time loud shrieks of laughter shook the old Ship's rafters and made them echo again and again.

Round the flickering fire, the first of the season, but a bright one, sat the Islanders, Joe Pullen, French, Cip de Musset, Granger, Gilbot, and a few others. They did not mix with the roaring, yelling crowd of seamen, but sat stolidly, drinking slowly, talking slowly, and enjoying themselves after their own quiet fashion. Now and again, perhaps, a young man would leave his seat to go over and split a joke and a pint with a sailor, but the majority kept themselves to themselves, neither objecting to, nor wholly approving, the noisy pleasure of the smugglers.

Hal, especially, was very taciturn. He stood quietly in a candle-lit corner, cleaning pewter, and spoke hardly at all. Sue, however, was in a very good humour; in her best kirtle, and her hair tied with a bow of scarlet ribbon which French had given her, she flew hither and thither carrying the liquor.

Anny had not yet appeared, and Blueneck nudged Noah Goody as they sat at the long table, when the time crept on, and still she did not come.

Little Red sat on French's knee keeping very still and listening to the conversation with the utmost interest.

Granger's remark called forth a chorus of "Ay's," some disconsolate, but mostly cheerful.

Gilbot looked at the reeling crowd out of the corner of his little red-rimmed eyes; then he chuckled:

"Nish," he said thickly, a weak, happy smile playing over his big, puffy face. "Nish, oh! very nish indeed. Letsh have a song," and he struck up "Mary Loo" in a thin, quavering voice.

At this moment the door was flung open and a wave of cold air blew round the stifling kitchen; several men from the table turned to swear at the intruder, but their mouths shut silently and they rose to their feet as they saw who it was.

Blackkerchief Dick stepped lightly into the room and, shutting the door behind him, stood smiling on the company, a slim, dapper little figure in black velvet.

Then he removed his black beaver and called loudly for liquor all round. His words were received with cheers, and once again the talk broke out and the singing restarted.

Dick perched himself on the end of one of the empty tables and looked about for Anny. The smile faded from his face when he saw she was not there, and a look of disappointment took its place. He had no doubt she was preparing to fly with him, but he had expected to see her waiting for him, her big eyes and wistful little face alight with expectation, and, he flattered himself, love. His vanity was hurt at her neglect. So his astonishment and anger when he saw her come in a few minutes later, in her usual kirtle and serving apron, an unwonted colour in her cheeks and a sparkle in her eyes as she fluttered to and fro from one knot of seamen to another, leaving a smile here and jest there, and a pert, stinging remark somewhere else, knew no bounds. He looked at her in amazement; she had not even glanced his way. The disappointed expression left his face and a smile returned, but it was not the same smile.

In the next half-hour Anny surpassed herself for gaiety. Her laugh rang out loud and clear, almost every other second, and the whole company was at her feet in ten minutes.

Even old Gilbot noticed her, and, wagging his head sagely, said that "good lashes "were "good business."

But for Dick she had no eyes; not once did she meet his glance, bring his liquor, or come within five feet of him.

At first his surprise kept him silent and grave, so that Blueneck observed in a whisper to Goody that it was wont to be the lasses and not the Captain who were grave when sailing time came, and that times had changed, but after a while Dick's smile grew more and more pronounced and he called for rum again and again.

Still Anny took no notice of him. Louder and louder grew her laugh, quicker and quicker her retorts, brighter her smile, and more numerous her admirers.

Hal looked up from his pewter cleaning and sighed.

"She was never so happy when we were sweethearts," he muttered.

Only Sue looked at Anny strangely; she was a woman and she knew that there was a false note in the girl's laughter, and that the light in her eyes was an almost desperate one. But she was an Islander, and therefore another lass's business was none of hers, and she said nothing to her nor to anyone else.

At last the Spaniard could bear this lack of notice no longer, and raising his voice called pleasantly enough:

"Mistress Anny!"

The girl started and the tray of mugs which she was carrying rattled nervously, but she recovered herself in a second, and smiled radiantly at him.

"Will your lordship wait till I put these down?" she said gaily, with mock deference.

Dick's smile grew broader, and Blueneck who was watching him whistled softly between his teeth and nudged Goody again.

"Not at all," Dick was saying, his voice very soft and caressing.

Anny put down the tray with a clatter.

"Oh, there now," she exclaimed brightly, "if I haven't spilt one half of Master French's sack; I must fill it up. Here, Hal, will ye go to the Captain for me while I do this? I know he likes being served quickly."

Hal went over to him obediently.

The Spaniard's eyelids flickered and his smile broadened as he ordered more rum, planking down a jacobus in payment.

The time went on and Gilbot and his customers grew more and more lively; still Anny avoided the Spaniard, and still he sat on the table steadily drinking rum.

Suddenly in the middle of a song Dick looked at the clock, and then rising to his feet, shouted:

"Get aboard, dogs!"

The singing died away immediately and all eyes were turned on the clock. The hands pointed to 8.15.

Then a murmur rose among the crew and one bolder than the rest said something about orders being a quarter to nine.

Dick sprang to his feet and his hand played round the hilt of his knife.

"A mutiny?" he asked softly.

Instantly there was a shuffle towards the door and they filed out one by one, and Gilbot, his fuddled brain just realising that the merriment had suddenly died down, began to pipe cheerfully:

> "Oh, no one remembers poor Will
> Who stuck by hish mate at the mill."

Dick laughed and took it up, and the crew, glad to find him so easily recovered, joined in eagerly, and they filed off down the road, singing in chorus:

> "He ground up more bones
> Than barley or stones,
> And more than old Rowley could kill.
> More bones, more bones,

More bones, more bones,
More bones than old Rowley could kill."

"Ah, well!" said Joe, rising to his feet, as the last man reeled drunkenly out of the doorway. "I reckon I'll be getting down to look to my boat."

The others laughed; it was well known that the smugglers would commandeer any rowing-boat that might come their way to take them to the brig, and like as not would set it adrift to be carried out to sea.

"I'll go with ye, lad," said Granger, and they went out together.

Most of the others followed, leaving only French, Red, and Cip de Musset sitting with Gilbot round the fire.

Anny and Sue stood by the door talking together, their backs to the Spaniard, while Hal went on cleaning pewter.

Dick swaggered over to French.

"Master French," he said softly, his beautiful voice very even and clear, "hadst thou not better go down to the brig and see to thy goods?"

French looked up puzzled.

"Goods?" he said wonderingly, and then added, as he met the Spaniard's steady gaze, "Oh! ah! maybe I had, maybe I had," and got up hastily.

Red caught hold of his hand.

"Take me," he whispered.

French looked down at him and laughed as he stroked his honey-coloured beard.

"Come on, then, young 'un," he said kindly.

Red whooped joyfully, and the big man and the little boy went to the door together.

Sue slipped her arm into French's as he passed her.

"I'll come a little way with ye, Ezekiel," she murmured.

French put his arm about her and they went out.

Cip de Musset then rose to his feet.

"Are you coming, Captain?" he said, as he picked up his stick.

Anny caught her breath as she edged round behind the empty table.

Dick smiled sardonically.

"I shall follow," he said.

Cip looked about him, and then smiled knowingly, and putting on his hat went over to the door, and out into the dark.

Blackkerchief Dick waited until he had gone and then turned and faced Anny, who was watching him fascinated. She felt that the time had come at last when she must shake him off for ever, or else go with him.

She had not heard from Nan since Red had taken her message, and she remembered the old woman's promise as the one gleam of hope on her horizon, and every moment she expected to see her hobble into the kitchen, but it was getting late, and Nan had not come.

Dick walked over to the table behind which she stood and seated himself upon it without speaking.

The desperate light crept into the girl's eyes again and she began to laugh. At least she must keep him in as good a temper as possible. She realised that. So dropping a curtsey she came a little nearer, and leaning over the table, asked him would he drink again. To her surprise he answered her very pleasantly that he would, and ordered rum.

Hal, who was still cleaning pewter, looked up from his work, and watched the little scene with a growing sense of despair.

To know that his love was lost to him was bitter enough, he told himself, but to see her happy in the Spaniard's company, to see her hang upon the Spaniard's words, and wait for his smile, was too much; he turned away quickly.

When Anny came back with the rum, Dick caught her wrist and held her firm with one hand while he raised the tankard to his lips with the other.

"Why are you not ready to come with me?" he whispered, as he set down the empty rumkin.

Anny began to laugh again.

"Lord! how you talk, Captain!" she said, trying to pull her arm from out his grasp.

The Spaniard's grip tightened, and his smile grew more grim.

"Ann, this is not the time to jest," he said, his voice growing softer and more musical at every word. "The brig waits us."

Anny noticed that his voice was gentle and began to giggle again.

"Well, Master Dick, let it wait," she said, tossing her head. "It can wait till Doomsday before you'll see me aboard," and she broke into a little nervous laugh.

To her surprise Dick joined in with her, and his long, low laugh echoed through the kitchen.

Hal looked up quickly and then turned away as though the sight had stung him, while Gilbot thinking that it was a signal for general joyfulness began to sing again:

"Pretty Poll, she loved a sailor,
And well she loved he——"

"Peace, damn you, peace," roared Dick, suddenly gripping Anny's arm so hard that she cried out.

Gilbot sat spellbound. Never had anyone so spoken to him in his life before and he was about to reply, but one look at the furious face of the little Spaniard calmed him and he subsided, muttering:

"No offensh, no offensh."

This outburst had surprised Anny quite as much as Gilbot, and she looked at Dick with new fear. If only Nan would come, she thought, if only Nan would come!

At this moment the door opened and she turned eagerly, her eyes alight with hope, but it was Sue who came in softly and sat down quietly by the fireside opposite her uncle.

Dick turned his head without letting Anny go, and called for more rum.

Hal brought it without looking at either of them, and set it on the table.

The Spaniard drained it at a gulp.

"So you will not come with me, my beautiful one?" he said, still smiling, and leaning across the table towards the girl.

Anny looked at him and her spirits rose; he was only playing with her after all, she thought, as she saw his dark eyes smiling at her.

Yet she wished that Nan would come, although she was still

vague in her mind as to what she expected the old woman to do when she did come.

"Nay, sir," she said smiling, "not this time."

The Spaniard laughed again.

"Not this time, my Ann? Not this time?" he questioned in an almost threatening note, which crept into his laughing tone.

"Here, boy, more rum," he called over his shoulder.

Hal brought the liquor; the Spaniard drew his knife from his belt and held it up by the blade so that the flickering light fell on its jewelled hilt.

" 'Tis a fair blade," he said admiringly.

"Ay, it is," agreed Anny, as she took the rum from Hal, who nearly cried out as he saw her bright, eager face lifted to the foreigner's.

Dick took the tankard and drained it; then he began to smile again and to twist the knife through and about his fingers with that peculiar, smooth movement his crew knew so well.

The girl watched him for a second and then looked up at the clock. Why had not Nan come, she wondered?

" 'Tis late, Captain, you will miss the tide an you do not hasten," she said.

Dick's eyelids dropped a little lower over his dark eyes, but his knife slipped through his fingers with a faster motion than before. Yet still he smiled, and when he spoke Anny thought that she had never heard so beautiful a voice.

"Ah! Senora, I would not leave the Island without that jewel which is mine by right," he said softly.

"Oh! I had forgot," said Anny, feeling in her apron pocket, "here is the ring, sir, I had it ready for you," and she drew out a little paper packet, and unfolding it disclosed the flowered ring which he had given to her. She held it out to him.

Sue, who had been watching them, gasped at the sight of such a jewel, and looked at Anny wonderingly.

The girl was over-lucky, she thought.

Dick took the ring and slipped it over the blade of his knife; it slid up to the hilt and there stuck, a band of gold and gems round the blue steel.

"You give it back to me?" he said half to himself. "You give it back to me? No other woman has done so much," he added suddenly, looking at her with that peculiar smile playing round his lips. Then his voice dropped, and he said, as though he had just realised something, "But to no other woman have I given so much," and he laughed again unpleasantly and yet so musically—while the knife fairly sped through his slim, delicate fingers.

Anny began to feel fairly sure of herself. Why should she wait for Nan to defy him, she thought? Here he was, laughing and playing; surely there would be no danger in telling him the truth.

She leaned a little nearer to him and said very softly so that none of the others could hear:

"I would you would go, sir; you have your ring; what else remains?"

The knife paused for a moment in its unending circle round the thin white hand, the dark lids flickered and the thin twisted smile vanished, but only for a second; then the soft voice said smoothly:

"One thing, Ann, my Ann of the Island, one thing remains that must come with me; that is my wife."

Anny began to laugh again nervously, but conquering herself she said sharply:

"Pest on ye, sir, will ye never stop teasing a poor girl's life out? I tell you, I hate you, sir."

Dick laughed softly, and there was a new note in his voice which no one could mistake, and Anny drew back a little.

"You said so once before, sweet Ann," he said, "and I did not believe you then, as I do not now."

Anny felt strangely irritated by his attitude and bending still closer to him, said in a sharp half-whisper:

"Oh! but, sir, you should; a man who woos unloved is a foolish sight in my eyes."

Dick slipped his arm round her waist and held her fast; he was beginning to realise that he had at last come up against a will which would not bend before his own, and a wave of uncontrollable anger surged over him; his smile almost vanished for a moment and the knife quivered in his hand.

Anny took his silence as a sign that her words were prevailing with him and determined to play her last card.

"I love another one," she said softly, drawing away from him as she spoke.

A ripple of laughter burst from the Spaniard's lips and he held her closer to him.

Hal looked up at the sound with a fierce light in his eyes; he made a step forward, but drew back again almost immediately.

"The lass likes it," he thought mournfully. "The lass likes it."

Yet he could not keep his eyes off the two.

Anny pointed to the knife, which was hanging before her, and looked into the dark smiling face so near her own.

"Put by thy knife, sir," she said pettishly. "It fears me."

Once again Dick laughed.

"Nay, 'tis a beautiful thing," he said, holding it in the palm of his hand, the point towards her, "Think you not so?"

The girl shrank away and he bent towards her. "You said you loved another, Mistress," he said suddenly, fiercely. "Is it truth?"

Anny smiled at him fearlessly.

"Ay, sir, truth!" she said quietly.

The Spaniard's smile returned, and the blue knife with the gold band on it seemed suddenly to have become part of his hand as with a deft movement he laid the bright steel against the girl's bosom.

Hal and Sue leaned forward to see this new foolery of the Captain's, each thinking that his love-making was a little too open to be decent.

"Oh! my sweet one, how fair my blade looks against thy white breast," said Dick, his eyes holding Anny's. "You gave me back my ring, but I am generous; see, I give it back to you." With the last words the knife seemed to suddenly quicken and spring from his hand, and Anny staggered back from the table, her hand clasped to her breast.

"Oh! how you hurt me, sir," she said simply, the smile still on her lips and her cheeks still bright with the excitement of a moment before. Then her eyes closed and she dropped on to the floor, the little thud her body made on the stone flags echoing all round the kitchen like a thunder-clap, and the knife Blackkerchief Dick held in his hand was red blood up to the hilt.

He looked at it dazedly, a horrified expression on his usually inscrutable face.

"Dead!" he said hoarsely, his voice sounding old and strained in the intense silence. "She is sure to be dead; we have never struck twice," but his voice sank to a whisper, "at last we have struck too soon."

He passed his hand over his forehead and gazed fixedly in front of him; some of the blood which had spurted off the knife on to his hand now smeared his forehead. Save for this, his face was ashy pale—then with slow, deliberate steps he walked to the door, opened it, and went out.

For a second the kitchen was in perfect silence, and then a scream as high and despairing as a woman's rang out loud and clear in the suddenly cold room, and Hal Grame, his boyish face distorted with rage and horror, flung himself across the kitchen and out after the Spaniard.

The night was an exceedingly dark one, and Nan Swayle stumbled once or twice over the loose stones in her path, as she strode over the rough track which ran from her shanty to the Ship.

Many strange thoughts came to her as she passed on through the darkness, her tall, gaunt figure straining against the wind, and her ragged garments flying like streamers out behind her.

The bitter memory of her last encounter with Pet Salt still rankled with her, and the thought of Anny's enforced marriage to the Spaniard made her hate the other old woman more deeply than before. She had sworn to Anny that she would prevent her sailing with Dick, and it was to fulfil this promise that she was striding through the night.

To prevent Dick from carrying off Anny.

Nan had thought over her self-allotted task very carefully, and to her there seemed but one way to accomplish it. She had decided to take that way. And as she hastened on, her thin brown fingers gripped her long staff fiercely, and from time to time she stopped to feel the heavy round stone which was bound to the top of it, making a once harmless walking-stick a formidable weapon.

On she went, her head held high, and her sharp eyes fixed ahead as if she were seeking to pierce the blackness which closed in all around her.

"They do not sail till eleven," she muttered, "and she would not go at once. I shall be in time to catch them as they come out of the yard. Ay, that is it, as they come out of the yard; it is dark there," and, mumbling to herself, she clambered through a gap in the hedge and stumbled out into the Ship lane.

She had now a very little way to go and her grip on her staff tightened as she hurried on.

A sharp bend in the road brought her in sight of the Ship. She could see the lights from the kitchen gleaming through the trees. She pressed on for a few more yards and then stopped suddenly, and holding her breath, stood rigid for a second, listening.

There was silence everywhere and the old woman shifted uneasily.

"No noise?" she muttered. "No noise? What has come to the Ship on sailing night that all should be so still?"

Keeping her eyes fixed on the lighted window she hastened on to the yard gates. There she paused again. The Ship was silent as before, and then, as she stood there watching, the door opened and a slim figure stood silhouetted against the bright background for a second and then staggered out towards her.

Without further thought Nan strode forward, her staff upraised.

Hardly had she moved, however, when Hal's terrible scream rang out through the open doorway.

The old woman sprang forward, a faint inkling of what had happened flashing through her mind.

Dick did not see her until she was almost on top of him. He came across the yard dazed and horrified, conscious of one thing only—that in a fit of rage he had killed the one woman he had ever loved.

The knife, still sticky and uncleaned, hung from his fingers, and the light from the window fell upon it as Nan came up to him.

When he saw her dark form and shining eyes rising up before him out of the darkness he started back, bringing his hands up before his face.

Nan seized her opportunity and without a thought of the possible consequences dropped her staff and darting forward wrenched the knife out of his nerveless grasp and plunged at his throat.

Nan was a strong woman, and the knife glancing on the Spaniard's collar-bone turned and slipped down into his neck, cutting the jugular vein.

A choking exclamation, "Donna Maria," fell from his lips, a rush of blood stifled all other words, and he dropped on the dry stones as dead as the girl he had left in the Ship's kitchen.

Nan heard them and laughed bitterly.

"Maria!" she muttered. "You may well call on her. Here, this is thine; take that with thee to hell, you slithering coward," and bending down she slipped the twice-stained knife into the slim white fingers.

Then she straightened her back and looking up, became aware of Hal Grame's tall figure standing not two feet away, his eyes fixed on her.

They stood quite still for several seconds, neither speaking, and then Gilbot hurried out of the door. The shock had sobered him for once in his life.

Seeing Hal, he broke out excitedly.

"Have you seen him, lad? Have you caught him? Where is the ruffian?"

Still Hal did not speak, but catching the old man by the arm he pointed silently to the still figure at their feet; the stream of light from the open doorway fell across the Spaniard's face and the white hand which held the knife.

Gilbot bent down for a moment and when he looked up his face was even paler than the boy's.

"Who?—What—what happened?" he whispered.

Hal looked silently at Nan.

The old woman faced him without flinching.

"As I come up the road, I see him come out o' the door waving his arms, and then suddenly drop like a sack; when I got up to him he was like this," she said. "He killed hisself, I reckon," she added carelessly.

Old Gilbot looked down at the huddled form.

"'Twas just what I feared when I come to the door," he muttered. "Lord! what things men do because o' wenches—and in my house too. What's to happen now?"

Chapter XXV

Ten minutes later, Joe Pullen, who stood on the beach watching the *Anny's* red lantern swing to and fro in the sharp breeze, was startled by the sudden appearance of Hal at his elbow. The boy's face showed livid in the faint light, and his eyes seemed to have turned dead and dull like those of a corpse. When he spoke, his voice was strangely high and uncontrolled.

"Where's Blueneck?" he said nervously, clutching the other man's arm.

Joe jerked his thumb over his shoulder to where a little group of men could just be distinguished in the darkness.

Hal gasped with relief and turned to go to them, still keeping his hold on Joe's arm.

The elder man suffered himself to be dragged after the boy without a murmur. He saw that something had happened, but until Hal volunteered the information, he was not the one to enquire for it.

Hal pushed unceremoniously through the little crowd, still pulling Joe behind him.

"Master Blueneck, will ye come up to the Ship at once?" he said, tapping the Spanish sailor on the shoulder and speaking in a whisper. Something in his tone caused the man to start back away from his fellows and step aside with the boy, and after a few muttered words of conversation the three set off up the lane at a brisk run.

A few seconds later they turned into the Ship yard; the door was still open, and a bright light shone from within the kitchen while all around was dark and very silent.

Running all round the paved yard, which was long and very narrow, was a wider one of beaten earth, and, as the three men turned into the gate, they could just make out the form of a tall woman standing well on their left. She was digging.

Old Gilbot met them in the doorway; he was very excited but quite sober.

On seeing Blueneck he seized him by the arm and dragged him into the room.

Joe and Hal followed slowly.

Inside the kitchen everything seemed dead and quiet; the atmosphere was cold and damp, and smelt of stale rum, the fire had died down to a few smouldering embers, and the steady ticking of the clock was the only sound.

Sue crouched in a corner shivering, her eyes wild with horror, and her teeth chattering. The two long tables had been dragged together and on this rough bier Dick and Anny lay side by side, the knife between them.

There had not been time to wash the tables even had anyone desired to do so, and the two lay among the dregs and sloppings of the night's drinking.

Blueneck walked across the kitchen and stood looking down at the bodies, without uncovering.

Gilbot followed nervously.

"What are you going to do?" he whispered anxiously.

The sailor said nothing for a moment or two but continued to stare down at the limp, blood-stained figure, whose white fingers held the thin red knife.

Gilbot stood trembling behind him, a picture of a wild crowd of captainless seamen sacking his inn rising up in his mind.

A strange light began to break over the Spanish sailor's face and he stroked his ill-shaven chin thoughtfully.

"Do?" he said slowly.

Gilbot swallowed painfully, his fat podgy knees shaking under him and his little reddened eyes shifting uneasily.

"He killed hisself," he muttered.

Blueneck bent over the table for a second and with his finger and thumb lifted one of the dark eyelids. He appeared satisfied, and straightening his back looked at the two critically.

"I knew it wasn't no usual affair with him," he said almost complacently. Then he turned to Gilbot. "She was a pretty wench," he said, nodding at the little white still smiling face on the table.

Gilbot did not speak, and the man went on: "I never thought he'd do for himself, though," he muttered, "but it's his stroke right enough; see," he dragged the lace ruffles from the small, gushing wound, "right over the collar-bone and down to the neck—he was a wonder with that knife of his; there wasn't another man in the country who could try that stroke on himself and hit so clean."

Gilbot nodded.

"Ay, he was a wonderful little fellow," he said, "though I never took much notice of him. But what are you going to do, sir?"

Blueneck faced the three men steadily, a smile breaking out on his lips.

"Put to sea!" he said deliberately. "The men are a mangy lot, God knows, but if they'd sail under him they'll sail under me, and be glad of the change."

He paused and Gilbot heaved a sigh of relief, and Blueneck, seeing that his decision was approved of, added: "And if ever I come near this accursed, God-forsaken Island again the devil scuttle my brig and carry off my canvas," and so saying he turned on his heel and strode to the door. "Good-night, good people," he said, turning on the threshold.

Hal stepped forward and took the little knife from out the fingers that were still warm.

"Will you take this?" he said, holding it out to the sailor. "It served him well and may you."

Blueneck drew back.

"Nay!" he said hastily, "I'll have none of it, and, mark my words, lad, you put it down; the thing is evil. The man there was harmless enough without it, but together, by God, they were devils. Put it down. Fare you well, my masters," he added, and went out.

They heard his footsteps die away down the road before anyone spoke; then Gilbot wiped his beaded forehead and turned to the two friends.

"You must get them out of here; get them buried," he said

jerkily, pointing to the table. "Sink them in the mud," he added, an idea coming to him.

Hal sprang suddenly forward, a light in his dulled eyes and his mouth half-open—but his words died on his lips for at that moment Nan Swayle, spade in hand, appeared in the open doorway.

"It is done," she said, her big booming voice sounding strangely hollow in the silent room. "Susan, are you ready? Come, help me."

The frightened girl crept out of her corner and went towards the table; the old woman followed.

Gilbot put his hand on her arm.

"What are you doing, woman?" he said.

"Burying my gran'daughter," replied Nan laconically.

"Not in my land," said the old man quickly. "I'll have no graves in my land."

Mother Swayle turned and looked at him steadily.

"The lass shall be buried in good Island earth, near the only home she ever had," she said determinedly, "and the grave is dug, and, thy land or no, Master Gilbot, there she shall lie."

The man hesitated for a moment, but little by little his wavering eyes dropped before Nan's bright ones, and, shrugging his shoulders, he drew back to let her pass.

Hal, who had stood motionless watching them, now stepped forward.

"I—I'll carry her for you, mother," he said, without looking up.

Nan stared contemptuously at him for a moment her bright eyes growing suddenly hard.

"Had you carried her off ere now all had been well," she said abruptly.

The boy winced, and something like a sob escaped him, but he turned and faced the old woman dry-eyed.

"May I take her?" he said again.

Nan made a gesture of impatience.

"Ay, take her, take her, boy, take her," she said bitterly. "None of your carelessness can hurt her now."

Joe, who had been watching the whole proceedings, now came forward and caught the old woman's sleeve, and drew her away; then whispered:

"The lad is wonderful over-wrought, witch; leave taunting him."

Nan looked at him fiercely, but she drew back, and the boy, stepping past her, picked up the light, cold form of his love and, holding her in his arms, her blood-stained corsage pressed against his breast and her pretty head with its long black plaits lolling heavily on his shoulder, carried her quickly out of the room.

Sue began to cry softly, and Nan stood leaning on her spade and looking down into the fast whitening embers in the open grate.

In two or three minutes Hal came back; he was very pale and there was blood upon his hands and clothes. "I have left her to you, mother," he said rather unsteadily, as he stood in the doorway looking across at the old woman.

Nan turned from the fire without a word and beckoning to Sue, who followed her, still weeping, she went out and shut the door behind her.

Gilbot looked after her.

" 'Tis a wonderful strange woman she is," he said thoughtfully, "talking about granddaughters and such like, and her never having had a child."

He shook his head and then turned to the table. "We must get him out of here," he said, suddenly growing nervous again, as he looked at the dead Spaniard.

"Here, Hal, Joe, take him down to the mud. It will do the old place no good if folks get to know he's lying here," and he began to drag the limp mass on to the floor.

Joe looked up at the clock.

"Half-past twelve," he said thoughtfully. "Twill be full dawn at five."

Then he turned to Hal.

"In four hours I'll risk going out with him, lad," he said. "Will you wait till then?"

Hal nodded.

Gilbot looked up.

"I had forgot," he said, "I had forgot; it is a long time since I went out on the mud—ah, well! Hal, bring me some rum."

The sky was a pale grey, in which two or three late stars still shone faintly, and there was a sharp twang of frost in the air, when two men, carrying the body of a third between them, and four great weights slung over their shoulders, stumbled out of the old Ship's kitchen, leaving behind them a girl asleep by the empty grate and an old man lying drunk upstairs.

As they came out into the yard, they both turned instinctively to a patch of newly-disturbed earth on their right, from the side of which rose a dark figure, who glided off into the greyness beyond.

The shorter of the two men spoke gruffly.

"The witch was fond enough of the lass," he said, "I wonder she didn't do more to save her."

The other answered him bitterly.

"It wasn't her place, Joe. 'Twas mine. And I did naught. God knows; I—I thought she loved him," he added, giving the slim little figure whose shoulders he held a violent shake.

Pullen shook his head, and a drop of pure sentiment crept into his bright blue eyes.

" 'Tis a wonderful pity," he said slowly, "a wonderful pity—poor little lass—and him too—he must have loved her, or he'd never have killed hisself."

The memory of Nan's upstretched arm and fierce blow came clearly to Hal and he opened his mouth to speak but thought better of it, and they trudged on in silence.

The mud looked very black, cold, and sinister when they at last reached the shore; the tide was well out, and the sea seemed a full mile the other side of the soft, greenish belt.

Joe dropped the Spaniard's feet and stood staring in front of him for a moment; then he stooped down and lifted them again.

"It's a bit further up," he said shortly, and they went on.

Presently he stopped again.

"Here we are," he remarked, as he sat down on the shingle, and, taking off his back a pair of boards specially cut for the purpose, he proceeded to tie them on to his feet.

Hal did the like and the two set out over the black, evil-smelling ooze.

The boards prevented them from sinking more than a few inches at each step, but it was not easy going, for the limp body of the Spaniard, although not heavy, was yet not light.

The two slipped often, sometimes almost falling.

After some fifteen minutes of this Joe paused.

"This'll do," he said, nodding to a circular patch of smooth, greyish mud which lay just in front of them.

Hal looked at it and at the white face of the Spaniard; then he shuddered.

"It's horrible," he said.

Joe grunted.

"Give us those weights, lad," he demanded, holding out his hand.

Hal slung them over.

Hastily, and with perfect calmness, Joe tied them to the Spaniard's feet; he had to bend nearly double to do this, as to kneel with the boards on was impossible, and he straightened his back with some relief on finishing.

"That's enough; now in with him," he said briskly, wiping his hands on his jersey. Then his eyes fell on the silver buttons on the black velvet coat and the rings on the white hands, and he pulled out his knife.

" 'Twould be a pity to leave him these," he said practically, bending down again.

"Let be, Joe Pullen." Hal's voice rang out clear over the windswept flats. "We'll have naught of his. Let the devil keep his own." He drew from his belt the thin two-edged knife, now brown and clotted with dry blood, round which was still the flower-ring, and threw it into the centre of the grey circle. It sank almost immediately.

Pullen watched him.

"Ay, maybe the knife, but not the buttons; there's no evil in them."

Hal shook his head.

"Nay," he said determinedly, "evil in everything he touched, everything he owned—sink it deep, Joe, sink it deep."

Pullen sighed and shrugged his shoulders.

"Maybe you're right, lad," he said, "maybe you're right," and added cheerfully, "and I don't know who'd buy them anyway. Come then, heave him in."

Hal bent down and together they lifted the once so gallant little figure, still clad in all its bravery, and dropped it gently into the grey patch; the weights hit the mud first and sank quickly out of sight, dragging the silk-stockinged feet with them; the ooze clicked and chuckled to itself as it sucked down its prey. Further and further in sank the body of the great little Captain, who twelve hours before was so gay, so sure of himself, so debonair.

The dawn breeze came stealing across the sea, and a sea-gull screamed lazily near by, while a faint yellow light began to glow over the mainland the other side of the bay. Now the mud had reached the Spaniard's breast; his head, still bound with his famous black kerchief, had fallen forward and his limp arms lay loosely on the soft slime.

Joe looked at him critically.

"I wonder now has he struck the hard?" he said thoughtfully, and leaning forward he put his foot on the black-coated shoulder and pushed vigorously. The mud sucked noisily and the body vanished rapidly. Now only the head and one arm was visible. Now the head was gone. The dark eyes, the terrible crooked smile, the white flashing teeth, the cold, silent mud had them all. Now only a hand was left; it lay for a second on the grey background white and shapely, and then it too vanished, leaving the grey circle as quiet and untroubled as before.

Joe turned away.

"Come," he said slowly, "it's all over now."

Hal looked up.

"Ay," he said, and his voice was heavy and toneless. "It is all over—Joe, all over in one night. Come."

And they toiled, slipped, and struggled back to their homes again.

The yellow light over the mainland grew brighter and brighter, turned to gold and then to crimson, and the rising sun rose once more over the Island as quiet and peaceful as if the Spaniard and his love had never been.

Chapter XXVI

One evening two or three years later, Big French and Sue, his wife, their young daughter, and little Red Farran, whom they had taken to live with them, sat round the fire in the Ship kitchen.

Gilbot was dead. It was said in the village that he had died singing "Pretty Poll." And he had left the old inn to Hal Grame, who proved himself a very able landlord. He had grown very taciturn, however, since the affair of the Spaniard and the girl, which had by this time been almost forgotten by the easy-going Islanders, and he had taken to tobacco, with which Fen de Witt was well able to supply him at a cheap rate, and he sat now in a haze of smoke on the opposite side of the fireplace to French, his pipe in his mouth and his head thrown back as though in earnest contemplation of the rafters.

Joe sat at his elbow drinking ale; they two were as friendly as ever, but Pullen had been known to aver that no word of Anny or the Spaniard had been exchanged between them since that cold September morning long ago when black mud had swallowed the last trace of the affair.

It was late and all the other company had gone; the dips were beginning to die out one by one, and tall shadows began to creep over the oak-beamed ceiling and dark, rum-fumed walls.

Presently French rose to his feet.

"Ah well," he said, "I reckon we'll go home, Sue. Good rest to you, Hal."

The landlord nodded.

"Same to you, Master French, and you too, Mistress," he said, without taking his pipe out of his mouth.

Sue smiled and picked up her baby, who was crawling on the long seat beside her.

"Good-night, Hal," she said, and then added, looking round the room affectionately, "it's almost like the old days to be all here together again."

"All?" murmured Hal bitterly.

Sue did not hear him, but went on gaily:

"Yet I would not change," she said. "These days are happier, I with my man and my little one."

Hal winced, and French who was watching put an arm affectionately round his wife's shoulders.

"Come, lass, we stay too long a-talking," he said, gently drawing her to him.

Sue looked up at him a smile on her lips. She was very proud of her handsome husband, and they went out together, little Red following, his hand clutching French's big coat skirts.

After they had gone there was silence in the room for a second or two, while Pullen helped himself to more ale from a pitcher at his elbow.

Hal stared into the blazing fire.

"Like the old days?" he said at last half to himself. "Like the old days? My God!"

Joe put down his tankard and wiped his lips.

"I reckon I'll be going home to Amy—damn her," he said, getting up.

Hal looked up frowning.

"Must ye so, mate?" he said wistfully.

"No, no, er—no, lad, no need," and Joe sat down again and refilled his pot.

The silence continued.

Suddenly Hal rose and standing on tiptoe reached down one of the old cracked cups on the high mantelshelf, and emptied its contents into his hand.

Joe heard the clink of coins and looked up.

His friend was leaning against the chimney-piece, his face half-hidden, and in his hand which he held open before him were two little coins.

Presently the younger man turned away from the fire and held out his hand to Pullen.

"Do you remember these, mate?" he said rather abruptly.

Joe looked at the money curiously.

"Groats?" he said. "Well now I can't say as I do, but"—he broke off suddenly—"that day we'd bin after fish?" he enquired.

Hal nodded.

Joe looked at him in astonishment.

"Why, lad, you don't go thinking o' that now, surely?" he said.

Hal clinked the coins together and looked round the kitchen ruefully. "I couldn't give her aught then—but now—if only——" his voice trailed off and ceased.

Joe shifted uneasily in his seat.

"Don't think on it, lad, don't think on it," he advised.

Hal laughed bitterly.

"You know not what you say, Joe Pullen," he said. "I must think on it; 'tis all I have to think on," and he puffed at his pipe almost fiercely.

Joe did not speak, and after a while the other went on again; he spoke jerkily and his voice was very low.

"Sometimes I think I see her come in crying and him after her. That's when I try to forget, but it's no use, I can't; she loved him, I reckon; I can't forget that."

Joe cleared his throat noisily.

"Why trouble yourself, lad?" he muttered. "She's gone and he with her, and you're here——"

"More's the pity," interrupted the other. "I have naught to make me want to stay."

Joe leaned back and crossed his legs.

"Oh! I don't know," he said, "there's the Ship; she's your love—after—after Anny."

Hal looked up quickly.

"The Ship?" he repeated slowly. "The Ship my love after Anny? Ay, maybe you're right, mate, maybe you're right; I had forgot her—ay, the Ship." A slow smile spread over his face and he forgot to smoke.

"My love after Anny," he kept repeating softly. "My love after Anny."

And after Joe had gone home he sat long looking into the fire, the slow smile still on his lips, but later still, when his eyes fell again on the two groats, he picked them up tenderly and put them back in the cracked cup upon the mantel-shelf, and then, after carefully bolting the door, he took his candle and went up to bed.

On their way home Big French and Sue had to pass Nan Swayle's cabin, and, as they came towards it, Red noticed the red baleful eyes of Ben the old tom-cat peering at them from behind the shed.

"Nan's at home," he said, hugging French's hand, "and Ben's bin whipt."

The big man looked across at the lonely shanty.

"God be wi' ye, Nan," he shouted; his voice resounded over the silent marshes, and echoed round about the hut, but there was no reply.

French went nearer and knocked at the door.

"Are ye well, Nan?" he called.

Nan's big booming voice replied and her usual greetings rang out through the door:

"Ay, God be wi' ye, good swine."

French laughed and they went on, and as they crossed the dark saltings to their home they heard her hail, expressing approval and friendliness, following them over the flats, loud, then soft, and finally trailing off into a long-drawn-out wail:

"Rum, rum, rum—m—m."

A NOTE ON THE AUTHOR

Margery Louise Allingham was born in Ealing, London in 1904 to a very literary family; her parents were both writers, and her aunt ran a magazine, so it was natural that Margery too would begin writing at an early age. She wrote steadily through her school days, first in Colchester and later as a boarder at the Perse School for Girls in Cambridge, where she wrote, produced, and performed in a costume play. After her return to London in 1920 she enrolled at the Regent Street Polytechnic, where she studied drama and speech training in a successful attempt to overcome a childhood stammer. There she met Phillip Youngman Carter, who would become her husband and collaborator, designing the jackets for many of her future books.

The Allingham family retained a house on Mersea Island, a few miles from Layer Breton, and it was here that Margery found the material for her first novel, the adventure story *Blackkerchief Dick* (1923), which was published when she was just nineteen. She went on to pen multiple novels, some of which dealt with occult themes and some with mystery, as well as writing plays and stories – her first detective story, *The White Cottage Mystery*, was serialized in the *Daily Express* in 1927.

Allingham died at the age of 62, and her final novel, *A Cargo of Eagles*, was finished by her husband at her request and published posthumously in 1968.